"Spud is going to be okay, right, Uncle Aiden?" George's voice shook as he blinked back tears.

Aiden crouched down, placing his hands on George's thin shoulders. "I'm going to do everything I can to ensure a competent vet treats that pup."

"His name is Spud," George said thickly.

The door to the exam room closest to the lobby opened. Aiden straightened and turned, half expecting the same sourpuss caregiver that had been so insensitive to him as a child. Instead, shock reverberated through him. The woman—whose blue eyes widened as she took him in—had grown up in the years since he'd last seen her, but he would have recognized Cassie Raebourn anywhere.

"Aiden Riley?" she breathed like she was looking at a ghost.

"I need your help, Cassie." There was no point in pretending he didn't know her. "We need to see a vet. It's an emergency."

"I'm a vet," she said like she couldn't quite believe it.

Dear Reader,

I can't tell you how excited I am to invite you to return to the world of Crimson, Colorado. Although fictional, Crimson is a town near and dear to me—to create it, I took the best parts of each of my favorite Colorado mountain towns. It's a magical place and the perfect setting for a love story between two unlikely friends.

Cassie Raebourn would consider Aiden Riley a friend, although when the book opens she hasn't seen him for nearly twenty years. But when Aiden shows up at the veterinary clinic where Cassie is working with an injured puppy, her heart immediately opens up to him again. Unfortunately, Aiden doesn't believe he has a heart—at least not one worthy of a woman as sweet and sunny as Cassie. It will take some canine matchmaking to help these two on the path to happily-ever-after, and I hope you enjoy their journey as much as I did.

While writing this book, we said goodbye to our ten-year-old Lab and a couple of months later, hello to a new puppy. My family can mark most of our big life events by the dogs we shared them with, and this four-legged devotion made *Love at First Bark* a joy to write. If you have a pup at home, please give them an extra hug from me.

Happy reading!

Michelle

Love at First Bark

MICHELLE MAJOR

HARLEQUIN

SPECIAL
EDITION

Recycling programs
for this product may
not exist in your area.

ISBN-13: 978-1-335-59429-7

Love at First Bark

Copyright © 2023 by Michelle Major

Harlequin Enterprises ULC
22 Adelaide St. West, 41st Floor
Toronto, Ontario M5H 4E3, Canada
www.Harlequin.com

Printed in U.S.A.

Michelle Major grew up in Ohio but dreamed of living in the mountains. Soon after graduating with a degree in journalism, she pointed her car west and settled in Colorado. Her life and house are filled with one great husband, two beautiful kids, a few furry pets and several well-behaved reptiles. She's grateful to have found her passion writing stories with happy endings. Michelle loves to hear from her readers at michellemajor.com.

Books by Michelle Major

Harlequin Special Edition

Welcome to Starlight

The Best Intentions
The Last Man She Expected
His Last-Chance Christmas Family
His Secret Starlight Baby
Starlight and the Single Dad
A Starlight Summer
Starlight and the Christmas Dare

The Fortunes of Texas: The Wedding Gift

Their New Year's Beginning

The Fortunes of Texas: The Hotel Fortune

Her Texas New Year's Wish

The Fortunes of Texas: Hitting the Jackpot

A Fortune's Windfall

Visit the Author Profile page
at Harlequin.com for more titles.

"Did you know that there are over 300 words for love in canine?"
—Gabrielle Zevin

This one is for all the dog lovers out there. Animal people are my kind of people.

Prologue

Eleven-year-old Cassie Raebourn stood in the waiting room of the veterinary office with what she could only assume was a pit of deep sorrow cracking open in her stomach.

Cassie was a happy kid with a happy life, so the unfamiliar pain that cut across her midsection felt like a physical blow as she watched the heaving shoulders of her classmate. Aiden Riley was clearly trying to keep his emotions in check. His will was an almost palpable force in the quiet of the empty lobby.

She didn't know him well, but since her family had moved to Crimson, Colorado, at the beginning of the school year, they'd been in the same fifth-grade class. And because their last names started with the same letter, Mrs. Donahue, their teacher, had seated them in the same row.

Aiden mostly kept to himself and didn't seem to have a lot of friends at school. He and his sister lived with their

parents on a ranch outside of town and took the bus daily.
Cassie's father had taken over running the largest local
bank in Crimson, and her family lived in a four-bedroom
Victorian-era house within walking distance of the elementary school.

Like her parents, Cassie liked living in the mountain
town more than she had growing up in Phoenix, their
previous home.

It had been on the playground just before the start of
winter break four months earlier that she'd seen snow
for the first time. The joy and wonder of it had almost
brought tears to her eyes.

That was when she'd first noticed Aiden watching
her with a kind of reluctant yearning in his dark gaze.
She had the feeling he watched her more than she realized. He sat behind her in class, so there was no way for
her to check her theory, but she'd catch him glancing at
her at odd times during the day—in the cafeteria or at
recess. They didn't talk much, but she felt a connection
between them.

His quiet, solemn demeanor was so different from
most of the obnoxious, loud boys she knew. And unlike
the girlfriends she'd made, he didn't seem to want her to
be anything but who she was on the inside. Most people
didn't look beyond her blond hair, blue eyes and perky
personality to understand she wasn't always the carefree kid they wanted to see. By the way Aiden watched
her at school, she had a feeling he knew but seemed to
like her anyway.

She hoped he wouldn't turn around now. She didn't
want him to know that she bore witness to his grief
and shared it in some unexplainable way. But she also
couldn't seem to leave him totally alone.

From what she'd gathered, a neighbor had seen Aiden

carrying his injured dog on the side of the highway and driven them to the vet clinic where Cassie volunteered a couple of times a week.

She adored animals, but her mom was allergic to any dander, so they couldn't keep anything other than Cassie's beloved betta fish and the leopard gecko her parents had reluctantly given her for her tenth birthday.

Aiden's dog was a scruffy mutt of indiscriminate breed that had to weigh at least fifty pounds. The animal had trembled in the boy's arms, clearly in pain, and Cassie had seen a trickle of blood staining the dog's muzzle.

She hated that Dr. Rooney wasn't in the office that day. Her favorite vet's partner, Dr. Smith, was competent enough, but he didn't care about his patients like Dr. Rooney. He didn't care the way Cassie thought a veterinarian should.

The office was near closing time, so the last scheduled appointment of the day had just left when the neighbor, an older man in faded Wranglers and a dusty flannel shirt, had walked in with Aiden.

Dr. Smith had ignored the boy even though it was clear he was the dog's owner. The vet tech had taken the injured animal. After speaking to the neighbor in hushed tones, Dr. Smith had closed the exam room door on both of them.

The neighbor had gone into Dr. Rooney's office to make a phone call, so Aiden was left standing in the waiting room with no one.

Cassie had never personally experienced the kind of desperate loneliness that radiated from the boy she considered a friend even though they probably weren't. It wasn't as if she didn't understand sorrow.

Her parents hadn't meant Cassie to be an only child,

but her mom couldn't seem to make it through a second pregnancy. Although they didn't speak of the repeated losses, Cassie understood what made her mom close herself in her bedroom and why her dad sometimes stared out the window with tears staining his cheeks.

She also understood it was her role to be extra happy and loving at those times, and she tried her best to make her mom feel better. Sometimes it even seemed to work, and Melissa Raebourn would slowly come back to herself, her sweet smile returning even if it was wobbly at the corners.

Cassie couldn't imagine what it would take to entice a smile from Aiden Riley.

No, that wasn't exactly true. She knew what he needed the same way she knew her own name. He needed his dog to recover and survive whatever had happened to it.

The two ladies who worked the front counter were whispering among themselves about the kind of man who would beat an animal so badly. They were talking about Aiden's father, and Cassie quickly understood that she could hate a person without ever having met him. Then she said a silent prayer that Dr. Smith would do better than she expected.

She also hated seeing Aiden's struggle to keep himself from breaking down. She'd seen enough people come into the vet office in the past four months to know that waiting was the hardest part. Waiting alone was simply wrong.

Without thinking about it, she walked over and stood beside him in front of the closed door, linking their fingers together. He didn't pull away as she might have expected. Instead, his hand gripped hers like she was the only thing tethering him to this world.

It felt like hours, but in reality, it was probably minutes later that the door to the exam room opened. Dr.

Smith appeared, and before he said a word, Cassie knew he hadn't been able to save Aiden's dog.

"Somebody hurt that animal badly," he said, and Aiden went rigid.

"It wasn't me," he said through gritted teeth. "I would never hurt Sam."

"He passed away naturally on the exam table," the vet continued, and Cassie wanted to scream at him to shut his mouth.

The words weren't going to help the devastated boy still holding her hand.

"It's a blessing," Dr. Smith said, "because I would have had to put him down and that costs money I don't think you have, son."

How was that supposed to help Aiden feel any better? Dr. Rooney would never have been so callous, but she could tell that Dr. Smith was blaming Aiden for whatever had happened to the dog. It hadn't been his fault. He was devastated by the loss of his pet.

Where was the neighbor? Where was somebody to protect him?

"Who did it, son?" the vet demanded. "Who hurt that dog?"

"Sam!" she yelled. The doctor's head snapped back. "He told you his dog's name is Sam. Sam was his friend."

The vet's bushy brows drew together. "This is none of your concern, Cassie. Why don't you go back to the kennels and check if any of them need to be cleaned?"

She felt tears sting the back of her eyes. She didn't want to be dismissed or to leave Aiden alone, but he dropped her hand suddenly, like the contact burned him.

"Aiden?" The sound of a woman's desperate voice had them all turning.

Cassie had never seen Aiden's mother, but there was

no doubt that she was standing in the clinic's doorway. She had his same dark hair and eyes, although hers looked haunted. Her upper lip was cut, and one cheek appeared swollen and red.

"Ma'am, was that your dog this boy brought in?" Dr. Smith demanded, totally ignoring her distress and injuries.

"Can we call the police?" Joanie, the receptionist, asked. Dr. Smith hadn't bothered to offer even though the dog hadn't been the only one who'd been abused that day.

"Sue, what's going on? Do you need help? Has Eddie been drinking?" The neighbor had come out of the office at that point, but Aiden's mother ignored his questions and kept her gaze on her son.

"Your sister's in the car. We're leaving for good this time."

No! Cassie wanted to shout. She might not have known Aiden Riley well, but her hand in his had meant something to her. It changed something between them. Although she was too young to understand the rapid beating of her heart, she knew it was important. He was important.

Aiden took a step forward, then turned and met her gaze. She could tell he didn't want to leave, either. He felt it—whatever was between them. He saw her for more than a happy smile, and she recognized a kindred soul in his dark, sorrowful eyes.

For a moment, Cassie thought he would tell his mother he wanted to stay. But he gave a slight shake of his head and walked away.

"We can help you, Sue," the neighbor said.

"Ma'am, I'm happy to call the police," Joanie offered again.

Dr. Smith just stood there looking uncomfortable. Dr.

Rooney would have fixed this mess. He would have made it so that Aiden didn't have to go.

Cassie refused to believe he was leaving for good. She wanted to get to know him. She wanted him to be her real friend.

Without looking back, he followed his mother out into the crisp April day. It would warm up in Crimson in a few weeks, but spring came late to the high mountains of the Rockies.

Surely she'd see him again. Somebody who had the potential to change your life even if you couldn't explain how couldn't just disappear from it. Or could they?

Chapter One

"You had no business hiding a dog from your mom and me," Aiden Riley said as he glanced at his eight-year-old nephew, George, in the rearview mirror. "That puppy is too young to be away from his mother."

"I'm his mother," George said, his jaw lifting in a stubborn tilt. One Aiden knew all too well from looking in the mirror.

"Buddy, you don't have the equipment to be that pup's mother."

"They were being mean to him." George snuggled the tiny mutt closer. "Gabe Tinmouth went home to get firecrackers to tie to his butt."

Aiden let out a curse that would have had his sister pointing at the swear jar she'd placed on the counter when he'd moved into the bunk house on their family's struggling ranch a few months earlier. He was fairly certain Lila would fund a Disney trip with his donations to that damn jar.

"Where does Gabe Mealymouth live?" Aiden demanded.

"On the other side of the valley," George said. "But that's not his name."

"I know his name, and I've got his number." Aiden turned down the gravel drive that led to Animal Ark Veterinary Clinic. It had been twenty years since he'd been inside the nondescript brick building, but his mouth still filled with bile. "After we get that dog on the mend, I'll pay wee Gabe a visit."

"He's also not wee," George stated. "He's the tallest boy in second grade. And he's real mean."

"Not meaner than me."

"That's true."

If his gut weren't churning with unwanted memories, Aiden would have smiled at his nephew's agreement. George was a gentle soul, just like his mother, and a straight shooter, the way his father had been.

A terrible thought crossed Aiden's mind. "Have I ever been mean to you, George?"

The boy seemed to consider the question. Aiden pulled to a stop in the one available parking space in the clinic's parking lot. Blood roared in his head. He'd accepted his surly disposition and quick temper a long time ago but believed he'd spared his nephew from the worst of it. He would never purposely hurt a child—verbally or physically. He would not turn into his father.

"No," the boy said after a moment.

"How about your mom?"

"She thinks you're funny."

Aiden's sister had a warped sense of humor.

"But I'd think you were nicer if you let me keep Spud."

"You did not name that puppy Spud." Aiden shook his head. "You can't name an animal that doesn't belong to you. It only makes you feel attached." And becoming emotionally attached to anything led to being hurt. Aiden had learned that lesson well.

"He belongs to me," George said simply. "I love him."

Love was the worst of all.

Aiden grunted instead of answering. What the hell was he supposed to say that?

"Let's get him checked out." He opened the car door so George could exit while still holding the tiny animal. The exterior of the clinic hadn't changed much from his ill-fated visit decades earlier. A few more shrubs were planted, mostly brown around the edges. Probably a result of too many patients lifting a leg.

A wooden wind chime hung under the eave in front of the window next to the entrance. Aiden remembered the last time he'd entered this building like it had been yesterday. He could still feel Sam's trembling body and his labored breath.

The dog had attacked Aiden's father when Ed Riley had gone after Aiden in a drunken rage. Aiden would have taken whatever beating his father had doled out if it had meant saving Sam.

But he'd been powerless to stop his dad.

As much as he didn't want anything to do with a stray puppy or a return to the scene of the lowest point in his life, he wasn't going to sit back and let George's tender heart break again after the loss he'd already suffered.

He might've been mean, but Aiden wasn't a monster. He wasn't his father.

The waiting room was crowded with people and animals of all shapes and sizes. A hush seemed to fall over humans and pets alike as he, George, and the puppy he refused to name entered.

"We need to see a doctor," he said as he approached the front desk.

"Do you have an appointment?" the young woman behind the computer asked.

"I have a sick puppy," Aiden answered, glancing at the furry bundle peeking out from the blanket his nephew held tightly. "Very sick."

The dark-headed woman with the pixie cut and a row of silver hoops on each of her ears frowned. She wore scrubs with flying pigs printed on them and stood to examine the dog.

"His name's Spud," George offered. "I rescued him."

"The dog is a stray," Aiden clarified. "My nephew has been trying to take care of him, but the puppy needs to see a vet. Right now."

"Sir, we have a full slate of appointments this afternoon. If you could wait in—"

"I'm not waiting." There was no way in hell that Aiden would stand in the same lobby he'd stood in while his dog died on the exam table.

"Jules, let me check with the doctor," another woman said from the office space attached to the reception area. "If it's a true emergency—"

"It is."

"Spud is going to be okay, right, Uncle Aiden?" George's voice shook as he blinked back tears.

"Don't cry. Crying isn't going to help that puppy."

"Okay," the boy whimpered.

Aiden could feel the people in the waiting room shooting daggers at his back. He'd managed worse disapproval.

Slowly, he crouched down, placing his hands on George's thin shoulders. "I'm going to do everything I can to ensure a competent vet treats that pup."

"His name is Spud," George said thickly.

"I know you tried your best to take care of him. I can't promise an outcome I don't control, but you did right by him, George. Know that. You saved him from a bully and took care of him."

"I love him."

If Aiden had a heart, the kid would be tearing it in two right about now.

The door to the exam room closest to the lobby opened—the room where they'd taken Sam years earlier. Aiden straightened and turned, half expecting the same sourpuss caregiver who had been so insensitive to him as a child.

Instead, shock reverberated through him. The woman whose blue eyes widened as she took him in had grown up in the years since he'd last seen her, but he would have recognized Cassie Raebourn anywhere.

"Aiden Riley?" she breathed like she was looking at a ghost.

"I need your help, Cassie." There was no point in pretending he didn't know her. "We need to see a vet. It's an emergency."

"I'm a vet," she said like she couldn't quite believe it.

Aiden could hardly fathom this turn of events himself. He'd been back in Crimson since the start of the new year and hadn't heard anything about Cassie Raebourn living in town.

Not that he did much socializing or that Lila would have a reason to share that tidbit of information with him if she even realized it.

Since her husband's death ten months ago, Lila had retreated into herself. She barely left the ranch or took part in life in any meaningful way.

"We've all got pets that need to be seen by the doc," a man called from the far side of the waiting room.

"The clinic is short-staffed today," Cassie explained with an apologetic smile. "Dr. Smith had a family emergency."

There were a few snickers and noises of annoyance from the people waiting to be seen.

Cassie's smile disappeared as she took a step closer. The subtle scent of lavender hit Aiden's nostrils. Damn if she didn't smell the same as she had as a kid. How was that possible, and why did he remember it so vividly?

"I don't want to see Dr. Smith," Aiden answered, and her cornflower-colored eyes gentled. He didn't want gentleness—not from her or anyone.

The urge to turn tail and run almost overwhelmed him. There weren't many people in the world who had seen weakness and vulnerability in Aiden.

He'd made a living on the rodeo circuit, competing in saddle bronc riding and barrel-racing events during his ten-year career. Weakness in the ring got people hurt.

Cassie had not only witnessed his soft underbelly, but she'd also stood with him at his lowest point. That gave her a power that he didn't like.

She took a step forward and sucked in a shocked breath when she got a good look at the animal George had wrapped in the faded blanket.

"Is this your sweet puppy?" she asked the boy, reaching out a hand to touch the dog's still form.

"Yes," George answered at the same time Aiden muttered, "It's a stray."

"May I take him to the back for a few minutes to check out what's going on with him?"

"They need to get in line," the same man who'd complained earlier shouted.

Aiden looked over his shoulder and glared.

"Fine," the man conceded immediately. "Let them cut."

"We'll be with you and Jellybean as soon as possible,

Darryl," Cassie said in that same sweet tone. Did she ever lose her sunny disposition?

Aiden couldn't imagine it.

"Can I come?" George asked as he transferred the dog into Cassie's arms. "I don't want Spud to be alone."

"It would be best if you stayed out here with your dad," Cassie told the boy. "As soon as an exam room becomes available, Jules will move you there to wait."

"My dad's dead," George answered. "This is my Uncle Aiden."

"Oh." Cassie's calm facade broke for a brief moment, although Aiden couldn't quite name the emotion that flashed in her eyes. She'd thought George belonged to him, as if he could possibly take on the role of parent.

It was the reminder he needed that Cassie Raebourn knew nothing about the man he'd become.

She disappeared behind the oak door that led to the back of the clinic, but Aiden didn't move from where he and George stood with their backs to the other waiting pet owners.

The boy crossed his arms over his chest and bit down on his lower lip.

A moment later, a woman with a meowing cat in a purple carrier came out from the door on the opposite end of the front desk.

The girl behind the computer immediately popped to her feet. "Tracy," she called, "can you take care of Lulu and her mom while I get the exam room ready for Dr. Cassie's current patient?"

"Of course," the other woman answered.

"Follow me," the girl named Jules said to Aiden and George.

She hurried out from behind the desk and led them to a room at the end of the hall.

As Aiden and George entered, she grabbed a box of cleansing cloths from one of the counters and quickly wiped down the exam table and cabinet behind it before exiting.

Aiden knew he should offer some words of comfort to his nephew while they waited but was too busy trying to strap down his emotions before they threw him off and trampled him like a raging thousand-pound animal.

It wasn't just Cassie who smelled the same as he remembered. There was an underlying medicinal tinge to the air that brought him back to that time twenty years earlier. Even the scent of the cleansing wipes seemed familiar in a way that affected him more than it should.

He pushed out the breath he'd been holding as the door opened and Cassie ducked in, closing it behind her.

"Is Spud going to be okay?" George asked, his voice thick with emotion.

"It's too soon for me to answer that question." Although the words weren't exactly encouraging, her tone seemed to placate the boy. "That puppy is lucky you found him," she continued as she sat down on the short stool next to the exam table, bringing her to George's height. "Can you tell me the circumstances of how Spud came to be with you?"

The kid has been less than forthcoming with Aiden's questions other than admitting the name of the bully who'd been hurting the dog before George had stepped in. But the floodgates opened as a result of Cassie's compassionate presence.

George explained not only how he'd found Gabe and his minions taunting the abandoned puppy but how the boy himself had been a victim of the bully's teasing since he and his family had moved to Crimson.

Aiden did his best not to react to his nephew's revelations as he tried to work out how to talk to his sister about her son's struggles. It would break Lila's tender heart to know George was enduring this.

The boy mentioned at least three times that no one needed to share what he was saying with his mother because he could handle it alone.

Aiden should have realized something was wrong before now. He studied George's slouch and the way he seemed to curl in on himself as he spoke and recognized those physical signs of a problem from watching Lila at the same age shrink under their father's constant berating and taunting.

It was evident that even though George spent the majority of his time building LEGO sets or reading in his room, he wasn't as oblivious to his mother's depression as he seemed. Kids picked up on things, whether tension or sadness or fear.

"I'm going to call Animal Control and have them pay a visit to Gabe and his family," Cassie said when George finally finished. Her voice had taken on a steely edge. "You're a hero, George. You saved Spud from being hurt by those other boys."

"But like Uncle Aiden said, I shouldn't have kept him in the barn overnight," George lamented. "It was cold in there, and he was alone while I slept and then went to school. I was scared to bring him into the house because Uncle Aiden doesn't like dogs."

Cassie blinked, her summer-sky eyes darting to Aiden's with a meaningful look.

"You did fine, George," Aiden muttered, hating that he had a role in the puppy's current trouble.

He didn't dislike dogs, he just didn't want to get close to any, but he would never hurt an animal. Not like his father had. Why did he feel the need to keep reminding himself of that fact?

"More than fine," Cassie amended. "I promise I'll do everything in my power to make sure Spud lives a long and healthy life with you, George."

"Not with him." Aiden shook his head. "George is not keeping that animal."

"Uncle Aiden, please." George turned on his big puppy-dog eyes full throttle. "If you talk to Mommy, she'll say yes. Maybe Spud could make her smile more."

There went that uncomfortable shifting in Aiden's chest again—the exact place his heart had once resided.

"Do you own a cell phone?" Cassie asked him, seemingly out of the blue.

"Of course I do. I'm not a dinosaur."

"I didn't say that." She took a cell phone out of her lab coat pocket and handed it to him.

It didn't surprise him that the phone had a pink sparkly case. He would have picked that exact one for her.

"Put your number into my contacts. I'll text you updates on Spud's progress. And, George, if you have any questions or want to know how the dog is doing, your uncle can message me or you can call anytime."

"You mean I don't get to take him home?"

Cassie shook her head, and a wisp of blond hair escaped the knot at the back of her neck. It grazed her cheek, and Aiden found himself jealous of a tendril of hair.

"We're going to keep the puppy here overnight. He's very dehydrated, so I want to make sure he responds to the medicine and fluids we're giving him. You have my word that I'll take care of him as if he were my own. I know how much a dog can mean to a boy."

Aiden felt his fingers tighten on the phone and quickly

punched in his contact information, then dropped it onto the exam table.

He wasn't going to take the chance of handing it back to her and their fingers touching. Not when he could clearly remember how the last time he'd held her hand had affected him.

"Let's go, George. Other people are waiting, and your mom will be wondering where we are."

George's shoulders perked up the tiniest bit. "Do you think she'll be up from her nap?"

Aiden swallowed back a grimace. He honestly had no idea. His sister slept entirely too much. "We'll wake her for dinner if not." He turned to Cassie. "Thank you."

"I'm glad I could do something to help this time around," she said as she stood.

Aiden opened the door but, before following George through, turned back to her. "This has nothing to do with that situation years ago. It's not the same thing, and I would appreciate it if you wouldn't throw out subtle references like you think you know me. A lot has changed in twenty years."

As if she couldn't help herself, Cassie looked him up and down. "Tell me about it."

He shook his head. "I'm not going to tell you anything because after you fix this dog, we're taking it to the animal shelter, and it's going to live its happy and healthy life with somebody more equipped to raise it."

"Your nephew has bonded with that dog, and it sounds like he needs Spud as much as the puppy needs him."

"My nephew has been through more loss than a boy his age should have to manage. The last thing he needs is the potential to have his heart broken all over again. Thank you for your time and help. But I'd advise you to stay out of my family's private business after this."

She looked wounded by his words, and he knew he was a jerk for saying them. He could deal with being a jerk—it eased the pain in his chest.

"I'll remember that," she agreed slowly. "Nice to see you again, Aiden."

"No one uses the word *nice* to describe anything about me, Cassie," he said and strode forward.

"I'm not shocked," she called as he kept walking.

Chapter Two

Cassie's four-legged alarm system sounded later that night. She checked her watch—nine o'clock—and got up from where she sat on the floor of the laundry room. Spud, the puppy, remained cradled in a blanket in her arms.

The puppy lifted its head and gave a soft yip as if wanting to join in the chorus of howls and barks from Cassie's trio of motley canine companions.

"It's okay, everyone," she said, although she supposed safe was better than sorry when it came to alerting her that someone was knocking at her front door.

Baby and Bitsy didn't pay one bit of attention as they circled the thick braided rug in the house's open foyer. Clyde stood on the sofa in front of the window, his paws on the back as he let out a series of staccato barks.

"Hush," she said with more force, and all three dogs went quiet. Spud snuggled closer to her with a sigh.

She peered out the peephole, and a shiver of awareness

rippled down her spine. Cassie might've been unable to control her body's inherent reaction to Aiden Riley standing on her porch, but she only needed to remind herself of how rude he'd been earlier to confirm that she wanted nothing to do with him.

Except she wasn't the type of person to ignore a knock at the door.

He knocked again.

She opened it to find him turned in profile, staring out toward the darkness surrounding her house. He had a straight nose, a strong jaw, and the same thick, wavy hair he'd sported as a boy. He was as handsome as any man she'd ever seen and had an air of trouble that made her toes curl despite not being a woman who typically went for the bad-boy type.

"What are you doing here?" She lifted a brow. "I'm guessing this isn't a social call since you don't do niceties."

He blinked and then pointed to the bundle she carried. "That's the puppy we brought in."

Spud wriggled at the sound of Aiden's voice, which Cassie found curious since he wouldn't admit a connection with the animal.

"His name is Spud," she said.

Aiden's mouth thinned. "You brought him home. Why? Is he in that bad of shape?"

Baby and Bitsy were nosing at the backs of her knees, and she gestured Aiden forward and out of the cool September night. "You should come in because I'm not in the mood to chase my dogs through the darkness."

"I don't think this is a dog," he said as Baby greeted him enthusiastically. "It's the size of a miniature horse."

"Baby is an Irish wolfhound. He's a hundred and fifty pounds."

"Baby," Aiden repeated dubiously.

"So named because he's timid."

As if to disprove her point, the dog stuck his nose directly into the crotch of Aiden's faded jeans.

"Yeah, he seems real timid."

Cassie stifled a laugh. Most people immediately tried to pet a dog that approached to greet them. It seemed to be human nature, from her observations. Aiden stood still, although he adjusted his stance so that Baby didn't have the best access to his private parts.

He dressed like a cowboy with faded jeans that hugged his muscled legs and a denim shirt, so maybe he knew from experience how to handle a timid animal or perhaps he remained standoffish because he truly had no desire to connect.

Either way, her normally shy gentle giant was immediately smitten. Bitsy, her eleven-year-old golden retriever mix had never encountered a stranger—not for long anyway. She circled and wagged her tail and rubbed up against Aiden.

Clyde, ever the distinguished gentleman at fourteen, watched from the couch. He was a terrier mix and had been abused so badly before Cassie had adopted him that he didn't trust anyone but her.

"It's okay, Bitsy," Cassie crooned as the dog's tail-wagging velocity increased. "I know you're excited, but don't—"

"Your dog peed on me." Aiden sounded shocked. "What the hell, Cassie?"

"Lower your voice, or you'll make her more nervous." She handed him the towel with Spud wrapped inside, and he took the dog before seeming to realize what he was doing.

"I don't want to hold this thing," he protested an instant later.

"Would you rather clean up Bitsy's nervous pee?"

"That's my other option?"

"On your bed," she said firmly, and all three dogs headed for the trio of fleece-covered dog beds in the corner of the room.

She grabbed a wad of paper towels and the disinfectant spray bottle she kept on the counter. The first thing she'd look for in a house to rent was that it had tile floors. Well, the second after finding a place that would accept her menagerie.

Aiden pressed himself to the wall behind the front door as she wiped up the mess. She disposed of the paper towels, washed her hands and turned back to him. He hadn't appeared to move a muscle, still rigidly holding the puppy in his arms.

"He's not going to bite, and to answer your question, I brought Spud here for the night so I can monitor him. Things can change quickly with such a small puppy."

"Is it going to die?" The harsh tone of the demand surprised her.

"He's doing much better. If he continues improving, I think he'll be fine."

"When can he go up for adoption?" This question was also delivered with so much force she nearly backed up a step.

"It's too soon to think about that. I'm guessing his age to be around six weeks, so in theory he shouldn't be separated from his mother. We can supplement with formula. He has to gain some weight, and I want to see him eating on his own."

"You'll keep him until he's ready to be adopted?"

"I hadn't planned on it. I can help you and your sister and George care for him. It's clear the boy has bonded with the puppy."

Aiden shook his head. "It's also clear that the more quickly we find this puppy a new place to stay, the easier it will be for George to get over the loss."

"Aiden, why are you here?" she asked. She could tell he expected her to take the dog from him now that she was finished cleaning up Bitsy's accident.

Instead, Cassie took a seat on the couch, curious how he would react when she didn't step in.

"I was rude earlier when you were only doing your job."

"I wasn't *only* doing my job," she countered, tucking her legs under her. "I was helping an old friend."

"We aren't friends, Cassie. We never were. You saw me in a moment of weakness years ago. I'm not that powerless kid anymore."

He definitely wasn't powerless. She reacted to his powerful body, even covered under a thick shirt. Despite his obvious physical strength, Cassie still saw the boy who had changed her life that day so long ago. She hated that he wanted to pretend like it had never happened.

"Being vulnerable isn't a weakness," she told him. "There were stories after you and your sister left with your mom about the kind of man your father was. I don't know if they were true, but—"

"If they were awful, then they were true," Aiden interrupted.

She swallowed and forced herself to continue meeting his gaze, which had turned nearly black. "They were awful. Maybe people knew what was happening before, but they refused to acknowledge it because then they would have had to do something about it. You trying to save your dog was a catalyst for change in this community, Aiden. It was one of the strongest things I'd ever seen anyone do, and I wish I could help you understand that."

"I understand plenty," he said, but his eyes gentled slightly. "Most importantly, I understand that you gave my nephew hope today, and he needs that. I appreciate it. I shouldn't have snapped at you, and I apologize. Will you take this puppy now?"

There was a desperate note in his voice, making her smile. "I think he's comfortable with you for the moment. Have a seat."

Cassie was almost positive he would have bolted if he hadn't been holding the little bundle. Funny because he'd sought her out. He had her phone number, so he could have called or texted with an apology.

But he was here now. That meant something—at least she wanted to believe it did.

As he slowly moved forward, she noticed the slight hitch in his gait for the first time. Curiosity flooded her veins. She bit down on the inside of her cheek to keep from asking what had caused the limp.

It was too soon. She knew enough about working with injured animals to understand some things were also transferable to people. Aiden had inspired her career that day, but she had a feeling he wouldn't want to hear that, either.

"When did you return to Crimson?"

"Just after the new year," he said as he sat at the opposite side of the sectional. Clyde let out a low whine. That dog fancied himself king of the couch.

She smiled. "Me, too. I'm surprised we haven't run into each other. This town has grown so much since we were kids."

He frowned. "I haven't spent much time in town. My sister and her husband took over my father's property a couple of years ago, and then Jason died last November."

"I'm so sorry."

"It was a brain aneurysm while he was out in the field. George was the one to find him."

Cassie's heart ached for the boy.

"My sister blames herself." He blew out a breath as he looked down at the puppy, who had begun to lick Aiden's hand gently. "She blames my dad, too."

"I'd heard that your father died a few years ago."

One of the first things Cassie had checked on when she'd returned to town was whether Aiden's dad still lived there. She hadn't wanted to take a chance on running into him.

"He left the ranch to my sister, but he also left her with massive debt. She and Jason should have sold the property, but they had some far-flung idea about turning it around. Jason was out mending fences the day he died. Lila thinks that if they lived someplace not so remote, he might have gotten immediate medical attention. Maybe they could have saved him."

"That's a lot of maybes," Cassie murmured.

Aiden glanced up at that point. "I'm here because she's struggling."

"It's hard to lose someone you love."

"Are you speaking from personal experience?"

"Not with a husband—nothing like that." Did she imagine the look of relief that flashed in his dark gaze? She certainly couldn't deny the way her heart seemed to skip a beat in response.

She cleared her throat and continued, "My father died last year. My mom took it pretty hard. She's doing better now, but those first couple of months were rough. He'd been sick for so long but taking care of him was the life she knew. They were together, and then she was alone."

"She's still here in Crimson? Is she the reason you came back?"

Cassie shrugged. "Not exactly, but she was part of my motivation. The senior vet at the practice here in town, Dr. Rooney, was my mentor, and I owe him a lot. He had hip surgery and needed somebody to fill in. I wanted a change from the emergency vet clinic in Denver where I'd been working, so I agreed to sign on up here for a couple of months."

"Not permanently?"

She made a face "I think that remains to be seen. I love Dr. Rooney, but Dr. Smith isn't exactly my ideal partner. What about you?"

She doubted he realized it, but Aiden had begun to rhythmically pet Spud's little head with one finger. The dog was perfectly content in his arms.

"I retired from the rodeo last year and immediately got hired on as a ranch manager at a big operation up in Wyoming. I'm due back there…well…they wanted me back at the end of summer, but I need to get Lila on her feet again."

"So if you work on a ranch and you spent some time on the rodeo circuit—"

"A decade," he clarified.

She nodded. "Then all this business about not liking animals can't be true. You're surrounded by them."

"I never said I didn't like animals. I said I wasn't keeping any as a pet."

"What about a horse?"

"A horse is a coworker, not a pet."

"But you have a bond with a horse."

"I'm not keeping this dog, and neither is George."

"What if he could make your sister smile like George suggested? I know it's not the same thing, but when my mother was struggling, she had a close circle of friends who forced her to get involved in the community again. Because of my dad's ALS, her life had gotten really small. Much like I can imagine it did when your sister and her husband were spending all their time trying to make your family's ranch profitable again. Crimson is not the same as it was when you left, Aiden. There are people who could help your sister."

"I can take care of her, but I need you to take care of this dog." He stood up—a clear sign he was done sharing for the night. He'd told her much more than she would have imagined he'd be willing to divulge, but she wanted more. "I didn't mean to take up your evening."

"I don't mind," she said softly.

He shook his head like he was coming out of some kind of trance. Was it possible she had that sort of effect on him? He dumped the puppy into her lap, taking pains to ensure they didn't touch. Interesting.

"I'll let George know that Sp…that the puppy will likely be okay. It'll help him sleep better tonight."

"Did you end up talking to the parents of the boy he mentioned?"

"Not yet, but I will."

Cassie didn't doubt it. "Bring George to the clinic after school tomorrow. I can give him some time with Spud, and then we can talk about next steps. Your sister is welcome as well."

Aiden ran a hand through his hair as a muscle ticked in his jaw. "I don't think she'll leave the ranch. She hasn't gone anywhere for months."

Cassie didn't like that one bit. "What time does George get done with school?"

"Three o'clock. The bus usually drops him off at the house by three thirty. I'll feed him a snack, and we'll plan to arrive around four, if that works for you? I think the sooner we can explain to him that he is not keeping that dog, the better."

"Yeah, you've mentioned that," Cassie said, charmed despite herself at his mention of a snack for George. Aiden Riley did not seem like the type of man to prioritize snacking. Despite his gruff exterior, Cassie was convinced Aiden was a good guy. She also knew his nephew needed the puppy just like Spud needed somebody to love him best of all.

"We'll see you tomorrow, Cassie." He took another step toward the door.

"Good night, Aiden."

Chapter Three

Aiden returned from his ride at three the following afternoon to see an unfamiliar white Jeep parked in the driveway.

He took his horse, Storm, to the barn, unsaddled and brushed him down and then strode toward the main house. As far as he knew, his sister didn't have friends in town—at least not any she'd stayed close to since Jason's death. He certainly hadn't reconnected with anyone he'd known as a child, except Cassie.

She remained a puzzle he couldn't quite piece together, mainly because his body and heart reacted to her in equal measure. It was silly.

She was a vet, and the puppy was her patient. She likely would have taken just as much of an interest in any animal brought to her in such grave shape.

He knew better than to think it meant something, but due to Lila's ongoing struggles, he often felt like he was on his own trying to make things okay for George.

And he might've been the least equipped man on the planet to help raise a gentle young boy. Cassie's concern made him feel not so alone, and Aiden had been alone for so long.

He wanted to get rid of whoever was at the house before George came home so they could get to the vet clinic. Aiden was also anxious to check in on the little canine and had to admit he'd started thinking of the puppy as Spud. Maybe whoever adopted the dog would keep that name.

He walked to the back of the house and entered through the kitchen door, apparently bursting in with more force than was necessary. His sister startled and dropped the glass of water raised to her mouth.

The glass didn't break but spilled on the table, sending liquid everywhere. Aiden was just as shocked when the guest who hurried to the paper towel roll on the counter turned out to be Cassie.

"That was unnecessary," Lila said. She also stood. "You made me make a mess."

"Water is easy enough to wipe up." Cassie offered Lila a bright smile. "Last night, Aiden literally scared the pee out of one of my dogs. That takes disinfectant to fix."

Lila pulled her sweater more closely around herself. "You ended up at Cassie's when you went for a drive?"

"Yeah," he agreed, not meeting his sister's suddenly assessing gaze. "I stopped by to check on the puppy."

"You didn't mention that part," Lila told him.

Well, he wasn't a complete idiot.

"That's why I'm here," Cassie said with a smile. "I thought your sister would like to meet Spud."

Aiden heard a high-pitched bark from a metal enclosure he hadn't previously noticed that was set up on the far side of the kitchen. It was like the puppy was responding to hearing the name, damn the little guy.

Lila's smile went soft. "It's the perfect name for him."

"I've already told George he can't keep a dog," Aiden assured his sister, earning a scowl from Cassie that looked almost comical on her angelically beautiful face.

"Why would you say that?" Lila asked, sounding legitimately puzzled.

"Li, you know I'm not staying here for good. A dog is a lot of responsibility."

"So is being a parent, Aiden," she countered, "but I've managed that for the past eight years."

He opened his mouth to respond, then closed it again.

Lila drew a harsh breath and shook her head before turning to Cassie. "I've had some issues with depression since my husband died," she revealed. "Aiden worries about me, and not without reason. But I can handle a dog if you think it would be good for George."

"I think learning responsibility by helping to take care of a pet benefits most kids," Cassie said.

"He can help me with Storm," Aiden said, earning arch looks from both women when the words came out as a growl.

"My son is afraid of horses," Lila told Cassie.

"He was very good with Spud. George has a big heart and a lot of love to give."

Lila bit down on her lower lip. "He takes after his father."

Aiden felt his chest tighten as Cassie placed a hand over his sister's. How was she so inherently empathetic?

"I don't want to force you to make a decision you're uncomfortable with, but I think George would love making Spud a permanent part of the family."

"No," Aiden repeated, feeling his control slipping away.

Just then, the front door opened and George ran in. "I need to eat my snack quickly so we can see…"

He stopped short at the sight of the puppy in the enclosure. Spud was wriggling like crazy. "You're here," George whispered, and the smile on his face stretched from ear to ear.

Aiden glanced toward his sister, who was gazing at her son like she'd just woken up from a long sleep. She was like that fairy-tale princess who pricked her finger on the spindle.

Lila was a real-life version of Sleeping Beauty.

He wasn't sure he'd even realized how bad off his sister was until he saw a glimpse of the woman she'd been before she'd lost the love of her life.

There was nothing he could say to change the fact that they were keeping the puppy. But it didn't make him happy because Lila's depression had been a weight on his shoulders since he'd returned to their hometown.

He knew better than to believe her issues would be overcome by one sweet moment with a stray dog.

It confirmed what life had taught him: Love could break a person, and the pain would never be worth the risk. Not for him. Cassie dabbed at the corners of her eyes as she watched the puppy and the boy interact.

The little guy certainly was a charmer, and even Aiden had to admit that. Lila opened up the door to the enclosure and lowered herself to the ground next to George.

She smiled as the puppy clambered up onto her lap.

"Can we keep him, Mommy?"

Lila didn't hesitate for a second. "Yes, we can keep him."

Cassie hadn't meant to manipulate Aiden or his sister into agreeing to keep Spud. By the way Aiden scowled at her from across the room, she could tell that was his opinion. But today's visit been more about her desire to meet his sister than anything else.

She vaguely remembered a girl who'd been several years ahead of them in school. Lila would have been at the middle school when Cassie had first come to Crimson.

Aiden's sister was a beauty, although she looked too pale and her shapeless sweatshirt seemed to hang on her thin frame.

"If you need more time to think about it, that's okay," Cassie said. "A dog is a big responsibility and a many-year commitment."

George's feathery brows furrowed as he studied his mother. "If it's too much, we don't have to keep Spud. I know Doc Cassie will make sure he finds a good home."

That kid was truly one in a million. Cassie's gaze flicked to Aiden, who rubbed a hand over his jaw like he was trying to absorb a punch.

"I'm up for the challenge if you are, sweetheart." Lila reached out to push a stray lock of hair from his forehead.

"You bet I am." George scooted over to his mother and threw his arms around her neck. "I'll do almost all the work, I promise. And I'll train him, and he's gonna be the best dog."

Lila hugged him tight and then peeled his arms away from her. "You're my best little man." Her voice cracked on the last word.

The dog had curled into a ball on her lap, and she lifted him off and handed him to George. "This is more excitement than I've had in a while. I'm pretty tired all of a sudden. I think I'll go take a little rest."

"Take all the time you need," Aiden said, and Cassie had never imagined that his voice could take on that gentle of a tone.

George watched his mother with a look of concern,

and then his attention was captured again by the puppy. "So he gets to stay here from now on?" the boy asked.

Cassie watched Lila quickly hurry up the stairs and didn't think she imagined the sheen of tears that stained the woman's cheeks.

"I'd like to keep him one more night," she told the boy. "Just to make sure everything is good."

"Sure," George agreed. He bent down and kissed the top of the dog's furry head. "That will give me and Uncle Aiden time to get the stuff we need." His honey eyes widened. "Will you help me, Uncle Aiden?"

"Yeah, bud," Aiden said. "I'll help you."

"I should be getting back to the clinic," Cassie said, checking her watch. She moved the crate she'd brought closer to George. "Do you want to put Spud in here for me and carry him to the back of my car?"

George's eyes lit up at the request. "You bet."

"You can keep this enclosure," she told Aiden. "At least until you can order one of your own. I'm not sure they'll stock anything similar at the local pet store."

"I'll find one or I'll build one. I don't need anything from you. You've done plenty."

Her stomach knotted painfully at this censure in his voice. "I can help with whatever Lila and George need."

"So now you're staying in Crimson permanently?"

"Nothing is definite. Definitely for the next couple of months."

"You're supposed to be a vet, Cassie, not a puppy pimp."

"That's not what I was doing," she argued.

"You didn't think my sister would have caved when she saw how George feels about that dog? You can't deny that."

"I truly believe Spud will help."

"Help send Lila crying to her room when the emotions overwhelm her."

"She was also engaged for a few minutes. That has to count for something."

His jaw worked, and she knew he wanted to deny her words. Instead, he smiled as George came forward with the carrier balanced in his arms.

"Uncle Aiden, can you get the front door? I don't want to drop Spud. I'm gonna be real careful with him, Doc Cassie. You'll see."

"I believe you, George." She met Aiden's gaze over the boy's head. "I believe in both of you."

He rolled his eyes and opened the door for George. "It looks like we'll be heading to town for puppy supplies before dinner."

"This is the best day ever," George said as Cassie followed him into the afternoon sun.

Cassie's stomach felt like a tight ball of conflict by the time she walked into the clinic's back door twenty minutes later. She'd just gotten Spud placed in his kennel when Bryan Smith popped his head out of his office door.

"Cassie, there you are. We need to talk."

"Can it wait a few minutes?" she asked, bristling at his tone. She didn't need another man getting in her face this afternoon.

"It can't. Martin is here, and we'd both like to speak to you, *Cassie*."

"Okay, *Bryan*." She put the same emphasis on his first name as he had on hers. When she'd first started filling in for Dr. Rooney, she'd joked about how strange it felt to call Dr. Smith by his first name. He'd looked down his nose and told her she was welcome to call him *Doctor* if that made her more comfortable.

It would have made it more comfortable if she had never interacted with him, but that wasn't possible. At least there was the silver lining of seeing her mentor, who she would always think of as Dr. Rooney no matter how many times he besieged her to use his first name.

As she entered the small office, he turned in the chair where he sat across from Bryan Smith's desk office and offered her a wide smile. When Cassie had been younger, Dr. Rooney had seemed bigger than life, a bear of a man with wide shoulders, hands the size of catcher's mitts and a thick mop of dark hair that had been perpetually falling into his eyes. That hair had turned salt and pepper now, and he didn't seem so Paul Bunyan–like in stature.

"How are you feeling, Doc?"

"I think I'm starting to drive Wendy crazy," he admitted, although Cassie couldn't imagine his sweet-tempered wife irritated about anything.

"I'm driving myself there as well, if I'm being honest. I'm not used to all this rest."

She smiled. "It's good for you, both mind and body."

"Let's get down to business," Bryan said, perching his reading glasses on the edge of his nose. "We've had some complaints about you, Cassie. I'm concerned that you aren't a good fit for this practice."

"I don't understand," she said as she tried to catch her breath from the shock of his words. She and Bryan hadn't become close during her time at the practice, but she'd believed there was a mutual level of respect between them. She'd assumed her future was secure.

"This isn't working."

"It is," she protested, then shifted to face Dr. Rooney. "Everyone I've met has been so nice. My patients—I mean, their owners—seem to genuinely appreciate the time I take with them. This doesn't make sense, Dr. Rooney. I promise I—"

"Did you cancel your appointments for this afternoon without approval?" Bryan asked.

Cassie felt like an irritated parent was scolding her. She swallowed and worked to regain her composure. "I rescheduled two appointments and wasn't aware I needed approval."

"We're professionals here. We don't get to go gallivanting around in the middle of the afternoon."

"Bryan." Dr. Rooney's voice was strained. "Is that necessary?"

"I wasn't gallivanting," Cassie told the two men. "A very sick puppy was brought into the clinic yesterday. He markedly improved overnight, so I took him to see the boy who'd rescued him."

"During work hours," Bryan reminded her. "Without permission."

She sat up straighter. This whole exchange felt ridiculous and reminded her why she did not like Dr. Smith and never had. "I am a professional, taking good care of Dr. Rooney's patients in his absence."

"You can't get personally involved."

The words felt like a pointed criticism. It was the same complaint her boss at the emergency hospital in Denver had made. Part of the reason she'd agreed to take on this interim role, even though she wasn't guaranteed a full-time position upon her mentor's return, was that she'd needed a change from the hustle and grind of being a vet in the big city.

She knew Dr. Rooney cared deeply about his patients. When she'd volunteered at the clinic as a girl and later worked there in her teens, she'd seen that with every creature he'd cared for. She'd wanted to do the same.

"I give everything I have to my patients."

"It's not professional," Dr. Smith told her. "You need some distance. I was told you treated an animal who did not have an appointment yesterday and regular patients were waiting."

"A puppy that was in bad shape. I made a judgment call, and anyone with half a brain and a sliver of heart would understand why."

"Okay, now." Dr. Rooney held up his hands. "We're on the same team here—let's remember that."

Cassie didn't feel like she was part of a team. She felt like she'd been shoved off an island with little more than a raggedy piece of driftwood to keep her afloat.

The truth was she loved working at the practice in Crimson and reconnecting with people in her hometown. The schedule was booked constantly, and she'd had every reason to believe that this temporary position would become permanent.

She hadn't mentioned her hope for that to anyone— not even her mother. But Cassie wanted to stay.

She wanted a home, and Crimson could be that for her.

But not if Bryan Smith ruined everything, just like he'd ruined things for Aiden years earlier.

There was no way to say this delicately, but she had a feeling he was coming after her because she was good at her job and he felt threatened. Since she'd been at the practice, she'd treated several animals who Bryan had previously misdiagnosed.

Cassie knew she was a good vet, and she recognized an incompetent one.

"Bryan, it was my choice to bring Cassie in while I recover, and I've heard only positive feedback about her."

"You're not hearing everything," the other man griped. "She can't just leave in the middle of the day."

"She can if appointments are rescheduled. She's allowed to have a life."

Only she didn't have much of a life at this point, which didn't matter. She loved devoting herself to her work, and as angry as she was at the unfounded accusations, they also hurt her.

First Aiden had accused her of manipulating his sister and her emotions, and now Dr. Smith had the audacity to suggest she was too involved.

Wasn't she supposed to care and try to do what was best for her patients? Why did the people around her insist having a big heart was a weakness?

She wouldn't know how to function without taking care of people. That was what she'd always done from a young age—first her mother and father, and then channeling her deep need to care for people and animals into her work. How could she turn off her desire to help?

Who would she be without it?

No one, unfortunately. Without giving everything, Cassie feared she was no one.

Chapter Four

"That's the most ridiculous thing I've ever heard. He had no right to say that to you."

"The people around here love you, Cassie."

"The next time Bryan Smith comes into the diner, I'm going to give him a piece of my mind."

Three days later, Cassie was smiling at the trio of middle-aged women who gazed up at her from the cozy arrangement of chairs in the back room of the bookstore her mom owned in town, A Likely Story. Her mother had a date with her beloved book club twice a month. At Melissa's request, Cassie had driven into town on her day off to visit with the ladies.

It was better than wallowing in the self-pity and doubt that pinged around her brain like sparring partners taking shots at each other.

In addition to her mother, there was Helen Tallien, who owned the diner in town—famous for their breakfast skillets and giant sandwiches served with homemade coleslaw and fries, and Genevieve Gott, the longtime secretary at the local high school.

She'd told her mom on the phone earlier about the conversation with the older vet, trying to sound casual about it so Melissa Raebourn wouldn't be upset on Cassie's behalf.

Her mom still seemed fragile after losing her husband last year. He'd beaten the odds to live for nearly fifteen years after his ALS diagnosis, the motor neuron disease progressing more slowly in him than was typical. But the end had been hard and messy and had taken a toll on her mother, his primary and devoted caregiver.

Cassie owed a huge debt to the women who surrounded Melissa now. They'd been the ones to help Cassie pull her mother from the depression that had seemed to engulf her like a wave after Tom Raebourn's death.

Did Lila have any friends to help her navigate the dark waters of her grief, or was the entire responsibility of support left on Aiden's strong shoulders?

"I'm sure it will all work out," Cassie told the women. "Dr. Rooney defended me."

"He should have replaced Bryan years ago." Helen, the eldest of the group in her late sixties, sniffed with disdain. "Dr. Smith had the audacity to tell me I was overfeeding Kitty." Helen's ragdoll cat was enormous, so Cassie couldn't fault Bryan for his advice.

"What's so wrong with overfeeding?" Genevieve asked with a laugh, then plucked one of the salted-caramel cookies Helen had brought for the group today off the tray on the coffee table in the reading nook. Melissa's freezer was still stuffed with meals Helen had delivered to her in the weeks after the funeral. Food was the diner owner's love language without a doubt.

"I do think the new food regimen is helping Kitty,"

Cassie said. She'd been shocked at the size of Helen's beloved cat the first time she'd seen the animal. Weighing in at nearly eighteen pounds, Kitty was a solid piece of work.

"I give *you* credit," Helen answered. "Not Dr. Smith. You explained the stress the extra weight takes on her joints and organs. I want Kitty to live a long, healthy life."

"You're inspiring her in other areas, too," Melissa added. "Helen has added a lighter menu to the diner's regular offerings."

"Who knew kale was so popular?" Helen looked generally perplexed.

Cassie laughed. "You make kale taste good, and that's no easy feat."

"And you have a way with animals beyond your book-smart knowledge," her mother said, her smile gentle. "Your father was so proud of you, Cass."

"God rest his soul," Genevieve said. "Now imagine how happy it will make Tom out there in the great beyond when Cassie signs on full time here in Crimson. Then we can find her a man."

Cassie immediately shook her head. "Yes to staying in town. No thank you to the man. I'm not interested in finding a man."

"Then a nice woman, maybe?" Helen asked. "My niece is—"

"I'm not interested in love in any form," Cassie interrupted quickly. She'd honestly never had a serious boyfriend, as supporting her parents through her father's illness had taken so much of her emotional energy. Sometimes she felt lonely or wished for a relationship, but she wasn't ready to make someone else a priority when she'd just started learning how to take care of herself. "I'm focused on me for the foreseeable future."

"You just need to find the right person," her mother counseled. "When I met your father, sparks danced in the air." The chimes above the front door rang, and she moved forward to greet her customers.

"Welcome in," she called, then looked over her shoulder at her friends and Cassie. "Even I'm feeling sparks at the moment." She made a show of fanning herself as she walked forward. "And I don't think it's a hot flash this time."

Cassie turned and felt her face immediately heat as she made eye contact with Aiden Riley, who had followed his sister into the bookstore.

His dark eyes flashed, and she felt the spark of awareness between them. Nope. Definitely not sparks, Cassie told herself, willing her body to believe the lie.

Lila glanced around in apparent wonder and tucked a lock of hair behind one ear. She wore loose jeans and a fuzzy pink sweater, her dark hair pulled into a clip on the back of her head. Although she was still pale, there seemed to be a bit more color to her cheeks.

"What can I help you find today?" Melissa asked as she approached the two of them. "We have some great new mysteries and a couple of romances I'd recommend if that's more your speed."

"No romance," Aiden said before his sister could answer. At least he and Cassie could agree on that.

Lila continued to take in the floor-to-ceiling shelves of colorful books as well as the other aspects that made the shop special. It wasn't a huge space, but her mother had added cozy touches, including upholstered sofas and chairs in quiet reading nooks and a children's area that invited investigation and play with beanbag chairs and several train tables. Lila's gaze finally landed on Cassie, and she waved and smiled.

"Hi, Lila. It's great to see you."

"Dr. Cassie, you're exactly the person we need right now."

Aiden's jaw went rigid. He apparently disagreed.

"How can I help?" Cassie asked without hesitation. Her mom had returned to her friends, and the three older women spoke in low voices behind her. She had the feeling they were discussing her and Aiden.

She hadn't mentioned him by name to her mother and hoped that Melissa didn't connect the dots of their shared past. Her mom certainly understood how upset Cassie had been as a child about the events the day Aiden's dog had died at the vet's office.

That had nothing to do with now, she reminded herself. He'd made that abundantly clear.

She focused her attention on his sister and ignored how her skin pricked as if she could feel him watching her.

"I'm not sure I'll be as much help as my mom, but fire away."

Lila bestowed a gentle smile on the bookstore owner. "I used to bring my son in here for story time before… well…when we first moved to Crimson."

Melissa stepped forward again. "I remember you. Your son is into dinosaurs, right?" She tapped a finger on her chin. "I seem to recall that he liked the herbivores the best, particularly stegosaurus."

"Wow, that's impressive." Lila seemed to relax. "I'll bring him back some weekend. He's the reason why I'm here. I thought I could pick up a book on puppy training to read with him."

"That's a great idea," Cassie said. "How are things going with Spud?" She'd dropped off the puppy two days ago, noticing that Aiden was conspicuously absent. The disappointment that had stabbed through her hadn't set well.

"Last night, he chewed a hole in my favorite pair of socks," Aiden said gruffly.

"You have a favorite pair of *socks*?"

He looked slightly abashed. "They're wool. Wool socks aren't cheap."

Lila rolled her eyes. "Ignore my brother. He wouldn't have a thing to say if he couldn't complain about something."

"That's not true. I didn't complain when you agreed to crate-train the dog. At least that's one step in the right direction."

"Spud is doing well," Lila shared as if he hadn't interrupted. "He's good company for me when Aiden's working and George is at school. He makes the house seem not so lonely."

"Be careful," Melissa said with a laugh, "or you'll end up like Cassie with multiple dogs and no real social life to speak of other than scooping poop."

"I have a social life." Cassie's cheeks burned as she noticed Aiden's quick grin out of the corner of her eye.

"I'm okay without a social life at this point." Lila reached out and squeezed Cassie's hand. "I appreciate you helping us with Spud. He's a good addition to our little family."

Take that, Aiden, Cassie wanted to say. Lila definitely seemed happier at the moment. It counted for something.

"There are a couple of puppy-training books I'd recommend. Mom, do you know if you have Marcia Brenner's book on training in stock?"

"I believe I do." Melissa seemed to be studying Lila. "Why don't you join me in the nonfiction section, and we'll see what we can find?"

Lila nodded, then glanced over her shoulder to Aiden.

"I'll be okay here if you have errands. You don't need to babysit me anymore, little brother."

He rubbed the back of his neck. "I'm not babysitting. We're hanging out, having fun, bonding and stuff."

Lila nodded. "And stuff. Got it. Do me a favor, Aiden, and bond someplace else for a few minutes. I'm going to get lost in this bookstore."

Cassie stifled a giggle at Aiden's shocked expression as his sister disappeared into the narrow aisle behind her mother.

"Bitter apple spray will deter Spud from chewing," she offered. "They stock it at the pet store."

"That'll be my third visit in as many days. The lady behind the counter will think I'm casing the place. I keep thinking I've got everything we need, and something else turns up."

"That's the way of puppies," Cassie told him with a shrug. "They're worth it."

"Babies are worth it, too, Cassie," her mother called. "Even more than dogs."

"Oh, my God," Cassie murmured under her breath.

"And you know good hips run in our family."

"Mom, are you joking right now?"

"Maybe a little," Melissa admitted as she peeked around the corner of a row of shelves, and Cassie laughed. She knew her mom was ready to be a grandma, even if Cassie wasn't ready to settle down at thirty-one. The thought that her mother would be extolling her virtues to Aiden Riley was hilarious in a weird sort of way. A man like him wouldn't be interested in a woman like Cassie.

"Would you like to walk with me to the pet store?" Aiden asked, surprising her with the request. One corner of his mouth tilted upward. "You could make sure I've got everything Lila and George need. That might save me another trip into town."

Cassie could feel Helen and Genevieve watching her. "At this point, I'd be happy to. Goodbye, ladies. Behave." She threw her mother's friends an arch look and then called, "I'll be back, Mother."

"Take your time. Love you, Cassie."

"Love you too, Mom." She shrugged when Aiden's smile widened as they walked out the shop's front door. "You can love a person even when they are sitting on your last nerve. Birthing hips," she muttered. "How humiliating."

"I thought it was funny," Aiden said as he led Cassie down the sidewalk. "You and your mom are cute together."

He didn't have much experience with joking with his mom. Even after she'd left Crimson with him and Lila, her relationship with his father had left a weight on her shoulders. Aiden knew she loved her children, but she'd been serious and watchful, ever on guard for any possibility of a new or familiar threat to her children.

"That was not funny," Cassie countered, unaware of the somber turn of his thoughts. "Only somebody with a warped sense of humor would find it so."

He inclined his head. "I take that as a compliment."

"I bet you do."

Several people said hello to Cassie as they walked down the busy sidewalk. She offered a sunny smile to every person—strangers or people she greeted by name.

"Are you sure you moved back recently?" he asked. "You seem very popular for being new in town."

"Occupational hazard. Regular people with regular senses of humor bond with their pets—and, by default, with the veterinarian who cares for them. I've seen many of Dr. Rooney's patients at this point and a few clients new to the practice."

"You must be doing a good job."

"I guess that depends on who you ask." Her tone had taken on an oddly sour tone.

"What does that mean?" Aiden was genuinely curious. How could anyone not like Cassie?

"Dr. Smith told me I'm too personally involved. He called Dr. Rooney in for a meeting to discuss how I'm not a good fit for their practice."

"Bull," Aiden said simply. "The other guy doesn't believe him, right?"

"I don't think so, but I thought you might agree given the Spud situation."

"Do you know the last time my sister went anywhere alone?"

Cassie shook her head. "No, but I'm guessing it's been a while."

"Too long. I came back here because George called and told me how bad things had gotten. He acted the same as when he spoke about taking care of the dog—like he was fine but just worried about his mother. Maybe that was true. Kids learn to make do in tough situations, and I know my sister loves that boy very much. She got lost in her grief and couldn't find a way out of it."

Cassie touched his arm—light as a feather, but the contact reverberated through him. "He called, and you immediately came."

He lifted a shoulder. "Of course I did. I didn't have a choice."

"People always have choices. It sounds to me like you made a selfless one."

"Don't try to pin me as some kind of hero, Cassie. That label won't fit no matter how much you want it to."

"I'm not calling you hero," she clarified. "But I do think you're a good brother and uncle. And if you've been to the pet store three times in as many days, then you're also a good puppy owner."

"I'm not Spud's owner, but George doesn't leave me a lot of choice. He loves that little thing already."

"A boy and his dog," she whispered. "Imagine that."

He expected to feel the pain that reminded him of Sam, but it didn't come today. He followed her into the pet store, and Aiden marveled at the way the customers swarmed Cassie like she was an animal-whisperer rock star.

It reminded him of some of the young guys he'd known after he'd been established on the rodeo circuit, the way they'd followed him through the barn at the end of the show, peppering him with questions about rodeo work and how to handle the buckle bunnies.

He'd done his best to advise the green cowboys, but Aiden had never had much interest in groupies. He'd dated a few women over the years—mostly women only looking for mutual pleasure. Never anyone who'd expected more of him.

Not when he understood that he had so little to give.

Cassie helped him pick out a few toys, a bag of training treats and the chewing-deterrent spray, and it surprised him that he didn't want the excursion to end. They were headed back across the street in the wide crosswalk when a car came roaring around a corner, swerving wildly. The driver was either distracted or under the influence.

Aiden didn't know which, and frankly, he didn't care. He yanked Cassie onto the sidewalk, tripping over the curb as he stumbled back. Her delicate curves plastered against him as they went down together.

He tried to catch his breath as his bad leg took the brunt of the fall.

"That guy was a maniac," he said through gritted teeth, then heard the squeal of brakes and a howl of pain, followed by a crash.

Cassie was out of his arms in a second, running toward the car that had crashed into a telephone pole. He followed, trying to ignore the pain shooting up his thigh.

As onlookers surrounded the car, a man climbed out, shouting and slurring incoherently.

"Call the police chief," someone in the crowd shouted. "Brett Barnard is driving drunk again."

"I swear I'm gonna throw his keys off the top of the peak," another person said.

Aiden stopped short, suddenly besieged by a memory from his childhood. His father prying the keys from his mother's hands after one of their fights brought on by his drinking and forcing Aiden and Lila into the car despite their mother begging him not to.

His father had sped along the narrow two-lane highway leading to the top of Crimson Mountain in their old Bronco, and it was the first time Aiden had understood his own mortality. He'd thought he was going to die at that moment, and something in him had shifted by the time they'd made it home.

For a moment, he hadn't cared about going over the side. He'd wanted his sister to survive, of course, but he'd been willing to sacrifice himself if it meant removing his father from their mother's life.

But now he didn't feel so self-sacrificing. He was pissed as hell at Brett Barnard, even though he didn't know the man. If it hadn't been for reflexes honed from years of dealing with unbroken horses, the man might have clipped Cassie. He might have killed an innocent woman, one Aiden cared about despite not wanting to.

"Aiden, I need you." Cassie's desperate tone broke through his dark thoughts. He turned and realized what that unearthly howl had been.

She was on the ground next to a scruffy animal, its fur brown and tan—the same coloring as Sam. This animal was larger than the dog he'd loved and lost.

"That idiot hit her," she said, blue eyes flashing as she glanced over her shoulder at the driver currently being corralled by the crowd. "Her leg is broken, and she could have internal injuries. I can't tell, but I've got to get her into the clinic. Can you stay with her while I get my car?"

"I'm parked a half a block away. I'll drive so you can sit in the back with her." The way Aiden had sat in the back with his dog when his neighbor had driven him to the clinic.

She nodded and turned her attention to the animal again. He sprinted toward his truck, the pain in his leg forgotten for the moment. What was happening to his life?

He'd spent over ten years working on ranching operations and the rodeo circuit and managed not to get personally involved in any sort of canine emergency. A return to Crimson, and he was up to his eyeballs in animals needing help.

He did *not* want to be the go-to dog rescuer—except he couldn't imagine letting Cassie deal with any of this on her own.

By the time he pulled alongside where she was crouched down next to the dog, two police vehicles with flashing lights had cordoned off that section of Main Street.

A smaller crowd of lookie-loos surrounded her.

"Get out of the way," he yelled, his tone forceful. "We need to get this dog to the clinic."

Cassie looked up at him as he made his way to her, and he wanted to take back those words about not being a hero right now. He wanted to dig deep and be her hero—foolish as it would be for either of them.

They loaded the collarless dog, still shivering, into the large back seat of the truck, and Cassie climbed in behind her. She quickly called the clinic and fired off instructions for what she would need upon arrival.

Then she dialed her mother, explained the situation and asked the woman to make sure Lila got home. His heart pinched knowing that amid all the craziness and confusion, she had the wherewithal to think about his sister.

They didn't speak on the short ride to Animal Ark, but his throat clogged with emotion listening to the gentle words Cassie murmured to the injured dog.

She instructed Aiden to pull around to the far side of the brick building, and she was out of the truck before he'd even come to a complete stop. He hopped out and then lifted the dog, which had to weigh at least eighty pounds, into his arms. Tears stung his eyes as the animal gave one soft lick to the back of his hand.

"Are you going to be able to save her?" he asked as he followed Cassie into the building.

"I don't know." Her voice was tight with uncertainty.

"We're ready for you, Dr. Raebourn," a woman said from outside the door of one of the rooms in the hall.

Cassie nodded. "Aiden, please put the dog on the exam table, and we'll get to work."

He didn't want to release the dog. When he'd let go of Sam, his beloved pet had died, but he knew Cassie would do everything she could to save this dog.

"Have you contacted the owner?" Dr. Smith demanded as he barged into the room. He was older and balder than he'd been two decades earlier, but his voice was just as grating and his demeanor spiteful. "Do we even know if it has an owner who is going to pay this bill? Cassie, you can't always—"

"I'm going to pay for it," Aiden said, taking a step closer. An intimidating step, which Dr. Smith understood by the way he stumbled back.

"I don't care how much it costs," Aiden continued. "I'll sign off on any guarantee you need. If this dog can be saved, you'll let Dr. Raebourn save it. She's going to try—unlike you did when I brought my dog here all those years ago."

The man was startled, and everyone went quiet.

Cassie gently touched Aiden's arm. "Thank you for that and for your help, Aiden. I'll call you when this girl is out of surgery."

He had a feeling Dr. Smith remembered him because the man scurried out of the room like the weasel Aiden believed him to be.

"I know you can do this, Cassie. I believe in you."

He regretted the words as soon as they left his mouth. They sounded stupid and sappy. Cassie knew she was a capable vet and didn't need his lame words of encouragement.

"Thank you," she said, squeezing his arm. "That means more coming from you. I'm going to do everything I can for her."

She released him, and he backed out of the room. He'd been so sure his heart was frozen forever, if he had one at all. Even his sister's sorrow hadn't managed to melt it. But Cassie had definitely been touched by the sun because she made his chest heat with an unfamiliar emotion—hope.

Chapter Five

Cassie woke with a start when her phone pinged. She rubbed her eyes as she glanced at the text that had just appeared on the device. It was nearly eleven at night, so she had no idea who would reach out so late and was surprised to see Aiden's name on her screen.

I see the light on in the clinic. Are you awake?

She glanced around, momentarily disoriented.

Yes.

She looked at the dog sleeping on the blankets she'd placed in the corner of her tiny office.

I'm awake.

She didn't bother to mention he'd woken her up. How did he know she was here?

Those three dots appeared on her screen a second after she'd hit Send.

I'm at the back door.

Cassie swallowed around her surprise. She stood slowly, not wanting to disturb Rosie, the name she'd affectionately given the injured dog. Despite Cassie posting on several of the town's social media pages a few hours earlier, Rosie hadn't been claimed.

She'd slipped off her shoes at some point, and she wiped the sleeve of her fleece pullover against her mouth. The clinic was typically quiet at this time of night. As she padded to the door, a few low whines and a soft yip sounded from the main kennel area where the overnight patients stayed.

Aiden stood on the other side wearing a CU Buffs sweatshirt, faded jeans and sneakers. The evening was cool and crisp with the distinct scent of fall in the air, but Cassie's body flooded with warmth as he offered a tentative smile.

"What are you doing here?" she demanded, off balance for a myriad of reasons. His grin topped the list.

"You said you were going to text me an update."

She blinked and looked past his shoulder, unable to hold his gaze. "Luckily there was no internal bleeding, and her heart and lungs were fine. But she had irreparable trauma to her back leg—the crash crushed too many bones. I couldn't save it."

He nodded. "My sister talked to your mom. She also said that you were spending the night here."

"I didn't want to leave the dog alone. We haven't

MICHELLE MAJOR 63

found her owner." She still couldn't figure out why he was standing before her.

As if he understood her silent question, he nodded. "I thought you could use some company." He held up a brown paper bag. "And I brought you snacks. Chocolate chip cookies."

"Did you bake for me?"

"I feel like I should say yes because that makes me seem like a better guy than I am. My sister and George made cookies. I watched and then did cleanup duty."

"It's nice of you to bring them." She reached for the bag, her fingers brushing his. "You gave up your night for me."

"Don't give me more credit for a social life than I deserve. Besides, you look like you've been run over by a truck, no pun intended."

"Wow. I've heard that cowboys were charmers, but you're exceptional with the compliments." She ran a hand through her hair as she turned and led him into the clinic, feeling self-conscious after his comment. She'd cared for Rosie for hours, and the surgery had been the most emotional she'd ever performed.

It hadn't been helped by the fact that Bryan had popped his head in several times to remind her that she was using precious resources to save an animal they didn't know.

"Maybe someone with more experience or talent could have saved her leg." She opened up the door to the office to reveal the dog sleeping in the soft light of the lamp that sat on the edge of Cassie's desk. "I tried so hard." She choked back a sob on the last word and covered her face with her hands when tears filled her eyes.

"Don't mind me," she said, her voice muffled. "I'm just tired, and I get too involved. There's no denying it."

She wasn't sure what response she expected from

Aiden but being pulled into a tender embrace with his big hand circling her back was not it. Yet it was exactly what she needed, although embarrassingly, his holding her didn't lessen her emotions.

His strength seemed to give them free rein, and she cried as quietly as she could manage against his sweat-shirt for a minute before drawing in a shaky breath and glancing up at him.

His jaw was steely, but his brown eyes remained gentle. "It's okay to care," he said.

"That's interesting coming from you."

"It's okay for *you* to care."

"I see how that works."

"I see, too, Cassie. I see that you are kind and generous and talented. You make a difference in people's lives." He smoothed back her hair, and his gaze intensified.

Was he going to kiss her right here in the office when she was pretty certain she smelled like sweat and anti-septic soap? Did she want him to?

Yes, she did. Despite everything, there was no denying it. Her breath hitched, and that one movement seemed enough to jar him back to reality.

"Are you worried about the dog surviving the night the way you were with Spud?"

"No. Rosie's going to be fine despite losing her leg. There were no other critical injuries."

"Rosie? How do you know—"

"I don't. I'm calling her that for now because she seems like a Rosie to me. It's silly."

"You're not silly, Cass. I once knew a three-legged dog. He belonged to one of the old guys on the rodeo circuit. He'd been trampled as a puppy, but that didn't seem to slow him down."

"That's what I wish for this sweet girl, along with hoping she has a loving family who comes to find her."

"What will happen to her if no one claims her?"

Cassie didn't think she mistook the concern in Aiden's tone.

"I'll reach out to a couple of rescues in the area. I know one in Denver that works specifically with tripod dogs."

"Tripods," Aiden repeated.

"Three-legged dogs."

As if hearing them talk about her, the dog woke, shifting on the cushion as her spindly tail wagged.

"I'm going to sit down with her again," Cassie said. "She needs the company. Don't feel like you have to stay."

"I don't feel like I have to do anything. I want to stay."

Cassie sensed something different in him tonight. There was a change she couldn't explain, but she wouldn't deny it sent her heart racing.

"I'll hang out with her for a while." Aiden moved toward the cushion where Cassie had been sitting earlier. "Do you want to head home and check in on your dogs? I can stay."

"My mom went over to feed them and let them out. She's going to go back early in the morning. But I wouldn't mind a potty break."

"Take all the time you need."

Cassie ducked into the bathroom at the end of the hall. She hadn't even thought about looking at herself in the mirror until Aiden had arrived.

When she did, she wished she hadn't. Her hair was matted to her head on one side and her ponytail sagged. There were mascara smudges under her eyes, although that might have been a blessing. Without that, the shadows under her eyes would have been more pronounced.

It didn't matter. She wasn't trying to impress Aiden.

She'd saved an animal's life today, which was what counted. She washed her face and brushed her teeth with travel-sized toiletries she kept in the clinic's bathroom.

When she returned to the office, Aiden looked utterly relaxed on the floor with the dog. Rosie had shifted toward him, and he cradled her head in his lap, stroking her soft fur.

"I don't think this dog has had an easy life," he said, glancing up at Cassie.

She frowned and lowered herself into the chair behind her desk. "She's a little underweight but nothing concerning."

"It's not about her physical appearance." Aiden returned his attention to the dog. "There's something in her eyes. She's been through stuff." Cassie swallowed down her response to his assessment. "Hopefully this is her chance for a better future."

"If her owners don't show up, I'll take her."

"Are you joking? Because that's not funny, Aiden."

He looked up sharply. "You don't think I can handle it?"

"I think you can handle anything you set your mind to doing. I'm surprised. You've been adamant that you will not bond with any animal. Your sister adopted a puppy, so she'll need your help still. It's a lot to take on."

"Your mom hired my sister to work in the bookstore."

"Really?" Cassie knew her mother had been looking for someone to help so Melissa could reduce her hours.

He nodded. "Her friends had left by the time you called, so Lila stuck around to help. They got to talking about losing people, and your mom offered her a job."

It was just like Cassie's mom to connect with Lila over their shared experience. It did Cassie's heart good to know her mom was genuinely recovering from the loss of her husband enough to support someone else who was grieving. "That's great, isn't it?"

Aiden seemed at a loss for words, his thick brows furrowed as he sighed.

"What's wrong?"

"Nothing. It's just that I would never have expected it. My sister has been lost. For her to agree to take a job— it's the best thing I can imagine. She's made herself a prisoner on that ranch as if she thought she owed that to Jason. As if she was held captive by our father's ghost. She believes the horrible things he did and the awful man he was somehow cursed her family."

"That simply isn't true," Cassie said quietly.

"I know, but she won't move on because her husband wanted the land. Now maybe she'll look at other options."

"Would you consider buying the property?"

His gaze went cold. "I'm not the settling-down type."

The hair on the back of her neck stood on end. She was disconcerted by the intensity of her reaction to his stare. "And what does my mom giving your sister a job have to do with Rosie?"

"I believe in paying my debts, and I think I owe this dog. If I hadn't needed to drive you to the clinic, maybe my sister and your mom wouldn't have started talking. Maybe—"

"You don't agree to adopt a dog out of some warped sense of payback," she told him, standing when the dog lifted her head to sniff the air. "She's going to have a long recovery. She needs somebody who can commit for her whole life. Are you willing to do that?"

He frowned, and she knew he was taking her question seriously. "I can if you'll help. Will you help me? I want to do the right thing. I'm trying the best way I know how."

Cassie walked over, bent down to check the dog's bandage and took Aiden's hand.

She got too involved, but this was the reason why. By getting involved, she could help people. It was why she did this work. The fact that the older vet wanted to push her out of a practice that already felt like home was a slap in the face.

But she would deal with that when she had to. Here was the glimpse of Aiden she'd almost given up hope of seeing again. Memories of the shy, sweet boy she'd once known pinged around her head.

"I'll help you," she told him. If she could do nothing else, she would make this right.

"I'm not getting involved," Aiden told his sister later that week. "There is no chance of me helping with any kind of fall festival. Also, your puppy is eating a dinosaur." He pointed to Spud, who had tugged one of George's old plastic toys out of the big wooden box and was happily chewing on the T. rex's leg like it was a juicy bone.

"We think he's teething," Lila said and popped up from the table. "Here, Spudsy, let me give you something better."

"Spudsy?" Aiden repeated as his sister grabbed a hard plastic ball with a hole in the center from the freezer.

She handed it to the dog, who gladly dropped the dinosaur and began licking the new toy like it was a doggie Popsicle.

Lila grinned at Aiden. "Cassie gave me the idea to stuff the toy with peanut butter and then freeze it because it'll keep Spud engaged longer. I also ordered fabric to sew him a Halloween costume. We're going to have him go as a french fry. Get it? Spud as a french fry. George will be a hamburger."

Aiden chuckled in amazement. "Who are you, and what have you done with my sister?"

She sniffed. "It's not that strange. I make a costume every year for George. I've always loved Halloween, and now I'm working in a bookstore, which is a dream come true. I love reading, too, unlike some people I know." She lifted a brow in his direction.

"I know I should read more. There are plenty of healthier habits I should be adopting." Aiden held up his hands. "I'm glad you're making these changes, Li. It's just such a radical switch from how things have been. I don't want you to overdo it and—"

"Spiral back into my black hole of depression?"

Aiden cringed. "I didn't say that, but yes."

"I also called the therapist my doctor recommended after Jason died," Lila said quietly, her eyes brimming with tears that made his heart stutter. "I'm still grieving and broken hearted." She swiped at her cheeks.

"I'm sorry. I didn't mean to make you cry."

"It's okay. Crying is better than the alternative of feeling nothing. I talked to Cassie's mom about emotions and how to feel them without drowning. That's been my biggest fear."

"Drowning in grief?" Aiden swallowed.

He'd known things were bad but hadn't realized how bad. Maybe he'd ignored the signs, just like he had with his father. Pretending things weren't as terrible as they were because that was easier.

Or at least it had been until that day when he'd lost Sam.

"Did you ever feel like you couldn't go on? Did you ever consider…" He couldn't bring himself to say the words for something so traumatic and final.

She shook her head. "I wouldn't do that to George. Without him, I'm not sure what would have happened."

"Don't say that."

"Part of me healing is not running from the truth anymore, Aiden. When I met Jason, I made him my whole life."

"You were his as well."

She flashed the barest hint of a smile. "He wanted to work the land, and when Dad died and left me this property, I thought that was the answer. I convinced myself it would be okay."

"Stop. We've been over this. You couldn't have known what would happen."

"I should have." She leaned forward. "Bad things happen to me at this place, Aiden. Coming back here…all of the memories…it was a lot. I wish that I had told Jason I didn't want it. We should have sold the property and given you half the profit. Not that there would have been much, thanks to Dad's second mortgage. It would have taken decades to crawl out from under that, adding to the pressure we both felt."

"Dad left this place to you. I don't want anything from it."

"Me neither, if I'm being honest," she said and wiped at her cheeks again. "But it was Jason's dream. I feel like I'll be letting him down if I let it go, but—"

"You have to do what's right for you and George. Jason would want that."

She sat across from him, tapping her fingers on the table before meeting his gaze again. "You could buy it from me and work it yourself."

"I don't want it, Lila. I'm not staying in Crimson. We've talked about this."

"Why? It was our home. It's a great town. I want you to be a part of George's life."

"I will be. I can visit."

"What about Cassie Raebourn?"

Aiden bristled. "What about Cassie?"

"You're adopting a dog from her."

"If no one claims Rosie, I said I'd step in. That dog is the reason her mother gave you a job. I owe that dog."

"I owe that dog *and* you." Lila smiled. "Plus Cassie and her mom. Melissa helped me see that getting through my grief doesn't mean I'll forget Jason."

"Of course not."

Lila inclined her head. "Just like letting go of the past and allowing yourself to get close to Cassie doesn't mean you're going to be hurt by her. Not everyone who you love will hurt you, Aiden."

"I don't think that. You never hurt me."

"It's not the same thing." She gave him her best big-sister stare. He hadn't seen that look of *I know better than you* in so long, and he'd missed it. "You're adopting a dog of your own, and you were against keeping Spud. I feel like that means something."

"Even geniuses like me make mistakes. I see now Spud is good for you and George. Adopting Rosie would be about making something right. I wouldn't wish that injury on any animal, but without it, who knows if you would have talked to Cassie's mom?"

"It also doesn't hurt that Cassie will be caring for the dog during her recovery. Lots of quality time between the two of you."

That wasn't why he'd made the offer, of course, but he wasn't going to complain about an excuse to see more of Cassie. Rosie was going to need to spend plenty of time at the clinic, and Cassie had already committed to helping with Rosie's transition to Aiden however she could.

"Can we stop talking about this?"

"Only if we can start talking about you helping with the Harvest Festival. The dog and romance talk distracted me."

"Seriously, Lila. No romance and no festival volunteering. I already told you—"

"I can't do this without you, Aiden," she said in a rush of breath. "I feel like I've just woken up from a grief trance. I understand that I need to do better for myself and George. But it's not easy."

She held out her hands and studied her thin arms. "I feel like people can still see through me to the sorrow in my heart. You make me feel safe. I know that nothing bad is going to happen when you're around. You'll keep me safe."

"There were plenty of times I failed at that, and we both know it."

"You were a kid. Kids aren't supposed to protect everyone around them."

His gut tightened with regret and anger at their shared past. "Maybe not." When the puppy trotted over, he reached down to scratch between Spud's floppy ears. "But there was no one else. How can you expect me to pitch in with something that benefits this town when no one did a thing for us?"

Lila shrugged. "Times were different then."

"Not so different."

"We're different people now. Older, wiser. I want to be happy again, Aiden. I'm not sure how to accomplish that. Right now, it's a fake-it-until-I-make-it kind of deal. My heart is telling me that trying to become a bigger part of this community is the next step. At least it will help George. Don't make me do this alone."

A growl rose in his throat, but he swallowed it down. Lila might've believed he shouldn't have been expected to save them from their father's temper, but Aiden still wished he'd been able to.

How could he say no to her now?

"A puppy, a three-legged dog and now a fall festival?" He mock shivered. "If I'm not careful, you're going to ruin my reputation."

"Maybe that's my ultimate goal."

He shook his head. "Don't set yourself up for failure, Li. I'm bound to disappoint you." He held up a hand when she would have protested. "But tell me what you need for the Harvest Festival, and I'll make it happen."

"Thank you." She stood again, scooping up Spud and leaning in to drop a kiss onto Aiden's cheek before holding the puppy up to his face for a few wet dog kisses. "You won't regret this."

He made a noncommittal noise in response, fairly certain he already did.

Chapter Six

The following Saturday morning, Cassie walked into her mother's shop downtown, only to come up short at the sight of Aiden reaching for a book on a high shelf.

George and a girl who looked to be the same age stood on either side of him, clearly waiting in anticipation.

"Crocodiles are so cool," George said in a reverent whisper as Aiden handed him the glossy photo book. "They're like modern dinosaurs."

"Did you know that birds are actual descendants of dinosaurs?" The girl leaned around Aiden, her focus on George. "But reptiles look more like them. This is my favorite book because it gives so many facts and pictures. I thought you'd like it."

She was a tall, lanky kid with two straight braids and round glasses perched on her nose. Aiden stared down at the two children like he was being faced with prehistoric creatures that he had no idea how to handle.

"Why don't you take the book to a table or something?"

Aiden suggested. "Your mom and I are going to some dumb meeting at the community center, so you need to stay out of the way until we get back."

"I won't be any trouble," George answered. "Allie, you want to look through it with me?"

"Sure." The girl shrugged like it made no difference to her. "My mom is in the romance section. Who knows how long she's going to be?"

The kids tromped off and walked under the rainbow arch leading to the children's section.

Cassie had helped paint the colors when she'd been in college, which was when her mother had bought the old building and taken over the bookstore. The shop had been a staple in the town for decades but had seen better days. Melissa's love for books and appreciation for readers was contagious. The fact that Crimson continued to grow in popularity thanks to the ritzier mountain towns around Colorado becoming more expensive to live in or visit didn't hurt.

She turned back to Aiden with a smile only to see him looking…well, the only word to describe it was *terrified*.

"What happened to you? Do you have a secret fear of crocodiles?"

"That girl said her mother was in the romance section," he said in a hushed tone like he expected a Jane Austen heroine to accost him at any moment.

"Don't tell me you're a book snob." She wagged a finger in his direction. "I have to admit it took me a while to get on the romance train, but my mom convinced me to try it. You know romance books sell more than any other genre. Cowboys are a whole deal in romance. Mom does a big display every year when the rodeo comes to town."

"I am not a snob when it comes to people's reading preferences," he said then glanced toward the back of the store. "I couldn't care less what somebody reads. That girl's mother is one of my sister's single friends, and she's in the romance section."

Cassie barked out a laugh. "So you think she's going to get inspired and pin you against a bookshelf? You fill out a pair of blue jeans nicely, but don't you think you might be overestimating your charms a bit?"

He held up a hand. "First, let's remember that your mother outright announced how fertile you were the last time we were here."

She grimaced. "Okay, good point."

"Right." A teasing glint crackled in his dark eyes. "But tell me more about liking how I fill out my jeans."

"I didn't say I like it." Cassie felt her face color. "I just said you fill them out. That's not an opinion. It's fact. But I don't think it's fair for you to assume a woman has designs on you just because she's single and reads romance."

"That's not what I'm doing. My sister has told me she wants me to meet her friend. Lila has some wild idea that I should stay in Crimson."

"Would that be so horrible?"

"It's not part of the plan."

"Plans can change."

He stared at her a long moment, almost as if he were deciding whether she'd be worth a change of plans. "I'm not staying in Crimson, Cassie. There's nothing for me in this town."

Ouch.

Okay, maybe she'd thought they were growing closer than was actually the case.

Aiden had come to the clinic every day since Rosie had had surgery. The dog was healing well, and she seemed to accept without question that Aiden was her person.

Dogs were a wonder that way. Cassie had warned him

not to get too attached since the local Humane Society required a ten-day hold on strays before an animal could be officially adopted.

Cassie had managed to fast-track the process for Rosie, convincing the shelter director to begin the countdown on the date of Rosie's injury and surgery. Rosie would stay at the clinic or with Cassie to avoid having to spend any time at the shelter. They did a good job with the animals in their care, but Rosie needed more attention.

The dog followed Aiden around the fenced-in yard in back of the clinic, hopping on her back leg, tail constantly wagging. Cassie timed her breaks so that she was typically available when Aiden stopped by.

They talked about Rosie's rehab and Aiden's work for a local rancher. Conversation flowed easily between them, and she didn't think she imagined the way his maple syrup-colored eyes gentled when he looked at her or the flashes of desire she sometimes saw there before he schooled his features.

Now she wondered if she had. Not that she thought of herself as a reason for him to stay in town. Heck, she still wasn't certain if Dr. Rooney would convince Bryan Smith to bring her on as a partner. But it was hard not to hope. Cassie might not have had much of a social life, but her imagination more than made up for it.

"I still think you're making too much of it," she said with a sniff. "You aren't that appealing."

He moved closer to her, one side of his mouth curving like she'd just thrown out a double-dog dare. "Is that so?"

Their eyes caught and held, and it felt as though a million butterflies took flight in Cassie's stomach.

"Hey, Cassie," Lila said, and Cassie took a quick step back, needing to remove herself from Aiden's gravitational pull. She never lost her head, especially over a man, so being so affected by one who'd told her he wasn't interested was particularly embarrassing.

"Hi, Lila." Cassie tried not to blush. "I thought we could walk over to the community center together."

"Great. I've convinced Aiden to help, too. He might just enjoy it."

"Doubtful," Aiden muttered.

Cassie breathed past the shock and admiration that filled her at how dedicated Aiden was to his sister. She could only imagine how it would feel to be on the receiving end of that type of devotion.

Lila gestured to the woman next to her. "Do you know Charlotte Bryant? Her daughter, Allie, is George's best friend at school."

The curvy redhead stuck out a hand, and Cassie shook it, noticing that the woman darted a surreptitious glance at Aiden. "It's nice to meet you."

"You, too," Cassie said, suddenly conscious of her very average figure. She'd never thought much about her lack of curves but felt decidedly plain in the face of Charlotte's fair-skinned complexion, big doe eyes and glossy lips.

Even worse, the woman's smile seemed genuinely kind. "Lila told me you saved the dog her brother is adopting."

"Yes, Rosie is a sweet girl." Cassie smiled, but it felt brittle as Charlotte turned her attention to Aiden.

"It's really heroic of you to step up for an animal in need." She squeezed Lila's arm. "Two animals, since you also helped ensure Spud got the care he needed."

"It was nothing," Aiden said. "Just doing the right thing."

"Spoken like a true hero," Charlotte told him.

Where was his denial now?

He wasn't putting up a fight with this woman, and Cassie hated to admit that it hurt her feelings.

"We should head over," she said, hoping she didn't sound as irritated as she felt, even though she could feel Aiden's dark gaze boring into her.

"Are you sure you don't mind taking George back to your house?" Lila asked her friend. "Melissa said he's welcome to stay here since she's sending me to the festival-planning meeting."

"Allie will love it," Charlotte said with a beaming smile. "I'm making roast chicken for dinner. Why don't you plan on coming by to get him and stay for a meal?" She glanced at Aiden and dipped her chin. "You're welcome to come over as well."

"Thanks, but I can't," he said without hesitation.

Lila blinked. "Why can't you?"

"I have plans. A date. We need to go."

Cassie tried not to appear as shocked as she felt.

"We really need to go," Aiden repeated.

"A date is nice." Charlotte didn't look like she thought it was nice.

"Why don't I know about you dating someone?" Lila asked with a frown. "Who is your date with?"

"It's with Cassie."

Cassie made a sound that might have been a gasp, a grunt or a groan because, right on cue, her mother appeared from the aisle across from them.

"I knew there was something between you two."

"It's got nothing to do with her hips," Aiden said, and Cassie sputtered out a laugh.

Her mother looked confused. "Okay, then."

Melissa must not have remembered her comment about birthing hips running in their family. But Aiden had, and now Lila and her friend were both staring at the area below Cassie's waist. She tugged on the fleece vest she wore.

"My hips are nothing to speak of. Nothing to see here," she nearly shouted. "I'm going to go to the meeting. You can join me if you want."

She walked out the door and headed down the street, her face and heart blazing equally.

"I'm sorry. I didn't mean to out the two of you," Lila said as she caught up, linking her arm with Cassie's. "I'm glad y'all are finally admitting what the rest of us already see."

Cassie felt Aiden behind them but refused to turn around and look. "Like I said, there is literally nothing to see."

"You guys have a connection. There's no denying it."

"I have a connection with all of my clients, four-legged and their two-legged people. Aiden is adopting Rosie."

"And now y'all are going on a date. Where are you taking her?" Lila asked over her shoulder.

"Italian," he said without hesitation. "It's her favorite."

Cassie's face flamed even hotter because he was right. Italian was her favorite, but how did he know?

"I don't want anyone to know about this," she said to Lila. Why didn't she reveal that Aiden had been making up the whole thing to put off the romance-loving single mom in the bookstore? "I've already been accused of getting too involved with my patients, which might be frowned upon."

"That's stupid," Aiden said from directly behind her shoulder.

"But the truth," she responded through gritted teeth.

"I get it," Lila agreed. "I won't say anything, and I'll tell Charlotte not to, either. She doesn't have pets, so most likely she's not going to talk to anybody who knows you. I'm sure your mom won't say anything."

"My mom." Cassie groaned. This situation was way beyond what she could deal with right now.

They'd gotten to the community center, and her breath started to hitch like she was having a panic attack.

"I need to return a quick phone call. I'll meet you guys inside," she said and hurried over to the far side of the building without waiting for an answer.

She placed her back against the cool brick and focused on breathing in and out. How foolish to be affected by Aiden's lie. He'd needed a quick out to avoid a potentially awkward situation with his sister's friend.

He and Cassie were friends of a sort. She'd been his excuse.

Nothing more.

Except she wanted more.

And she didn't think she'd be able to engage in a fake-dating relationship with Aiden and come out the other side with her heart—or pride—intact.

She would simply have to tell him they couldn't do this, and he'd have to admit the lie to his sister. And Cassie's mom. And anyone else who happened to hear about it.

That was the part that had her practically hyperventilating. The thought of public humiliation because most people—her mom included—would probably easily believe the whole thing had been a ruse.

Aiden and Cassie would not be a match in anyone's mind.

Only in Cassie's secret fantasies.

She let the cold from the bricks seep into her bones, standing there alone until she felt in control again. After the conversation with Bryan Smith and Dr. Rooney, her focus needed to be on her job and the partner position, not the distraction of Aiden Riley.

Why did he have to complicate her life at every turn? she wondered as she headed into the community center. Things had been a lot simpler before him. There was a lesson in that fact, one that she would do well to heed.

Chapter Seven

Aiden moved closer to where Cassie stood at the back of the meeting. He still wasn't sure how he'd gotten into this predicament, somehow going from an uncomplicated post-rodeo retirement life to not only being back in the town he said he'd never return to but joining a planning meeting for a festival he'd rather stick a fork in his eye than attend.

Okay, maybe that was overstating it. But he certainly hadn't planned to get so involved or to use a date with Cassie as an excuse to get him out of a potential setup.

He should have just said no. He'd made a habit of saying no to plenty of requests but had somehow turned into a pushover in the past few weeks. So much for his reputation as a hard-nosed, rough-and-ready cowboy.

"We need to talk," he whispered as he came to stand behind Cassie.

She had positioned herself on the opposite of the room

to Lila and him, which he knew was on purpose. The meeting wasn't that crowded.

"I'm listening to what the people are saying," she said, her lips barely moving.

"Colorful leaves, bales of hay and pumpkin decorations. That's the gist. I didn't mean to say we were going on a date. It was a mistake."

"A mistake," she repeated, her voice devoid of emotion. "Of course it was a mistake, but I appreciate hearing you admit it."

"You don't sound appreciative."

"I guess cowboys don't understand sarcasm."

He rubbed the back of his neck. "We do. I'm just surprised to hear it from you. You're not a sarcastic person, Cassie. You're sunny, not sarcastic."

"That shows how well you know me." She glanced over her shoulder and leveled him with a glare. "Not well at all."

But he felt like he did know her. She was a grown-up version of the amazing girl who'd given him a brief glimpse of hope when she'd stepped in to be his champion at his lowest moment. Only now he felt like he knew her even better. He spent almost every afternoon at the clinic exercising Rosie, who was becoming increasingly comfortable getting around on three legs.

The staff had become familiar enough with him that he could come and go in the back as he wanted, at least when Dr. Smith wasn't around. Because of that, he got to see Cassie in action—how she took time with her patients and their humans. She remembered details of a person's life or how a skittish dog liked to be scratched behind the ears.

She made every patient feel like they were the most important in her life.

Not to compare himself to a dog, but she made Aiden feel unique and valued, which was probably why he'd blurted out what he had about the two of them having a date.

If things were different—if he were different—that was what he would want. Although Aiden didn't consider himself an expert with emotions, he knew that his declaration had hurt her somehow.

He didn't like that. He didn't want that.

He'd learned his lesson about wanting things he couldn't have a long time ago, but being around Cassie made him want to change the future. She made him want a lot of things he wasn't willing to name.

"What do you think, Aiden? Are you willing to take it on?"

He blinked and quickly glanced around to see everyone in the meeting staring at him. The woman at the podium in the front of the room—he thought her name was Olivia—studied him, clearly waiting for a response. If only he knew what his answer should be.

His scalp began to itch as heat crept up his neck. Cassie was glaring at him even harder now. His sister watched him from the other side of the room with a look that could only be described as pleading.

How was he supposed to admit he had no idea what the question had been?

"I'm up for it," he agreed with a nod.

Cassie sucked in a harsh breath.

"That's perfect." Olivia clapped her hands and smiled broadly. "I think we've gotten a lot accomplished today. You all have your assignments, and I'll email out a recap. The next step will be for committees to get together. We've got a month to go. I know we can make this the best Harvest Festival Crimson has ever seen."

As the meeting adjourned, several people patted him on the back as they walked by.

"What were you thinking?" Cassie demanded, turning to him.

He opened his mouth and tried to find a way to answer that wouldn't make her think he was a bigger idiot than she already did.

Too late, he realized because her mouth dropped open before she snapped it shut. "You don't even know what you volunteered for, do you?"

He shrugged and tried to will away the sudden nerves blooming in his chest. Aiden Riley didn't do nerves, not even when he climbed onto the back of a horse intent on bucking him off.

"I assume it's to build something. I'm handy. I can handle a few power tools."

"Can you handle being in charge of the barn dance that's the culminating event of the festival weekend? It's the biggest moneymaker for the town's community center. I agreed to help because Dr. Rooney's wife usually oversees it and is busy taking care of him. Olivia was trying to lessen my workload by finding a cochair. Your sister threw out your name, and you weren't paying attention."

He blew out a breath and tried not to cringe.

"I knew you'd agree to volunteer since you and Cassie are dating," Lila said as she approached.

Several people glanced toward them, and Cassie quickly shook her head. "We're not really… It isn't…"

"Remember that Cassie wants to keep things under wraps," Aiden told his sister.

"Right," Lila agreed, cringing slightly. "Sorry. I won't say another word. But I'm happy you're helping, Aiden."

"You know I love a good dance."

His sister laughed, and Aiden couldn't regret the lie because her amusement was so good to hear. It had been so long since she'd seemed this content. He hadn't been certain he would ever see her this way again.

"I understand," she said with a wistful smile. "Jason and I kept things quiet when we got together."

She turned to Cassie. "It was my first year at Mesa over in Grand Junction. Jason was a junior and played football, but he'd just broken up with his high school girlfriend. When we met, he wasn't in the market for love, and I didn't believe in it. Some things are just destiny."

"This isn't the same." Cassie shook her head. "Aiden said we were having dinner because—"

"I miss him," Lila said, her dark eyes turning misty.

Cassie darted Aiden a look that clearly said, *Fix this*, but before he could respond, Lila rolled her shoulders and flicked a hand across her cheeks.

"I'm grateful for the memories," she continued, "and I'm learning to be grateful that our time together brought us back here. He would be happy to see me again in the world. He'd want me to be happy. Thank you both for reminding me of that."

Once again, Aiden was reminded that everything he was going through and whatever he had to endure—even if it meant being in charge of some ridiculous dance—was worth it. There was no price too high to pay for his sister's healing. He hoped Cassie would understand.

"Aidan said you're doing Italian for dinner. Does that mean Basil?" Lila asked as she fell in step with Cassie, who'd started for the door.

Aiden knew Cassie probably didn't want company, at least his, but he kept up with the two of them.

Cassie shook her head. "We're not—"

"We're going to Basil," he interrupted. "I haven't been

to the new ski resort since I've been back, but the restaurant is supposed to be nice."

"That's a perfect choice," Lila agreed. "It's romantic. Jason and I got a babysitter for George and went there last year on our anniversary."

"I wasn't aware you kept up with the town hotspots," Cassie said to him, her voice distinctly cool.

"Now you know I do," he said.

Lila gave the two of them a funny look. They certainly didn't sound like two people who were newly dating, but he hoped his sister would blame that on his well-known propensity for grumpiness. She wouldn't like knowing he'd made up the whole thing.

"Don't stay out too late," she said, wagging her finger with a laugh.

Cassie's spine went even more rigid if that were possible. He should come clean, but he didn't want to—only partially because it would disappoint Lila, who seemed so thrilled that he'd made a love connection.

He liked the idea of dinner with Cassie. Maybe he wouldn't call it in official date, but they were friends. She couldn't deny that, could she? He sure hoped not.

"My car is this way," Cassie said, placing a hand on Lila's arm. "Thanks for taking the lead in the bookstore's festival participation. It's a lot of work for my mom, and I know she's happy to move some of it off her plate."

"Your mom has helped me more than I can say." Lila leaned in and hugged Cassie. "I owe you, too, Cassie. Spud makes our house feel happy again. Aiden and I both owe you."

"Don't forget I'm adopting a dog, too," he added. "I'm contributing."

Lila released Cassie and patted his cheek. "Don't be fooled into thinking Rosie needs you more than you need her. This is definitely a situation where that dog is rescuing you."

He didn't know what his sister meant by that.

"I don't need to be rescued," he grumbled, then realized Cassie was walking away.

He excused himself from Lila and hurried after her. "I'll call and see what time Basil has available for reservations tonight. Will seven work for you?"

Cassie whirled on him. "What are you talking about, Aiden? None of this works for me. You saw how happy your sister was, and I had to lie to her. You've made me into a liar."

He shook his head. "You didn't confirm or deny anything."

"It's a lie of omission. That's still a lie."

"You're reading too much into this. If you think about it like—"

"Oh, no. You aren't going to mansplain me right now."

"I don't know what that means."

"You don't have to. You're still doing it."

He had the strangest urge to smile at the consternation on her face. It was like being reprimanded by a kitten. Cassie was adorable in a temper, although he knew she wouldn't appreciate that observation. Truly, he hadn't meant to make her angry.

"Come on, I owe you, and now if we don't go, Lila will think something is wrong."

"Something *is* wrong," Cassie said, holding up her hands. "We're not dating."

"But we're friends."

"Are we? I'm not sure a friend would lie about his relationship with me."

He didn't like the note of sadness that had crept into her sweet tone. "You're right. I shouldn't have said that."

"And you shouldn't have agreed to cochair the barn dance."

"I'm a hard worker," he told her. "I'll pull my weight. We can discuss plans for the dance tonight. A working dinner. It won't be awful, I promise. I'm not in your league, Cassie, but we can have fun together."

She opened her mouth, then closed it again like she didn't know how to respond. What had he said now to make things awkward between them?

There was no doubt he was messing this up big time. Dating had been easier on the rodeo circuit, where the women had just thrown themselves at him. They hadn't even cared if he'd spoken as long as he'd looped an arm around their shoulders in front of their friends.

"I know I screwed up. I'm sorry. I would never hurt you on purpose, although I suppose that doesn't count for much when I managed to do it not on purpose." He took her hands in his, surprised at how soft yet cold her skin felt, especially when he associated her so much with the sun.

"Please have dinner with me. Not because I made some public declaration but—"

"Why, Aiden? Why do you even care?" She yanked her hands out of his grasp. They'd reached her car, and she hit the fob to unlock it.

"Because you're important to me," he said, which was as much as he'd allow himself to admit. "I'll talk to my sister and tell her the truth tomorrow. Just be with me tonight."

She turned away from him for a moment, which he didn't like because he couldn't read in her sweet eyes what she was thinking and he desperately wanted to know.

He didn't push her to answer or say anything that would

be construed as mansplaining, which he did understand if he was being totally honest.

She glanced toward the peak of Crimson Mountain like she was searching for an answer from the snow-capped peak.

"Okay," she said finally, turning back to him, color high on her cheeks. "But just so we're clear, I'm going to order an appetizer and the most expensive entree they have on the menu and a dessert."

A little bit of sparkle had returned to her blue eyes. He didn't realize how much he'd missed that shimmer until it was gone.

"Two desserts," he told her with a wink.

She rolled her eyes. "No need to go overboard."

He had a feeling there was a need where Cassie was concerned. Something in the way she'd reacted to his recklessness in the dating comments made him think that she hadn't had an easy time regarding love and relationships.

He didn't like that thought.

She was kind and beautiful and perfect. Aiden didn't know what sort of white-picket-fence fantasies Cassie harbored, but she deserved every one of them to come true.

Chapter Eight

"Don't be nervous. There's no reason to be nervous."

Bitsy whined and nudged Cassie's knee as she stood in front of the full-length mirror hanging from her closet door.

"I'm talking to both of us," Cassie said as she patted the dog's head. "You don't need to pee on him, and I'm not going to fool myself into believing this night means something. It's not a real date."

Baby trotted into the room and gave a series of sharp barks, which felt like a dog version of a lecture.

"Don't act that way." Cassie wagged a finger at the bossy Irish wolfhound. "He feels guilty because he put me in a bad position. That's all this is."

She glanced at her reflection again. "Stop talking to the dogs," she commanded the woman in the mirror. "You aren't Dr. Doolittle."

She needed friends—ones who were her age. Since she'd been back in Crimson, most of her time had been spent working or taking care of her mom, which often involved being an honorary member of Melissa's close-knit group of friends.

Cassie felt older than her thirty-one years. She suddenly realized she looked older in the schoolmarmish, boxy sweater she'd chosen to go with her denim skirt and ankle-high western boots.

Without giving herself time to second-guess the decision, she yanked it off and grabbed the scoop-neck silk blouse in a deep burgundy color that lay discarded on her bed. She'd initially tried it on, then deemed it too suggestive. Now she shoved her hands and arms through.

It didn't matter what clothes she wore. Aiden thought of her as a friend. For her part, she could be covered by a potato sack and imagined most people would still be able to read the yearning in her gaze when she looked at him. She doubted anyone would guess it went beyond something purely physical.

He was an attractive enough man to garner attention from just about every woman he encountered. She glanced at the mirror again. Color had risen to her cheeks, and the new blouse revealed a bit of cleavage, humble as it might be.

Maybe this was too much. Perhaps the whole outfit made it look like she was trying too hard. The doorbell rang, and both Bitsy and Baby rushed to greet the visitor. With a final finger comb through her hair, Cassie followed.

"The welcome committee is out in full force," Aiden said when she opened the door. The ends of his hair were still damp, his jaw freshly shaved.

It bolstered her confidence slightly that he'd made an effort, but it still didn't mean anything, she reminded herself silently. Then he glanced up from greeting the two dogs who demanded his attention, and her breath caught in her throat.

His eyes widened and lowered to the scooped neckline of her shirt before quickly lifting again.

Maybe she had made the right decision with her outfit. She commanded Bitsy and Baby to their dog beds. "I just need to grab my purse," she told Aiden, turning away.

"You look beautiful, Cassie."

"Thank you." She glanced over her shoulder at him. "You, too. I mean, not beautiful. You look handsome. And clean."

"I showered."

Bitsy gave her a woeful look as Aiden grinned. The dog had managed to keep control of her bladder, but Cassie hadn't been able to rein in her nervous blabbing.

"Me, too," she blurted, then turned and hurried to the hook near the garage where her purse hung.

Aiden moved toward the couch to greet Clyde. Her little man was the shyest of the three dogs but moved closer to sniff Aiden's outstretched hand, then gave it one dignified lick.

"That basically means you're now his best friend. Clyde has no problem ignoring people he doesn't like, and he doesn't like many people. My mom has never been able to win him over. He senses that she wants it too much."

"I'm honored," Aiden told the dog. "I can appreciate being discerning. Nothing against your mom, of course. She's great and has made a huge difference in my sister's life in a matter of days."

"It goes both ways." Cassie smoothed a hand over her skirt. "Maybe it's my mom you should be taking to dinner. She's the one you want to thank for helping Lila."

He gave Clyde a final ear scratch and then stood, his

expression almost comical. "I don't want to take your mom to dinner."

She let out a nervous laugh. "I didn't mean it like you'd be interested in her romantically. I know this isn't a date."

"Two people shower and put on nice clothes. One of them looks beautiful, and the other is clean." He tapped one long finger against the tip of his chin. "It seems like a date to me."

Cassie's stomach swooped and dipped like she was on an amusement park ride. The tenor of his voice made goose bumps rise along her skin, and his maple-colored eyes had gone bittersweet-chocolate dark.

Perhaps this was more of a date than she'd let herself believe.

Cue more nerves.

They walked out of her house, and she locked the door behind her. Aiden opened the passenger door, placing a hand on her waist as she climbed in. His touch felt like a flame licking her body, and the air in the truck's cab felt charged with a heavy awareness.

They were both quiet as he drove toward the other side of town and up the mountain road leading to the ski resort.

"Do you ski?" she asked, and her voice sounded strangely loud in the silence between them.

"No." He shook his head. "We didn't have the money for it when we lived here. Once Lila, my mom and I moved to Phoenix, there wasn't much opportunity for cold-weather sports."

"Your mom is still there?" She realized they'd never discussed the topic despite spending plenty of time together.

"Yep. It took a while for her to feel like she was safe, but now it's her home. She has a job she loves at the front desk of a local day spa and a boyfriend who treats her well. She's happy, which she deserves, given what she went through with my dad."

"Did he ever try to contact her or you and your sister once you left?"

He shook his head. "It didn't surprise me he wouldn't put forth that much effort, but Mom spent years looking over her shoulder. I think she knew it would be bad if he ever came to find us. She made us keep a backpack ready to go in the closet. That thing sat there until I was a freshman in high school."

"What a scary way to live." It didn't surprise her that he would try to play it off.

"It was better than our life here," he told her. "Living with the potential for violence is an improvement over living with an abuser any day."

"I'm sorry that was your reality." Cassie looked out the window. This town had felt like home even when she'd moved a couple of hours away. Crimson was a safe place for her.

She hated that it hadn't been for Aiden. "I'm sorry you had to go so far away to escape your father. It's not fair. I can see why this town doesn't mean the same thing to you as it does to me."

He shrugged, and she wanted to reach out and try to take some of the tension from his broad shoulders.

"My sister adores Crimson, even if it was Jason who wanted to take over the ranch. I think she'll stay no matter what she decides to do with the land."

"But you won't." An unexpected ache bloomed in her chest at the thought.

"I'm not one for putting down roots. That's why I acclimated to life on the rodeo circuit so easily. Drifting is second nature to me. Certain aspects of a solitary life suit my personality."

She didn't agree with that. It might've suited the man he'd forced himself to be, but that wasn't who he was at his core. He related to people too well to be a loner. "Now you'll have Rosie," she reminded him.

"Have dog, will travel," he replied, pulling into the parking lot of the ski resort complex. "That's the nature of being a cowboy for hire. I think Rosie will adapt."

"Sure she will," Cassie agreed, tamping down her disappointment. Was it so wrong to want Aiden to want to stay in Crimson? She knew his sister would agree.

"Somebody has dumped a ton of money into this place," he said as they got out of the car. "Aspen, look out. Crimson is coming for you."

Cassie laughed and took in the renovated chalet that was the center of the complex as well as the additional buildings that had been added in the past couple of years.

They'd been fashioned after a quaint alpine village with burnished wood exteriors, wide sloping roofs and overhanging eaves. Trees and native grasses grew around the structures, while planter boxes filled with fall flowers lined the walkways.

"I can't quite imagine our little town with an influx of the rich and famous, but this is a fun family mountain. They offer ski classes for everyone from beginners to experts and sponsor plenty of events to attract locals and tourists. They even host an Oktoberfest celebration that coincides with the fall festival in town."

"That's interesting," he said as they headed toward the restaurant near the edge of the resort complex. "I wonder if they'd be willing to distribute flyers to publicize the dance. If they're still getting a decent crowd for weekend activities like mountain biking or hiking the trails, maybe we could do a couple of happy hour events where we bring in a musician or offer some impromptu line-dancing classes to get people excited about our event."

"Look at you with your marketing savvy," Cassie said because she couldn't hide her shock. The dance would take place at the event barn at the Crimson Ranch property outside of town. They'd already sold plenty of tickets, but additional publicity would garner more interest. "Who's going to teach those dancing classes?"

He made a face. "I suppose I could."

"You can line dance and well enough to teach it?"

"I can line dance. I can two-step. Sweetheart, you have no idea the range of skills I have."

Her heart seemed to skip a beat in reaction to the flirty note to his words, and she yearned to know more about him. To have Aiden trust her. "I don't think anybody does because you keep them well hidden."

"It's easier that way."

"Why?"

They'd made it to the restaurant's entrance. Cassie placed a hand on top of Aiden's when he went to open the door. "Tell me."

"I don't want to set expectations that I'm not willing to live up to. Avoids pain all around."

His words were like a gut punch. She shook off the impact, refusing to believe he was talking about the two of them. She wouldn't hurt him. He was speaking from a place of fear about things that had happened in the past.

Cassie appreciated Aiden's past and the part they'd shared, but she was ready to draw him into the present and hopefully the future.

"Then I expect you to have some smooth moves on the dance floor," she said.

"That I can manage."

She squeezed his fingers, and they entered the restaurant. The interior could best be described as *mountain chic*, with exposed beams, copper tabletops and iron accents. There was a large fireplace at one end with a river-rock hearth, and the rough-hewn wood planks of the floor added to the rustic ambiance.

The hostess showed them to a table, and Aiden quickly ordered a caprese-salad appetizer along with stuffed mushrooms. After a lengthy conversation with the restaurant's sommelier, he chose a bottle of wine.

Cassie found herself staring at him in surprise. "Okay, the two-step I can believe, but explain to me how a retired cowboy and rancher for hire knows so much about grape varietals?"

He grinned boyishly. "One of my buddies on the circuit grew up in Northern California. His family owned a vineyard, although he was the black sheep for choosing the rodeo as a profession. But he was also a wine snob even though we barely made enough to afford cheap beer. That didn't stop him from sharing his knowledge. He liked to make wagers with liquor store owners where if he could guess the origin of the wine and specific flavor notes, they'd give him a free bottle."

"That's ingenious," Cassie murmured.

"I drank some fancy wines back in the day, and I managed not to pay for a sip of it."

"You've done so much in your life," she said wistfully. "You make me feel boring in comparison."

"Cassie, you are anything but boring. You're an actual hero without a cape."

She rolled her eyes. "Okay, that's pushing it."

"Dr. Cassie?" A man in a crisp white shirt and black tie approached their table.

"Robert?" Cassie smiled. "Hello. I'd forgotten that you were the general manager here. This is my friend,

Aiden. Aiden, this is Robert. He's the proud owner of three adorable lop-eared bunnies."

"My five-year-old daughter is the owner of the bunnies. I'm the funding, and you would not believe how much money it takes to keep three rabbits in hay."

Aiden looked stricken. "I'll take your word for it."

"How's Petunia doing?" Cassie asked.

"Very well." Robert glanced at Aiden again. "One of the bunnies—the feistiest one—got into my daughter's Halloween candy, and we weren't sure she was going to make it. It happened on a Sunday morning, and Cassie met us at the clinic and spent all day making sure Petunia was okay."

"Of course she did."

Cassie wasn't sure what to make of the amusement mixed with affection in Aiden's tone.

"Have you ordered?" Robert asked, glancing between the two of them.

"Not yet," Cassie said.

"Are you celebrating something special?"

"No," she answered at the same time Aiden said, "Our first date."

She glared at him, her mood suddenly sullen again.

"We're friends," she clarified.

Robert's mouth kicked up on one side. "I get it." There was no way he could when Cassie couldn't begin to understand any of it herself. "Let me put together a tasting menu for the table."

"You don't have to do that," Cassie said immediately.

"I'd like to, as a thank-you to our favorite bunny doc."

Aiden tipped his head. "How can we refuse?"

Robert clapped his hands together. "Perfect. I'll get things started."

"Why do you look so disgruntled?" Aiden asked as the manager walked away. "You're a famous bunny doctor."

"You said we were on a date."

He blinked. "We are."

"It's not a real date, and we both know it. This is how gossip starts. I don't want people talking about us when we're just friends."

She watched as he absorbed her words. Surely he'd understand. His shoulders went rigid. "Is being on a date with me embarrassing?"

It was her turn to blink. "That isn't what I meant."

"Trust me, I get it. You're a professional. Educated, refined, and well on your way to being a community pillar here in good old Crimson. I'm the kid you felt sorry for once upon a time. Nothing but a washed-up cowboy with a bum leg."

"I didn't say any of that." She tried to wrap her mind around the change in his mood. "I don't think you're below me. I think…"

She searched her brain for the right words. Cassie knew how to deal with conflict. She was the person who smoothed over rough edges and made other people feel more comfortable.

It was the role she took on with her mother or with the friends she'd made in college, vet school, and even in her professional life.

If people were having trouble, she made it better.

But as she looked across the table at Aiden, she realized she didn't want to capitulate or smooth things over. If he were going to like her, it would be the person she was on the inside, not the woman who gave up her wants and needs to make other people happy. It was odd that Cassie refused to put on an act with Aiden, when pretending came so easily in other areas of her life.

"I think this was a bad idea," she said, secretly hoping he might disagree. "We can't force a square peg into a round hole."

He looked genuinely confused. "Who's the peg, and who's the hole?"

"It doesn't matter. I'm not a superhero or even a person with much experience dating. I can't flirt or bat my eyelashes or whatever the women you normally date do."

"I don't care about your eyelashes," he said, shaking his head.

She laughed softly, knowing eyelashes were the least of her worries. As much as Cassie wanted to be herself around Aiden, she couldn't imagine that woman would be someone he'd want to know better. "I returned to Crimson to help Dr. Rooney because life in the big city didn't work for me. Crowds make me nervous. I get social anxiety and feel more comfortable with dogs than people most of the time."

She paused as the waiter brought the appetizers Aiden had ordered. Cassie had lost her appetite. "No one is going to believe that you and I would be dating," she continued when they were alone again. "We aren't a match, and it has nothing to do with my education level. If you want to tell yourself that, I won't stop you, but I'm the problem here."

"You're perfect." He sounded so sincere it made her knees go weak.

"I'm not perfect, not even close. But I'm trying to accept who I am. I imagine I'm not your type."

The sommelier brought the bottle of wine to the table, but Cassie held up a hand before he could present it. "I'm sorry, but there's been a change of plans and we're going to need to cut the evening short. Is there any chance you could box up the food and cancel the remainder of the order?"

The man darted a glance toward Aiden, who gave a tight nod. At least he wasn't going to argue with her. She appreciated that he could respect her wishes.

Their waiter returned to the table as the sommelier gestured him forward. "We'll split the check," Cassie said.

"The hell we will," Aiden muttered.

"Robert comped the meal," the waiter explained, offering Cassie a weak smile. "Are you sure you don't want to enjoy more of it?"

She bit down on the inside of her cheek. "I need to go."

The young man nodded and picked up the two appetizer plates. "I'll get these packed up for you."

Aiden kept his gaze on the table, frustration rolling off him in waves.

"I'm sorry this evening didn't work out," Cassie said, wishing the evening had gone differently. Wishing she could be confident and lighthearted, someone who wouldn't ruin the potential for a perfect night.

Only nothing was perfect about faking anything—from a date to the way she dealt with patients at the clinic. It was past time Cassie started being true to herself, even if she broke her own heart in the process.

"You don't need to apologize," Aiden told her, his voice barely above a whisper. "You've done nothing wrong. I shouldn't have put you in this position."

"We're both doing the best we can." She offered the steadiest smile she could muster and started counting the minutes until she could close the door to her house, cuddle on the couch with her pups and indulge in a big, fat cry.

Becoming authentic and taking care of herself was harder than Cassie had imagined. She just hoped it would be worth the effort.

Chapter Nine

A square peg into a round hole.

Cassie's description of the two of them had tumbled around in Aiden's brain like loose rocks kicked off the side of a mountain trail, ripping through leaves and branches into the vast space below.

Three days later and he still didn't understand what she'd meant. Was he the square or the hole in the metaphor?

Aiden considered himself a simple man by most standards and returning to Crimson had reminded him of why he kept his life free of complications.

And women. Women were complicated and hard to understand.

By the time they'd gotten to dinner, Aiden had become accustomed to the thought of the evening being a real date with Cassie. Yes, it had started with him blurting out a lie, but that didn't matter.

Who cared how they got to a place? The critical part was enjoying it once they were there.

A dinner date was simple enough, or at least to his mind, it should have been.

Cassie hadn't agreed. The drive back to her house had been silent as he couldn't think of a damn word to say to fix the apparent mess he'd caused.

He also hadn't wanted to be accused of mansplaining again, especially when he had no clear explanation for his disappointment and dismay over her decision to end the date before they'd even ordered their entrees.

Emotions were as complicated as women, which was why he tried to steer clear of them as often as possible.

Cassie was all feeling. She led with her heart. Maybe that made her the square peg.

He drove the clamshell digger into the rocky soil again, grateful for an entire week of building a new fence near the edge of the ranch where he'd started working part time once he'd gotten things under control at his sister's place. Physical labor was a sure way to release some of the tension that he couldn't quite shake.

He glanced toward his truck to where Rosie watched him from the padded bed he'd placed in the back. He'd officially completed the paperwork to adopt the dog yesterday afternoon, embarrassed when the staff at Animal Ark had celebrated Rosie going home with an impromptu party, although Cassie had been noticeably absent.

Aiden didn't want to be the center of attention or given accolades for doing the right thing, and it had become clear that adopting Rosie was right for both of them. After he'd lost Sam all those years ago, he'd never expected to take on the emotional responsibility of a dog again, but the sweet tripod made him want to try.

Cassie made him feel the same, although he wasn't sure if she'd appreciate being compared to a dog. Maybe if she would communicate with him in more than perfunctory responses or when other people were around, he'd be able to ask.

He should have known better than to wish for something more when he wasn't cut out for close personal relationships.

Rosie barked once, and he turned to see Morgan Walten, the owner of the cattle operation, approaching on horseback.

"Son, no one expects you to have that whole fence line dug in record time. You're putting in the effort of a whole team of men."

Aiden took off his leather work gloves and wiped the sweat off his brow with one sleeve of his denim shirt. "Sir, I appreciate you hiring me on here, knowing it's only temporary. I'm going to do my best for you."

"I like hearing that." The older man, who wore a western shirt under a canvas jacket with the ranch's logo, climbed down off his chestnut bay and moved closer. He held out a hand for Rosie to sniff, and the dog politely lowered her head and allowed herself to be petted.

"What happened to her leg?" Morgan asked, turning to Aiden.

"Car accident shattered it."

"You have her since she was a puppy?"

Aiden shook his head. "I adopted her yesterday."

"Even with her injury?"

"She's not the only one with a bum leg. I figure we're a decent fit for each other."

"She looks at you with the adoration of a dog that's found her person."

Aiden laughed. "She looks at everyone that way. She's a good dog."

"Sometimes a dog is only as good as its owner."

"Sometimes the owner needs to work to deserve the dog."

Morgan laughed, a deep chuckle that made tiny lines fan out from his blue eyes. "I have a job for you."

"You've already given me a job, sir." Aiden gestured to the vast expanse of sky with the mountain rising up in the distance, decorated with swaths of yellow aspen interspersed with green pines. The beauty of it settled his soul and made him believe in something bigger than himself. No small feat for Aiden.

"I need help with a horse. Isaac is a beautiful palomino. He was a stallion for many years, but some fool woman with more money than sense decided she needed this golden god. She bought, gelded, and sent him to training where he was severely mishandled. I took him because she realized he was too much horse for her, but he's difficult to approach and a loner. He needs someone special to bring him back to the world."

A flutter erupted in Aiden's chest. He had relegated himself to being on the low end of whatever pole he hung his hat on. He'd been a big deal for a while on the rodeo circuit but hadn't tried to get a job working with horses after his accident.

What the hell kind of expert was he when he hadn't been able to keep himself out of harm's way?

Building fences was simple.

"You know my history," he told Morgan Walten.

The older rancher touched two fingers to the brim of his Stetson. "I do."

Aiden didn't like to talk about the freak accident that had led to his horse going down on him, ending both of their careers.

"Then I'm not sure why you're asking me to work with a damaged animal. Storm had been with me for nearly five years. The horse was in his prime, and the accident took that from him."

"It took something from you, too," Morgan reminded him.

"If I'd been more careful during practice, maybe his foot wouldn't have got caught in that roping sled."

"The way I've heard it, his entire weight landed on you, son. You were the one with the shattered fibula."

"My bones healed. Storm's spirit was broken in that fall."

"You still have him," Morgan said quietly.

"Of course I do. I'm not going to get rid of him just because he can't perform as he once did. I owe that horse."

"Accidents happen even to the most talented riders. Back when I was just out of high school, I lost a horse when his leg twisted in a badger hole. I put him down myself, which was one of my saddest days."

"You can find somebody better qualified to train a horse," Aiden said quietly, hating to say the words even though he believed them to his core.

"I can find a dozen qualified cowboys who can train a horse," Morgan said, his gaze piercing into Aiden like he could see all the way to his soul. "I need someone to help me heal a horse."

"What makes you think I'm that person?" He should have just said no but couldn't seem to form the words. He blamed Cassie. He'd been able to turn off his emotions easily enough before reconnecting with her.

Now it was like the dam had been opened, and he couldn't shut it again. He didn't want to, even though that would be easiest for everyone since he had no intention to stay.

"This ranch has been in my family for four generations, Aiden. I remember you, and I knew your father."

"I'm not like him," Aiden said automatically.

Morgan laughed again. "I know. I wouldn't have hired you if I thought you were anything like Eddie Riley. You might not have known me until this job, but I followed your career. I know several guys on the circuit, and I kept tabs on you."

"Why?"

Morgan sighed. "I remember the day your parents came to town after your grandfather died and they took over the ranch. Your mom was young, pretty, and so excited to be a bride." He shook his head, looking out toward the peak like he was asking permission to reveal some of the secrets it had seen over the years.

"I watched the joy drain from her eyes over the next few years. Like a lot of people around here, I told myself it was none of my business. To be honest, we didn't know how bad things were until she left with y'all. I know it's not an excuse, but—"

"I don't want your pity," Aiden said through clenched teeth, amazed at how the memories still haunted him.

"I'm not giving you pity, and that's not why I hired you. It's not why I'm asking for your help now. I'm asking for it because I've heard you have a way with animals."

"It's nothing special." It was the line Aiden had been using for years because if he admitted he had a connection with animals that would mean he'd have to admit he cared about them. If he cared, he could be hurt. He did *not* want to be hurt.

"Did the joy return your mother's eyes once she took you away from here?" Morgan reached out to scratch under Rosie's chin.

Aiden bit down on his lower lip and let his gaze settle over the open field. The land went on for miles in all directions, with scrub oak and pine trees dotting the high plains.

He hadn't expected to come back here but couldn't deny that this place felt more like home than anywhere he'd ever been. "Eventually," he said. "She's happy now."

"I'm glad. I hope your sister can find that happiness again as well."

"She will," Aiden answered, sure of it thanks to Cassie and her mother. "Jason was a good man, nothing like my father. Lila has a broken heart but not a broken spirit. She'll heal."

"I want that for the horse I'm asking you to meet as well."

Aiden narrowed his eyes. "I've seen scars on several of the horses you have on this ranch. It seems to me that you have a propensity for taking in wounded animals."

"Somebody has to. Most of them just need a little TLC, but every once in a while…" He shrugged. "Come on down to the barn when you're finished here. At least take a look at Isaac."

"If I say no is my job here at risk?"

"You're a hard worker and you know your way around ranching like you know your way around a horse. I want your help, but I'm not going to blackmail you into giving it to me. The choice of what happens next is yours. All I ask is that you meet him."

"Thank you, sir." Aiden inclined his head. "I appreciate that as well."

The rancher saddled up and galloped off in the direction of the barn. Aiden did not want to get involved in someone else's business but found himself hurrying through the rest of his work, nerves tingling as he thought about what might be on the horizon for him if he took a chance now.

"Cassie, we need you in back. It's an emergency."

Cassie nodded at Laura, the vet tech, and reached out to place a hand on the shoulder of the eighty-year-old self-proclaimed "dog mama" cradling the scruffy animal in her arms.

"You have my cell phone number, Marilyn. If anything happens and Pooh Bear needs me, I'm only a phone call away."

Marilyn Johnson's rheumy eyes filled with tears. "Thank you, Doc Cassie. I know Dr. Smith thinks I should accept Pooh's fate, but I'm not ready yet. She ain't, either."

Cassie forced a smile even though frustration pulsed through her. Her colleague had refused to make time for Pooh Bear when Marilyn had phoned that morning, distressed that the dog was having trouble standing and had lost her appetite.

Pooh Bear was a fifteen-year-old rez rescue, and according to Marilyn, the other vet had suggested it was time for the dog to die.

Cassie understood there was always a time to say goodbye, but she'd agreed to examine Pooh Bear when Marilyn had showed up at the clinic despite not having an appointment.

Luckily, Dr. Smith had already left for the day. Within a few minutes, Cassie had realized that the dog was dehydrated with a mild UTI and had given the scruffy animal fluids and antibiotics. With proper care, Pooh Bear was likely to make a complete recovery. And the senior vet would have simply allowed the dog to die without seeing her.

"Dr. Smith means well, but you know best when it comes to Pooh Bear. You'll know when it's time. Now that we have her stabilized and rehydrated, she should be feeling much better."

"You're a real blessing, Doc." Marilyn shuffled toward the door the vet tech held open.

Cassie breathed out and tried not to let her frustration at Bryan overwhelm her. Laura had mentioned an emergency. Cassie was the only vet and had a full schedule of appointments for the afternoon. If she canceled to take care of whatever crisis was waiting, she would incur her potential partner's wrath, which she did not want or need at the moment.

She put aside the thought and headed out of the exam room into the hall leading to the clinic's staff-only area. Several people were crowding the door to an exam room, so she made her way there and then felt her mouth drop open at the sight of Aiden in a chair with a blanket on his lap, surrounded by the three women working with her today at the clinic.

Color stained his cheeks as if he didn't quite know what to do with the attention he was receiving.

"What's going on?" she asked, the words coming out more harshly than she'd planned.

"Kittens," he murmured. She wouldn't have been more surprised if he'd told her he had an elephant in the back of his truck.

"What are you doing with kittens?"

"They're just babies," Laura said. "I'm getting the incubator ready and mixing up some formula."

"I found them in the barn at Walten Ranch," Aiden said. "I'm guessing the mama was taken by a coyote."

"We fixed all the barn cats out on the ranch." Cassie was aware that couldn't be true because these kittens hadn't just appeared out of the blue.

She drew closer and crouched in front of Aiden, lifting one corner of the blanket. Three fuzzy balls of fur snuggled in his lap. "How long do you think they've been without their mother?"

"I don't know. We barely heard them today. Thankfully the little black one was making enough noise to be noticed. Can you take care of them?"

She frowned. "I'll do my best."

"So I can leave them with you?"

"Oh, no." She shook her head. "We're going to need your help. These three need to be bottle-fed, and we're already short-staffed. Given the number of appointments I have for the rest of the afternoon, I'm going to put you to work."

Aiden looked genuinely terrified. "I don't know anything about bottle-feeding baby kittens."

"You'll learn," she told him. "How is it that a man who wants nothing to do with animals keeps rescuing them?"

"Maybe it's just an excuse to see you again."

She heard Laura's titter of laughter, and her heart pinched and then plummeted to her toes. His words were clearly a joke, but she couldn't even manage a smile this time.

"Mary, bring the next patient to Exam Room One. Jules, keep things moving out front. I can't get behind schedule. Laura, stay in the back with Aiden, and we'll handle the regular appointments. The most important thing is getting nourishment into them and ensuring they're warm enough. I'll check back when I can."

"You can't leave me here," Aiden muttered.

"You'll manage," she said, patting him awkwardly on the shoulder. She hated that her body felt soft and melty at the sight of him cradling the three babies. "It's for the good of the kittens."

He wrapped his big hand around her arm, thumb tracing over the delicate flesh on the inside of her wrist. "I *am* glad to see you again," Aiden told her, his voice pitched low enough so only she could hear.

"Okay, then. Thanks for sharing." Her stomach in nervous knots, she quickly pulled away and left the room to tend to her other patients, unwilling to allow herself to consider that his words might hold a deeper meaning.

Chapter Ten

"I heard you had more excitement at the clinic," Dr. Rooney said the following morning over breakfast at the diner in town.

Cassie ran a hand through her hair and nodded. "Kittens," she confirmed. "They couldn't be more than a month old, but they're fighters, all three of them. I'm still worried about the runt, but we'll do the best we can."

"Have you thought about calling the Humane Society and turning them over?" he asked, his gentle expression telling her he already knew the answer. "There are also a couple of good rescue organizations in town."

Jabbing her fork into the spinach omelet in front of her, she felt her face heat with consternation. "I know, and I assume if you've heard about the kittens that Bryan called you. Jules made the mistake of telling him when he called the clinic, and he's already complaining that we're wasting resources by caring for them."

She lifted a bite halfway to her mouth and then dropped

it again. "Why do people have such a problem with me wanting to help animals in need? Isn't that the whole point of this job?"

Dr. Rooney offered her a knowing smile. "One recent study claims over eighty-six percent of vets admit to suffering from burnout. The reason that burnout happens is that, like you, they've given too much of themselves. It's called compassion fatigue."

"Who's to say what's too much?" She shook her head. "I have plenty to give. This is my life."

"It's your job."

"They're one and the same to me," she countered.

"It should not be both, Cassie."

"When I was volunteering at the clinic and then when I worked there in high school, I remember showing up plenty of times on a Saturday morning to clean out the kennels and you would be there checking in on different animals. I know you were often the last one to leave. So why is it okay for you but not me?"

"I don't know that it was okay for me." Dr. Rooney held up a piece of toast in her direction. "It was not my plan to have my first marriage end in divorce. Or to have a heart attack at age fifty-five. I'm not blaming my dedication to the clinic for every problem I've had, but I should have had more balance. You can't do it all, Cassie."

"I can do more than Bryan Smith. The only patients he spends time with are the ones willing to spend money on the special, costly treatments he recommends." She held up a hand. "I'm not saying that some of them don't work, but I believe every patient who comes through those doors deserves the attention of a skilled veterinarian."

"I agree, but you have to take time for you."

"Or what?" She gripped the table's edge, feeling like

her world had lost its center. "If you don't want me to join the practice as a partner once you return, I deserve to know now, Dr. Rooney."

"I didn't say that."

"You didn't say it with your words, but your tone and the fact that you won't make eye contact with me tell a different story." She leaned in closer. "Is Bryan Smith going to blackball me in Crimson so I won't be able to get a position?"

"You're a talented vet, Cassie. Any practice would be lucky to have you."

"I want to work at Animal Ark."

"I want that, too." Her mentor sighed. "It's not only up to me."

"Thank you for breakfast, Dr. Rooney." Cassie scooted back in her chair. "I have a lot to get done on my off day."

"You barely ate a thing. Come on. Don't be like this. I want you to stay, but I need you to play nice with Bryan."

Play nice. That was what Cassie had been doing her whole life. Making sure the people around her were taken care of and comfortable without prioritizing herself or her needs.

She'd thought it would be different coming back to Crimson. She'd thought the vet practice where she'd first started working with animals would be a perfect fit.

Once again, she was reminded of the square-peg-and-round-hole analogy. She would fit if she contorted herself into whatever shape someone else demanded of her.

Heck, no one even had to make demands on her. Compromise and denying her own needs were second nature.

"You're right," she said as she stood.

"Bryan isn't so bad once you figure out how to deal with him."

"Not about Dr. Smith," she clarified. "I'm a good vet,

and any practice would be lucky to have me. If you decide not to offer me a partner position after my temporary contract, I'll find another clinic to work at. Or maybe I'll start my own."

Dr. Rooney sat back in his chair, bushy brows lowering over his kind brown eyes. "Is that what you want?"

"I want to be valued for what I have to offer and the contributions I make. I hope we can work together—that's been my dream. But I'm not going to be told how to practice."

"Fair enough." Dr. Rooney picked up a slice of toast and began to slather grape jelly on it. "I'll respect whatever decision you make."

She nodded even though she wanted to scream in protest. Had she honestly expected him to put up a fight? Expected, no. Hoped for, yes.

Was it too much to ask that someone fight for her?

She hooked her purse on one shoulder, thanked the older man for the meal she hadn't eaten and then walked out of the diner.

The sun was bright in the robin's-egg-blue sky. A slight breeze blew, and the air was crisp but quickly warming. It was a perfect high-mountain autumn day, and she had no idea how to fill it.

Before the conversation with Dr. Rooney had gone so far south, Cassie had planned to stop by the clinic and check in on a few of her patients, even though she was technically off for the day.

The older man had been right. She didn't have a life other than working and caring for her mom. She glanced down the street. Several merchants were sweeping the sidewalks in front of their respective businesses, all of which were decorated for the season with displays of pumpkins or colorful fall foliage.

Maybe she could wait for her mom and offer to help out around the bookstore. There was always inventory or new shipments of books to shelve, although Melissa had specifically mentioned how much having Lila working with her was helping lighten the load.

In fact, her mother was planning a weekend away to Santa Fe with her girlfriends to celebrate one of their sixtieth birthdays. Cassie's mom had more of a social life than she did.

She should head home and hang out with her dogs. How pathetic was it that her closest friends in life were canines? She pulled her phone out of her purse, scrolling through apps as she walked down the street. She paused on the dating app that she'd downloaded on a particularly lonely night when she'd first returned to town.

When she'd still been living in Denver, she'd blamed her lack of social life on her demanding job and the fact that she wasn't a big-city girl at heart. But the truth was she'd done nothing to change her solitary lifestyle now that she was back in Crimson.

She saw people she'd known from high school when they came into the clinic or in passing around downtown. And yes, she was volunteering to help with the Harvest Festival. But she didn't know how to get to know people outside of work or volunteering.

She knew that some vet techs and front office staff hung out on the weekends. When she'd first gotten to Crimson, they'd invited her along a couple of times, but she'd always had a reason not to go. First her mother, then not wanting to leave her own dogs alone when she already worked long hours. Plus, there were always animals staying at the clinic overnight who needed extra attention.

She was loath to admit that Dr. Rooney might have had a point about the lack of balance in her life and potentially burning out if she didn't find a way to become more well-rounded.

The past few weeks with Aiden, George and Lila had given Cassie the false sense—maybe she could go so far as to admit a false hope—that she was branching out a little bit. She should have just enjoyed the dinner with him instead of making it mean more.

Part of why she didn't have close friends was because in the past she'd always mothered them in the same way she cared for her own mother and her patients. She was the designated driver or the one somebody would call when they needed help moving or with a project at their house.

She was the shoulder to cry on for breakups or other life hardships, but she was never the person the few friends she allowed herself to have thought of when it came to having fun. She wasn't willing to share her own issues or rely on anybody else.

Her finger hovered over the dating app. She'd set up her profile but chickened out before matching with potential men. She didn't even know if there would be anybody available in Crimson, but she was desperate to prove, mainly to herself, that there was more to her life than work and caring for the people around her.

"You look like you're solving some monumental problems on that device."

She glanced up to see Aiden standing directly in front of her. He wore another pair of faded jeans, a T-shirt and a denim jacket.

Her pulse fluttered, and without thinking, she released her grip on the phone and watched it drop it to the sidewalk with a clatter, like it had suddenly burst into flames. She glanced away from Aiden's startled gaze and realized the phone screen had shattered.

Aiden muttered a curse and bent down to pick it up at the same time she did, their heads slamming together.

Could this morning get any worse? Cassie wondered. She immediately understood that it could when her eyes filled with tears. On the list of the last things she wanted in the world, crying in front of Aiden Riley definitely topped it.

But he didn't run as fast as he could in the other direction. "What's wrong?" he asked, gently taking her arms in his strong hands.

Even through the corduroy jacket she wore, she could feel his warmth.

"Nothing," she lied.

"Cassie, come on. I know I'm not your favorite person at the moment, but don't shut me out."

She didn't want to shut him out. She wanted to draw him closer. "It hasn't been the best morning. I don't think they're going to offer me the partner position at the clinic. Bryan Smith doesn't like me."

"Bryan Smith is ten kinds of an idiot," Aiden said, and she laughed despite her upset. "You'll get the job."

Maybe if she allowed herself, she could have friends. Maybe Aiden could be there for her if she let him.

"Lately I wonder if I'm the idiot for trying so hard. I don't need to work as much as I do." She shrugged. "The problem is I don't have anything else to do. It's my day off, and I don't have plans. It's sad."

"You are the opposite of sad," Aiden told her.

"You don't need to say that."

He pressed a hand to his chest like he was ready to repeat an oath. "Let's spend the day together."

"Aiden, I've already told you I'm not doing a fake relationship. You'll have to fight off the hordes of single women interested in you on your own." With a sigh, she shoved her broken phone into her purse. At least getting a new one would give her something to occupy her time today.

"Please," he said, then flashed a sheepish smile. "Don't make me beg. Hang out with me. It's not fake, and we don't have to call it a date."

"Don't you have work?"

He shrugged. "I'll let them know I have important personal business to take care of. My boss will understand."

She should say no. Get a new phone and tap on the dating app or call someone. But who? Her mother? That only ratcheted up the level of pathetic to new heights.

And she couldn't deny wanting to hang out with Aiden. "Okay," she said after a moment. Her heart melted a little at the look of satisfaction that lit his dark eyes.

"Perfect," he told her. "It's going to be perfect."

Anticipation fizzed through Cassie's veins, making her feel lighter than she had in a long time. She didn't believe in perfect, but Aiden made her want to try.

Chapter Eleven

"Are you sure you've never been here?" Aiden asked as he followed Cassie up the rocky trail an hour and a half later.

She paused and turned, her chest rising and falling in rapid breaths. "Positive. I would have remembered scaling a mountain."

"We're hiking a trail," he countered. "It's not the same thing."

"At least I know one way to add balance in my life." She pulled out the water bottle from the side pocket of her pack and took a long drink. "I need to start exercising more. I'll be too exhausted to worry about work or care that I have no social life."

Aiden's breath caught in his throat as he watched a droplet make its way down her throat and under the collar of the quarter-zip fleece jacket she wore. Jealous of a drop of water. That was a new one for him.

Every time he was with Cassie, he discovered something new—a subtle unfolding of emotions and desires he hadn't realized were part of his makeup. He'd gotten so used to not letting people in that he lived his life on autopilot.

Cassie managed to slide past his defenses without even trying. He'd been an idiot to make that claim about their dating, but her resistance had sparked something inside him.

He wanted her, and even more, he liked spending time with her. Aiden had been careful to keep desire and affection separate in his heart. Hell, most of the women he knew would confirm he didn't have a heart in the way a man was supposed to.

He didn't care.

But he cared about Cassie.

"I thought everyone who grew up in Colorado was outdoorsy." He grinned at her and gestured to the forest that surrounded them. "I think there's some rule about that when living in the mountains."

"I like the outdoors." She patted a nearby pine tree much like she would a dog's head. "I love living in the shadow of Crimson Mountain. But growing up, I spent time at the clinic and school and helping at home."

"Because your dad was sick?"

She wrinkled her nose. "Yes, but I didn't think of it like that. ALS is a brutal disease. He was confined to a wheelchair from the time I started high school. We played a lot of board games, and I read books to him. It was hard because he'd been a strong, independent man. He was a bank president, with lots of people looking up to him. The disease changed that."

Aiden hadn't given much thought to Cassie's life when they'd been younger. She'd been so happy and sweet at school, and he'd mistakenly assumed things were perfect in her family. He'd looked at her like a ray of sun-shine brought to life.

The teachers had loved her, and she'd been popular with the other students, although now that he thought back, in the time that he'd known her, she'd never had a best friend that he could remember.

He'd been too busy surviving to think about anybody but himself. Now he realized he'd done something simi-lar as an adult.

Yes, he took care of his sister and George. Otherwise, he didn't have close relationships other than casual friends he could grab a beer with after a big event.

"It's never too late," he said, wondering if the advice was meant more for her or him, "to be the person you want to be. It just takes effort, not that I have a right to be handing out advice."

She leaned in and wrapped her arms around the tree trunk. "It's good advice. I'm taking it. I want to be a tree hugger."

From a drop of water to a tree, Aiden was now jeal-ous of a thousand silly things—and all of them involved Cassie.

She straightened again. "I've caught my breath. But now I want you to take the lead for the rest of this forced march."

"It'll be worth it," he promised, realizing he was defi-nitely talking to himself this time. Even though he didn't believe he had much of a heart to give, he also knew Cassie's was big enough for both of them. She would give her all to anyone who needed it without taking care of herself or making herself a priority.

She'd said as much to him, and he knew it was true because he'd been on the receiving end of her care. His sister was doing better, so now he had time to help Cassie.

He would help her learn how to put herself first—how to enjoy life. If he got the benefit of her happiness in the process…he might've been a fool, but he wasn't fool enough to say no to that.

They'd been hiking along the path that paralleled the creek bed for nearly a mile, and the slope evened out as the roar of water got closer.

"You'll have to come back here in early summer," he told her as he began to lead her across a field of boulders. "We've had enough summer rain this year that the water is still flowing, but it's even more impressive in the early part of the year."

"Good to know," she said. "I'm surprised we haven't seen more people."

"It's a weekday and there are falls that are more accessible in the area. That's what made this one my favorite as a kid."

They came to the viewing spot, and Aiden reveled in the wonder on Cassie's face as she took in the beauty of the water thundering over the cliff and down into the pool below.

She reached out and squeezed his hand without turning her gaze from the waterfall. "Thank you for bringing me here. It's incredible."

"Yes," he agreed, but he wasn't looking at the falls. "I used to come up here when I was younger."

"You'd do this hike by yourself even as a kid?"

He nodded. "Lila would come sometimes, but she wasn't as into it as me, and she was better at staying invisible at the house. That was the trick with my dad—staying out of his way. The easiest method for that was hiking, and I wasn't alone." He pressed two fingers to his chest when the familiar ache bloomed, although not as sharply as before.

"I had Sam with me," he told Cassie. "That was another reason I hiked so much. Sam had a lot of energy, and if I could wear him out, he'd settle at the house and wouldn't bother my dad.

"I joined the baseball team when I was ten. I'd saved money from doing odd jobs for neighbors all summer to pay for the fees. Of course, I couldn't bring Sam to practice, and he got bored and started barking. My dad…"

She linked their fingers. "I know what happened next."

Right. He let her warmth soak into him, pushing back the shadows. "It's happening again," he said after a few moments when he finally felt like he had control of his emotions.

"What's happening?" Cassie asked, genuinely confused.

"This excursion is supposed to be about you. I'm trying to make you feel better and help you forget your worries. But I'm unloading on you. Again."

She grinned almost shyly. "You're helping. It's kind of hard for me to remember my troubles when I'm focused on breathing so I don't pass out on the trail."

He drew her closer. "So you're saying I take your breath away?" he asked, purposely misunderstanding her comment.

She lifted a hand toward the falls. "All of it takes my breath away, Aiden."

But she wasn't looking at the surrounding beauty. She was focused on him. His gaze dropped to her full mouth for a moment, then lifted again. Had her blue eyes always contained those flecks of gold, or were they produced by the flame that seemed to spark between them?

Aiden wasn't sure, but he wanted more. More spark. More connection. More of everything with Cassie.

He leaned in, refusing to deny himself any longer.

The first brush of his lips against hers sent sparks racing along his skin. "You taste like sunshine," he murmured against her mouth.

She laughed, the sound vibrating through him. "Sunshine doesn't have a taste."

"Warm, soothing, sweet." He cupped her cheeks between his palms. "You are all of those things, Cassie."

"Listen to you being a sweet talker."

"It's not talk." He nibbled his way over her jaw. "It's the truth."

She wound her arms around his neck as he claimed her mouth again, and when she drew her tongue along the seam of his lips, Aiden felt a low groan escape his throat. He wasn't thinking about sunshine now.

He was thinking about a different kind of heat, one that built low and made his body feel out of control. Despite wanting to draw her even closer, Aiden pulled back.

He didn't lose control. He always remembered who he was and what he needed to do to keep hold of his life. Falling for Cassie was not in the cards.

"Tell me that wasn't a pity kiss," she said, her delicate brows drawing low over the blue eyes that had lost their spark.

Not worrying about how he might shock her—wanting to shock her—Aiden grabbed her hand and pressed it low over the evidence of his arousal. "I don't pity you, I want you. Make no mistake about that. But that wanting has nothing to do with your past or my past. It's strictly about right now."

"Then why did you stop?"

"Because right now is all I can offer, and you deserve more." The truth was he'd wanted to shock her—to show her that he was too rough and ragged for someone as kind as her.

A woman who had so much love to give should be with a man who knew how to accept it and could give it back to her in return.

Aiden was neither of those things. But even when he lifted his hand, hers stayed on the button fly of his jeans. She didn't make an aggressive move, but she didn't need to.

What had he been thinking to make her touch him in that way? Apparently he was destined to be surprised by the connection they shared.

She inclined her head to study him for a moment, and he didn't allow himself to move. If he did, he was pretty damn sure they were going to end up naked on a rock, and he had more class than that.

At least he liked to think he did. It was hard to think with Cassie's hand on his pants.

Slowly she dragged her palm up over his waist and his ribs. Then her cool fingers trailed along his neck until she reached behind him and fisted his hair in her grasp.

She pulled him closer and kissed him soundly. He would never have guessed that Cassie Raebourn would take control of a kiss like she did.

But he loved it. She slowly released him, but not before taking a quick nip of his bottom lip.

If he'd wanted her before, now he was beside himself with need.

"Maybe what I want is now," she said, and he released a little breath.

"Is that true?"

Before she could answer, voices echoed up from below them on the trail.

"It looks like we're not alone," she said, taking a step back. She hadn't answered his question, which might've been for the best.

He needed time to gather his thoughts, along with his willpower. There was no way a woman like Cassie could be satisfied with what he had to offer, even if he tried to give her everything.

He wasn't built for the kind of relationship she needed. He'd gotten swept away today—in the memories the hike had brought up and the spark in her blue eyes.

She made him feel like he was more than the man he knew himself to be.

The last time Aiden let emotions take over, he'd wound up in the hospital with his leg broken in three places and the horse he'd trained for years unable to function at the level he needed to as a rider. Even more was at stake here.

He let Cassie set the pace on the way down. They mostly walked silently, but when they got to the trailhead, she stopped and whirled around.

"My life has a lot of uncertainty in it right now. I don't know whether I'm staying in Crimson, and if I do, I don't know whether I need to find a job at a different clinic. Mom has relied on me for years, and now she's finding her own way in the world."

She laughed without humor. "It's a pretty sad state when your widowed mother has a better social life and sense of herself. But that's what I'm dealing with—it's a lot. You have a lot you're dealing with, too. Despite what you might think, I'm not the kind of girl who would think a kiss…"

She glanced down the front of him, and he felt his face flame.

"Think that a kiss means something more is going to happen or represents a long-term commitment. I'm a practical adult, and I have my own life. You might think an aversion to commitment makes you an anomaly or less desirable in my eyes, but it's the opposite. I have plenty of people and animals depending on me. I'm not looking for something more."

"What are you looking for, Cassie?"

One side of her mouth quirked. "For the first time in my life, I want a good time. You think about that and decide if you're the man who can give it to me."

"If I'm not?" He didn't mean the words to come out as a growl, but they did.

"That's good information for both of us. But it's not going to stop me from finding someone who does."

Hell no. If Cassie had an itch to scratch, she wouldn't do it with anybody but him.

Aiden didn't say that, though. He wasn't sure if those words would fall under the auspices of mansplaining, but he wasn't taking any chances.

"I… That's good to know…yes."

"Yes," she repeated, her smile widening. "Also good to know." She leaned in and kissed him again. "Thank you, Aiden. You've turned my day around."

And she'd turned around his whole world.

Chapter Twelve

Aiden wasn't sure what he expected to happen next, but Cassie hopped into the front seat of his car like they hadn't just agreed to…not exactly a relationship…but it was something.

Something more than physical, although he wasn't going to be the one to point that out to her.

"Let's get together Friday night after the meeting about the dance," she said as he drove toward town.

Like it was that easy.

"Sure," he agreed. Was it that easy?

"You should plan to come to my place because it might be awkward if George notices my car outside the bunkhouse at the ranch."

"We wouldn't want things to be awkward," he said.

"Are you okay?" Cassie looked legitimately concerned.

"A little dehydrated," he lied. "I forgot to pack water." Another lie.

She grabbed her bottle from the pack that sat at her feet. "Do you want a drink of mine?"

"I'm okay." He held up a hand. "I don't want to…"

"Share germs?" She threw back her head and laughed. "Aiden, we just swapped spit and plan to do a lot more. I don't think you have to worry about drinking from the same water bottle."

"It's not that… I just…" He shook his head and took the bottle from her, guzzling down gulps of the cold water. His thirst wasn't as big a worry as his need for Cassie. He was supposed to be concerned with not letting her down or leading her on, and he was the one who wanted to balk at her no-strings attitude.

He pulled up to her house and handed back the water bottle. "I guess I'll see you Friday, unless—"

"Friday is great. I'm going to be slammed until then. But call me—"

He nodded. "I will."

She gave him a funny look, then continued, "If you have any issues with Rosie. She should be good to go now that her incision is healed, but I'm here to help if you need it. Or with Spud, for that matter."

"Spud is a menace but a healthy, happy menace."

"The best kind." She leaned over the center console and quickly kissed his cheek. "Thanks again for today. I feel like a new person."

"Same," he murmured as she bounced out of the truck.

He forced himself to drive away because it was too movie-of-the-week to sit in her driveway pining. No, not pining. Aiden didn't pine.

Boundaries and limits made him feel safe. He'd set them with Cassie but hadn't expected her to agree so quickly.

He had a few days to get himself in check. Self-control came naturally to him. Why did this feel so different?

He drove back to his sister's house after checking in with his boss at Walten Ranch. No one seemed bothered by the fact that he'd called in, probably because Aiden had been working seven days a week since he'd agreed to help at the ranch.

Staying busy at the cattle operation and on his sister's property kept his mind from dwelling on the past. Now he just needed to figure out a way to keep his mind from dwelling on Cassie.

That might be a more difficult task.

The door to the farmhouse opened, and Spud and Rosie, fast friends, came out to greet him along with George.

"You're home early," Lila said from the doorway.

"Am I?" He'd lost track of time completely.

"I thought you'd be working longer hours helping with the horse Morgan wants you to rehab."

"I wanted to get home and make sure everything was okay."

"I got an A on my spelling test," George said, pumping his fist. "Stupid Gabe got a C-plus."

"Don't call people stupid," Lila told her son.

"Even if they act it," Aiden added, earning a laugh from his nephew.

"Rosie's helping me teach Spud his manners. Want to see?"

"More than anything," Aiden answered, ignoring the speculative look his sister shot him.

They went into the house, and George demonstrated the two dogs' obedience skills. Spud had a bit of trouble dropping his bottom to the ground.

"You might have a future career as a dog trainer." Aiden ruffled his nephew's hair.

"Or an astronaut," George countered. "Or a guy who does crafts." He pointed to the kitchen table, which was filled with paper supplies and various markers. "I make real good bows."

The dogs started to wrestle on the braided rug. Rosie was patient with Spud, gently correcting the puppy when he got too enthusiastic.

"An astronaut or a crafter." Aiden tapped a finger on his chin. "So many options."

He glanced at Lila, who seemed to be smothering a smile as she nodded in agreement. "Are you also taking up crafting?" he asked his sister.

"I'm making bookmarks to sell at the bookstore's booth for the Harvest Festival weekend. Melissa thought it was a good idea, and I get to keep all the profits."

"Nice." Reality snuck into his consciousness at thoughts of his sister finally being willing to consider selling the ranch. "Are the payments on this place—"

"It's fine, Aiden."

"But if you need help…"

"I'm managing things for now." She inclined her head toward George, busy with the dogs but still within earshot. "We can talk about the future another time."

"Got it." He hadn't imagined it would be difficult to say goodbye to the land when he'd first returned to Crimson, given the memories that lingered in the house. But now other, better memories were replacing the bad ones, and he could remember some of the good times he'd had here.

"Did you know there's gonna be a dance, too?" George asked as Spud curled into his lap, tired from his play session.

Rosie came to stand at Aiden's side. "I did. Did you know I'm helping to plan the dance?" He scratched behind one of the dog's floppy ears.

George doubled over with laughter. "That's a good one, Uncle Aiden."

"What's so funny?" Aiden demanded.

"You can't dance."

"Why does everyone think I can't dance?" He thought about Cassie's disbelief. "I'm a great dancer."

Lila crossed her arms over her chest. "I'm with George. I don't think you can dance."

"I can dance," Aiden insisted.

His sister cocked a brow. "Come on. You volunteered because you weren't paying attention at that meeting."

"You could have saved me," Aiden told her, narrowing his eyes.

Her expression went soft. "It isn't often that I see my stalwart brother at a loss. I enjoyed it more than I should have."

"No way you can dance," George said.

Aiden glanced around the farmhouse's interior. "Lila, help me move the coffee table. We need room. I'm going to teach my nephew the two-step."

"What's that?" George sounded intrigued.

"A dance," Aiden told him. "One all cowboys worth their salt should know." He pointed toward George. "Astronauts and crafters, too."

He and Lila placed the coffee table to the side, leaving an open space just big enough for this impromptu lesson.

"Do you have a Bluetooth speaker?" he asked his sister, suddenly realizing that in the months he'd been back, he hadn't heard music playing in the house.

She shook her head. "The old CD player still works. I don't think Dad touched any of her stuff, and we only cleaned out the upstairs closets when we moved in."

Their mother loved music, particularly female country

artists. She'd repeatedly listened to a few of her favorite girl-power anthems for months after they'd left Crimson.

He checked out the row of CDs on the entertainment center along the far wall and chose Martina McBride, one of his mom's favorite artists.

Although he hadn't done this in over a decade, the movements of placing the shiny disc into the player and listening to it whir to life felt achingly familiar. He swallowed back his emotion and turned as the music started.

"You ready, George?" Aiden held out his hands as he walked toward the boy.

Rosie and Spud had taken up residence on the couch like an attentive audience. He noticed Lila dab at the corner of one eye. Clearly Aiden wasn't the only one who remembered.

George made a few disgruntled noises like he was too cool for dancing in the family room with his uncle but slunk forward and took Aiden's hands.

"First thing you want to do is straighten your shoulders. Nobody wants a slouchy dance partner." George nodded and threw back his shoulders almost comically, realizing this was serious business.

Aiden had been taught to two-step by a feisty barrel racer when he'd joined the rodeo circuit. At that point, he'd been young and angry, not sparing much thought to anything outside the arena. He hadn't grown up with the training or pedigree that many rodeo stars had, but what he'd lacked in experience, he'd made up for in grit and blind determination.

He'd taken to dancing the same way, especially when he'd realized that women liked a man who could dance. He might not have been able to offer his nephew the level-headed guidance his late brother-in-law would have, but he could make sure George knew the important things and learning to dance was essential in his mind.

He showed George the basic steps and how to follow the song's rhythm. The boy scrunched up his mouth as he concentrated and for the first half of the song did a bang-up job of treading all over Aidan's shoes.

Eventually he picked up on the beat, and Martina's words about her baby loving her just the way she was faded into the background as Aiden and George moved around the small area.

"You're getting it, kid. Fred Astaire, eat your heart out."

"Is Fred Astaire a cowboy?" George asked. "'Cause I'm adding *cowboy* to my list of jobs since I can dance like one."

"Fred Astaire was not a cowboy," Lila said from where she watched in the doorway. "But he was an excellent dancer, just like you and your uncle."

George glanced over his shoulder at his mother but continued to follow Aiden's lead. "Was Daddy a good dancer, Mom? I can't remember."

Aiden's gaze darted to his sister, wondering if the question would trigger a lapse into her sorrow.

That was how it had sometimes been with their mother when they'd first moved away. She'd have days and weeks of good moods, focused on her new life and the future she'd been building away from her abusive husband.

Then there would be a random noise or car backfiring outside the house. Or Aiden would knock a glass off the counter, and it would shatter the way things often had when his dad had been raging through the house.

The dark cloud would envelop his mother for another period. He'd hated those moments, and he'd done his best not to trigger them.

Aiden's first instinct was to snap at George and tell

him not to bring up the topic of his late father, but that wasn't right, either. Tamping down feelings of sadness or pretending like a loss hadn't happened wouldn't help.

It might bury the wounds, but they'd still be under the surface. Lila closed her eyes and swallowed.

"Your father was a terrible dancer," she said. "He didn't care. Anytime there was music or a band playing, he'd be the first one on the dance floor, George. He looked ridiculous, but he kept dancing anyway. He used to dance around the kitchen with you in his arms when you were a baby."

George squeezed Aiden's hands as the song faded, then turned to his mother. "I think I remember that," the boy said and started to hum the famous John Denver son about the Rocky Mountains. "That was the song he sang."

"You're right. He dreamed of living in Colorado. He couldn't dance." Lila offered her son a watery smile. "But your father had a beautiful voice."

"Do you know how to two-step, Mommy?" George asked.

She nodded. "I learned from watching my parents dance together in this room. Do you remember, Aiden? Do you remember any of the moments when they were happy?"

A new song started, a slow ballad, and the fiddle's sound felt like it was plucking at Aiden's heart.

"Now that you mentioned it," he said gruffly. "I do remember them dancing." Even if he didn't want to.

"How about a dance with your mom?" Lila asked her son as if realizing Aiden was at the edge of his ability to withstand any more emotional sparks at the moment. His chest felt like it was on fire.

"Yeah, but not this boring, slow music," George told her. "Uncle Aiden, can you turn on something fast again?"

"I can do that, buddy." He stepped toward the CD

player, shuffling the music until a song came on that met with George's approval. Aiden watched his sister and her son laugh as they twirled around the family room and thought back to when he'd watched his parents in the same way.

Before his father had lost his job and started making whiskey his preferred breakfast. Before Eddie Riley had made a habit of taking out his disappointment in life on his wife and children. If Aiden could remember the good times, maybe the bad ones wouldn't feel like they might swallow him whole every time life got difficult.

Maybe he could open himself up—not to love—that would be asking too much. But a little happiness couldn't hurt. Could it?

Chapter Thirteen

Cassie ignored the knock at the door early Friday evening. She sat on her sofa, Bitsy and Baby draped across her lap, staring forward but not really seeing anything.

Clyde, her oldest dog and king of the couch, had passed away that morning, and while Cassie had counseled countless people through the loss of a pet, somehow she couldn't manage her own sorrow.

At least the tears had stopped. She'd held them back most of the afternoon while seeing patients because Bryan Smith had told her she shouldn't leave the clinic mid-shift.

It wasn't as if he were her boss. Okay, maybe he was a senior partner, but if he wouldn't change his mind about offering her a position at the end of her temporary assignment, what did it truly matter?

But she didn't leave because, despite her grief, she was professional and her patients needed her.

The floodgates had opened as soon as she'd gotten to

her car at the end of the shift. Jules had offered to drive her home when it had been obvious that Cassie's composure had hung by a thin thread, but she hadn't wanted to inconvenience the other woman.

Even in the midst of her grief, Cassie had asked the receptionist to call her mother and explain that Cassie wouldn't be able to attend the meeting about the harvest dance. There was no way she could hold it together for that.

Another knock. "Cassie, I know you're in there. Answer the damn door."

Bitsy gave a mournful woof and Baby whined in response, but neither dog left the sofa.

"Go away," Cassie called without emotion. "I'm not fit company right now."

She glanced toward the door when it opened, and Aiden stepped through. "I don't want fit company. I want to be with you."

"You need to leave." Her voice broke on the last word.

"You need to lock your door."

He wore a heavy canvas jacket over a thick sweater with jeans, and a gust of cool fall air blew in with him. She shivered, feeling so cold.

"Aiden, I can't do this right now. It's been a day from…" She bit down on her lower lip. "I just can't."

"Sweetheart, I know." He moved across the small room, and Baby sat up and shifted to make a space for him.

Her dog was as big of a fool as Cassie.

"I'm sorry about Clyde," Aiden said as he sank down and wrapped his arms around her.

"He was fourteen." Cassie held herself rigid. "He had a good life. It was fast and painless. He just woke up and then climbed into my lap, and I knew something was wrong. I took him to the clinic to run some tests. Suddenly he was gone. He passed away on the exam table."

"That doesn't make it easier." Aiden rested his chin on the top of her head. "It's still hard to say goodbye."

"I'm not ready to say goodbye." She squeezed shut her eyes so tightly her head started to pound. When she could no longer resist, she let herself curl into Aiden's strong embrace.

"Why didn't you call me?" he asked gently. "I would have come over earlier. You shouldn't be alone right now."

"My dog died," she said with a sniff. "It happens to people all the time. It's not traumatic, and I couldn't have called you even if I'd wanted to. I was at work when he passed away."

"Why didn't you leave?"

"We had patients. It's the end of the month, and billing is important right now."

"Hell, Cassie, you're important. Your feelings are important."

"How did you even know about Clyde?"

"Your mom called my sister to come in after the clinic called so she could go to the volunteer meeting. I talked to her, and she would have come over, but I asked her to let me be the one.

"You were there for me when I lost Sam. And you've been amazing with the animals I've had you treating since my return."

"That's my job."

"It's more than your job, and we both know it. Losing a pet, whether from old age, injury or something else…"

She knew what he meant by "something else."

"It's okay to be sad, Cassie."

She wiped her face on her sleeve and pulled back. "I've never felt like it was okay to be sad for myself because—"

"You were too busy taking care of other people."

"Somebody has to."

"Not tonight. For the record, I'd like to string Dr. Smith up by his bony toes."

She huffed out a laugh. "How do you know he has bony toes?"

"I don't, but he looks like the type. You're allowed to depend on other people. I'd be honored if you'd let that person be me for a little while."

Baby shifted again and shoved her wet nose into the crook of Aiden's neck.

"Looks like it's not just me you're going to have to contend with right now."

"I know you like my broad shoulders," he said, smoothing the hair away from her face. "They can handle you and your dogs."

She smiled at the humor because that was what he was trying for, but secretly she wondered if he could handle the weight of her heart.

Right now, she was too exhausted by the emotions she was letting out and those she'd been trying to keep in. So she leaned against Aiden and matched her breathing to his.

"Just for a few minutes," she promised, and he held her tighter.

When she opened her eyes, Aiden was carrying her through the dark house. Cassie wasn't sure how long she'd slept, but darkness had fallen outside the windows and the rest had done wonders to soften the edges of her grief.

"Thank you for staying with me," she said, breathing in his clean scent as she nuzzled her nose into the crook of his neck.

"No place I'd rather be."

His words made her feel unbalanced, so she grounded herself by pressing closer to his solid chest.

Her rental wasn't big, and he lowered her to the bed far too soon. She didn't want to be alone, but more importantly, she wanted to be with Aiden.

The proposal she'd given him seemed ludicrous now—a straightforward good time. Not that she doubted the "good" part, but she couldn't deny there was more to her feelings for Aiden than purely physical.

But as he kissed her gently, then started to pull away, her physical need took over and made her braver than she felt. Possibly reckless, but she wouldn't focus on that.

She slid her hands up his torso and gripped his shoulders as she ran her tongue along his throat, thrilled when he uttered a muffled curse.

"I don't want to take advantage of you, Cassie." He seemed to be holding himself purposefully still above her. "This isn't about—"

"I want you," she interrupted and nipped at his jaw. "Here. Now. Tell me you want me, too, Aiden."

"More than my next breath," he said with a hoarse laugh.

"Then stay," she said, surprised by her own commanding tone.

Instead of answering, Aiden leaned in and kissed her, achingly slow and measured. It was as if he was still giving her time to change her mind. He trailed kisses along her jaw, then sucked her earlobe into his mouth with a gentle tug.

She moaned and shifted, her body pulsing with need, tempted by the promise of pleasure he offered.

His talented tongue and calloused hands and the weight of his arousal pressing against the apex of her thighs made her body hum with need.

"All night, Cassie," he said against her skin. "This is going to take all night. Are you ready for that?"

She had a feeling deep in her soul that one night wouldn't be nearly enough, but she was tired of living with one eye on the rearview mirror and the other worried about what the path ahead would bring.

Now was the important part when it came to Aiden.

"I'm ready for all of it," she answered, and he made a rumbling sound in the back of his throat, somewhere between a growl and a moan like her words were exactly what he wanted to hear.

He pulled away from her but only long enough to toe off his boots, impatiently yank his sweater over his head and strip out of his jeans and boxers.

Cassie probably should have been doing the same with her clothes, but she was too intent on watching him.

"You like what you see?" he said with an almost boyish quirk to his full mouth.

"It's not a bad view," she answered with a shrug that she didn't think was fooling him.

"You like it." His grin widened.

"A lot," she agreed as heat pooled low in her belly.

"Not as much as I like you. You are such a bright light, Cassie. Like sunshine come to life." He moved toward her again, and she sat up when he lifted the hem of her sweatshirt. He tossed it aside and then reached around her to unclasp her bra, his chocolate-colored eyes darkening to the color of dark coffee in appreciation.

"So beautiful," he murmured, and Cassie felt beautiful in a way she never had.

Desired. Treasured. Admired.

Wanted.

It made her pulse quicken to realize that Aiden might want her as much as she did him.

He kissed her again, then reached for her pants, sliding them down and over her hips along with her cotton panties.

She expected to feel self-conscious being naked in front of him, but her need drowned out any anxiety.

And when he fused his mouth to hers, Cassie could barely remember her own name. His hands were everywhere, lingering in sensitive places that had her trembling with need.

Their tongues mingled, and she fell back against the sheets as he positioned himself between her legs. But he didn't appear to be in any hurry because he turned his attention to her breasts, giving each of them equal attention—open-mouthed kisses and light tugs with his teeth that turned her into a puddle of yearning underneath him.

"I need you," she whispered when she thought she might climax just from his careful ministrations. "In me, Aiden. Now."

He reached for the wallet he'd placed on her nightstand and plucked a condom packet out of it.

She spread her legs wider as he rolled the condom over his length.

"I want you so much, Cassie."

The words were simple and direct, but the reverence in his tone made them feel like a vow.

She bit down on her lower lip, hoping the sharp sting would remind her that Aiden wasn't the type of man to make a vow, not to her anyway.

She'd agreed to mutual pleasure, and there was no way she would regret that decision. If only she could turn off her silly emotions where he was concerned.

As if she'd spoken her worries out loud, he paused and looked deep into her eyes. She could still feel his thumb tracing circles on her hip where his big palm gently gripped her, and that light touch almost drove her out of her mind.

"I want you, too," she told him because that much was true, just not the entire truth.

He held her gaze as his hand moved, and one finger dipped into her wet center. "I like the way you want me." He kissed her deeply as he centered himself over her and slid inside, inch by glorious inch.

Cassie's breath stole from her lungs, but it didn't matter because she could breathe Aiden in like he was all the oxygen she needed. She rolled her hips against him, their rhythm aligned as they moved together. It could have been minutes or hours because it felt like Cassie's body had been made to join with Aiden's.

When the pressure built so much that she thought she might shatter from it, she whispered a plea and he thrust into her harder, giving both of them exactly what they needed to spiral over the edge together.

She felt herself break apart as Aiden buried his face into the crook of her neck and shuddered his own release. Holding him tightly, their bodies like one, was the most intimate experience Cassie could imagine.

He didn't pull away as she might have expected but flopped to the bed, drawing her close in the circle of his embrace.

Brushing a kiss on the tip of her ear, he sighed. "You are incredible."

"We're incredible," she countered, and he tightened his grip on her like he didn't want to let go.

"We are," he agreed, and Cassie relaxed more deeply against him, her worries sated for the moment. This moment was everything, and she let herself simply enjoy it.

Three days after the morning Aiden had left her bed, Cassie walked into her mother's bookshop. Aiden stood next to the front counter with his sister behind the register.

"Hey, Cassie," Lila called. "Aiden was just telling me about your recent adventures."

Cassie blinked and tried to keep her expression neutral even as shock pounded through her. Would he have told his sister about them being together?

"I explained that the resort is willing to sponsor the dance," he said, raising his brows like he understood Cassie's worries.

"Excellent work." Lila smiled. "I figure it was your doing. I can't see my brother going to bat for the Harvest Festival."

"It was actually Aiden's idea." Cassie forced her mouth to curve into a smile. "I followed up with the marketing manager at the resort, but it's a mutual win."

"You guys are a great team." Lila seemed elated.

"I like staying busy." Not that Cassie had needed assistance with her task list for the dance. Sorrow from missing Clyde and nervous energy over what had transpired with Aiden had propelled her forward the past few days. She could have handled the planning of every detail of the weekend's activities on her own.

"Then you and my brother are one and the same because, as I'm sure you know, he's now helping build the festival grandstand for the town square. Plus, he's practically living over at the Walten ranch now that he agreed to help train the horse, but you probably know that as well. You probably know more than I do."

Cassie felt like she didn't know anything. She couldn't help but think the reason for Aiden's sudden foray into community involvement was to have an excuse not to see her.

Although she had to admit she'd been keeping herself

extra busy. She'd taken on several volunteer jobs doing free vaccinations at a local pet rescue located on a different ranch outside of town and worked for the county Humane Society.

Her days now started well before dawn and didn't end until after dark, which was why she told herself it didn't matter that she hadn't seen him.

She didn't have time, yet doubted his motivation was the same as hers. He looked uncomfortable at his sister's attention, and Cassie told herself not to get too worked up.

He had no right to be freaked out by her or thinking of their night together. She hadn't asked him for anything. She hadn't expected anything from him.

"I think I'm going to skip the meeting today." Lila glanced at the computer. "We have a new shipment arriving, and I don't want to have your mom start unloading things on her own. You two walk over together."

"All right," Aiden said.

Cassie wanted to protest, but she didn't. That would draw unwanted attention to them, which was the last thing she needed.

"Cassie, is that you? Cassie Raebourn?"

She turned at the sound of her name. "Hey, Cameron," she said, recognizing one of her high school classmates.

"I heard you were back in town." The woman came forward and gave Cassie a hug, which she returned. "My gosh, girl. You should have reached out."

"I meant to," Cassie mumbled.

"You're not on social media, are you?"

She shook her head. "No, not at all."

"I looked for you. I've been meaning to come by the vet clinic and talk to you. We've got a group of girls—the old crew—who gets together every week. We wanted to invite you."

"You did?" Cassie wasn't sure why she found that so difficult to believe, but she did.

"Yes, of course. You're one of the girls."

"One of the girls?" Cassie did not see herself that way. In high school, she'd been a part of the dance team and a student council and honor society member. She'd led the high school's annual canned food drive each Thanksgiving.

Yet in many ways, she'd been keeping herself busy and involved to appear normal, the way she'd felt before her father's ALS diagnosis. So her mother wouldn't worry and her father wouldn't feel guilty that his illness and frequent hospital stays hadn't robbed her of having a regular teenage life.

But she'd only been a typical teenager on the outside, and when she'd left for college, she hadn't stayed in touch with her high school friends.

She'd driven home every weekend from Fort Collins during both undergrad and vet school and then most weekends when she'd started working for the emergency vet clinic in Denver. But those weekends had been dedicated to her family, and she'd purposely kept a low profile so she wouldn't have to explain herself or disappoint people.

Old friends had stopped calling, and since she'd made no effort after moving back to Crimson, her social life had centered around her dogs and her mom. How sad.

"I'd like that," she said, realizing Cameron was waiting for an answer.

"That's great. Give me your phone, and I'll put my number in there." Cassie pulled the device from her purse and gave it to the woman.

Out of the corner of her eye, she saw that Lila was

busy with a customer and not paying a bit of attention to Cassie—unaware of how extraordinary this moment was.

She was making an effort to have an adult friend, embarrassed that she hadn't already. Of course, she considered Lila a friend and Aiden as well, if she were being completely honest.

He stood next to the register, watching as if he knew what this inconsequential exchange meant to Cassie. She didn't like that he could read her when she had absolutely no idea what was going on in his handsome brain.

"Hey, I just had a thought." Cameron returned the phone and leaned in like she was sharing a state secret. "Do you have a boyfriend, Cassie?"

"What have you heard?" Cassie refused to look at Aiden.

"I haven't heard anything," Cameron said with a little chuckle. "I was thinking about my older brother. Do you remember Henry?"

Cassie nodded. "He was a few years ahead of us in school. He played basketball, right?"

"Yeah, that was him. He's working on the ski mountain as one of the resort managers. It's a steady position. He went to school to play ball in California and got a fancy finance degree, but that didn't quite work out. For the past couple of years, he's been hanging out in Aspen, mainly couch surfing and hitting the slopes. We thought he would be a failure-to-launch ski bum for his whole life, but he's doing well now. Really has his life back on track."

"That's great."

"It is. I asked because he's not seeing anybody, and I thought if you weren't seeing anybody, maybe I could reintroduce the two of you. Wouldn't it be fun if we reconnected and then became sisters-in-law?"

Cassie heard a noise coming from the cash register's direction and forced her features to remain neutral. "Wow, that would be something."

Cameron grinned. "I know I'm putting the cart before the horse, but you never know what might happen. I could give him your number. He's not creepy or anything. I can vouch for him."

Cassie didn't know what to say, especially with Aiden staring at her. They'd just slept together, so what was she supposed to do—let herself be fixed up right in front of him?

Except he'd spent the night with her after making it very clear that he didn't have anything long term to offer, and she'd told him that was fine.

She believed it was fine, but that didn't mean she wasn't interested in more with somebody who might be willing to give it to her.

"I'll text you," she told Cameron. "And I'd love to join the next girls' night out. You could arrange for your brother to stop by. That would be less pressure on him or—"

"What a great idea. I should have thought of that. For sure. This is going to be so much fun. The girls will flip when I tell them you're joining us. You were so much fun to be around in high school. You always had a smile for everybody. I remember that about you. By the way, I'm sorry about your father."

"Thanks." Cassie nodded. "I have to get to a meeting. I'm helping with the Harvest Festival."

"Of course you are." Cameron smiled again. "You were always so helpful and sweet—a real sunshine girl."

Sunshine girl. The description reminded her of Aiden's words when he'd been kissing her, which she should not have been thinking about now. Yet he was the only one who'd seen past her mask of helpful congeniality and liked her anyway.

"Okay, great to see you," she told Cameron. "We'll get together soon."

"Perfect. See you later, friend."

Cassie turned for the door without waiting to see if Aiden was ready to leave. She needed some fresh air.

"You're going on a date with Henry McKerlie?"

In a few long strides, Aiden caught up to her.

"No, but I'm willing to meet him."

"He's not your type," Aiden said.

"How do you know?"

"He's a party guy."

"Oh."

"And an adrenaline junkie."

"I'm not sure a former rodeo cowboy has any right to use the phrase *adrenaline junkie* like it's a bad thing."

"I didn't mean it was a bad thing in general. It's a bad thing for you. You're not like that."

"I like an adventure."

"You know what I mean."

They'd almost made it to the community center, and her heart was beating like a dull weight in her chest. She turned to face Aiden.

"I *do* know what you mean. I also understand that now you don't need me for help with Spud or Rosie or…" She looked down at the ground. "Or help to scratch an itch. Things have changed between us."

When he didn't respond, she continued, "It's okay. Your sister was right. We make a great team working together. It doesn't have to be anything more, and you don't have to feel bad about it or like you need to warn me off other men because—"

Suddenly she was silenced in the most surprising way

possible when his lips pressed against hers. Without hesitation, she relaxed into the kiss. She couldn't imagine there would ever be a time when she wouldn't respond to Aiden. It wasn't as if she were proud of her weakness when it came to him, but there was no denying it.

Still, she couldn't believe he was willing to make such a public declaration because that was what this was. They weren't the only two heading to the festival meeting.

"Get a room," someone called good-naturedly.

"Oh, Michael. Leave the kids alone. You remember when we were like that."

Aiden released her slowly like he knew she might need a moment to regain her balance. "I'm not trying to let you go or get away from you," he said. "I'm trying to give you space. I don't want space. I also don't want you going on a date with Henry McKerlie with this thing still between us. You aren't an itch to scratch, Cassie. You're a full-blown total body rash."

She made a face. "That's not the most romantic thing I've ever heard."

He rubbed a hand over the back of his neck, looking adorably uncomfortable. "I'll work on some romance if that's what you want."

"What I want is you." She didn't say for how long or demand specifics because she understood neither one of them was ready for that. "We need to get to the meeting."

"You're right. We have work to do. After that's done, I'm going to fix dinner for you. If you and your dogs want to come over."

"You cook, too?"

"I have all kinds of skills."

Her face and other parts of her body warmed at his words. "I just bet you do. But right now, my mind is on the meeting."

Luckily, Aiden didn't call her out on the lie.

"Then far be it from me to distract you." He held open the door with a grin, a glint of a challenge in his eyes.

"I am getting a little hungry," she murmured. The idea of Aiden cooking her dinner was sexier than she would've guessed. Her heart lifted at the prospect of spending the evening with him even if she knew it was dangerous to her soul.

Chapter Fourteen

Aiden might have overstated his ability in the kitchen. He had no discernible culinary skills. His mother had spent too much time hustling to make ends meet to focus on home cooking, not that he'd cared.

He'd cared even less once he'd joined the rodeo, and since he'd returned to Crimson, he'd mostly eaten at his sister's table.

But he wanted time with Cassie and to show her she was worth the effort since he'd messed things up by not calling after their night together.

He figured grilling was safe, so he bought a couple of steaks from the grocery, a bag of salad, and a store-bought container of mashed potatoes. Keeping it simple was his best bet.

When the doorbell rang, Rosie popped up from her dog bed, and Aiden followed her to the front of the house, cradling his phone against one ear.

"Bob, I've got to go," he said, speaking to the manager of the ranch where he'd been working in Wyoming prior to returning to Crimson. "Can I give you a call tomorrow?"

He opened the door while simultaneously holding the phone away from his ear as the man on the other end started screaming about loyalty and knowing where your bread was buttered.

"I'm not a loaf of bread," Aiden said as frustration spiked in his gut. "I'm going to call you tomorrow, and I expect to have a civil conversation without you hollering at me. That's not going to get either of us what we want, and I know what you want, sir."

He pocketed his phone and tried to release the unexpected stress the conversation had elicited. He didn't like being yelled at or called out for his character. Aiden prided himself on his loyalty.

"Come on in." He gestured Cassie forward. She was staring like he was a puzzle she wanted to solve. "I'm sorry you had to hear that. I didn't anticipate the call going to hell." He ran a hand through his hair. "My boss in Wyoming got wind that I'm doing some horse training for Morgan Walten. He's not pleased about it."

Cassie frowned. "Why would he care?"

"He's a little possessive with his workers. I told him I would only be taking care of my sister and nephew during my stay in Crimson. He expected me back in Wyoming a few weeks ago, but that didn't happen. Now he understands part of the reason."

What his boss didn't understand, because Aiden could barely fathom it, was that Cassie was a more significant part of the reason he didn't want to leave.

He refrained from mentioning it because that would only get him into more hot water with her if he couldn't live up to the expectations he set.

And he was reasonably confident he couldn't.

"Are you still planning to return to Wyoming?" she asked, bending down to pet Rosie.

Wasn't it just like Cassie not to beat around the bush? She might've looked like an angel and had a smile that made him think of sunshine, but he appreciated her being a straight shooter.

"I suppose I am, but I don't like being told what to do."

She flashed a quick grin. "I wouldn't have guessed that about you." She was joking with him, which worked wonders for his mood.

"Here." She thrust a bag into his hand. "I know it's tradition to bring flowers or something along those lines, but I went for a gift that felt more appropriate for you."

He opened the bag to find a half dozen of what looked like muffins made of wood shavings.

"They're homemade fire starters. I noticed you have a lot of wood stacked near the bunkhouse and thought they'd come in handy."

"Thank you. That was very thoughtful."

"There's also a bone for Rosie. My dogs love the brand. They smell terrible, but that's part of the charm."

"Thank you for all of it and for agreeing to dinner." He leaned in to drop a kiss on her mouth, but her eyes went wide.

"I think your grill is on fire."

"Oh hell, the steaks." He ran toward the patio.

When he'd taken the phone call from Bob, he'd just cranked the heat on the grill to sear the meat. Instead, he'd transformed the filets into hockey pucks.

He quickly turned off the gas as smoke filled the air. His phone rang, and he picked it up after seeing his sister's name on the screen.

"It's fine, Lila. Everything's fine. No, I don't need to

come over for dinner tonight. Yes, Cassie is here. I'll figure it out." He drew in a deep breath to get his irritation over the situation under control. It wasn't his sister's fault he'd made a mess of the whole thing. "Thanks for the offer. Yes, I can take George to school tomorrow."

"It *is* going to be fine," Cassie said as he turned to her after he finished the call. "I'm sure you have the ingredients in your pantry to make something yummy."

"I don't have a pantry. I have a cupboard with cereal, a jar of peanut butter, and half a loaf of bread."

"I love peanut butter sandwiches." She smiled. "They're my favorite."

"You don't need to make this better, Cassie. I'm supposed to be taking care of you tonight. I'm supposed to be the one making an effort."

"You did make an effort." She pointed to the charred pieces of meat on the grill. "For the record, even if the steaks had turned out beautifully, I'm a vegetarian. Sorry I didn't specifically mention it before now."

Aiden couldn't help it. He threw his head back and laughed. "I can't get anything right where you're concerned, Cassie."

"You got a lot right the night you spent at my house."

He ignored the heat that welled deep within him at her words. "I'm good for more than a decent time between the sheets."

She shook her head. "First, we both know it was more than decent, and second, you are more than a good time, Aiden. If you're fishing for compliments, I have plenty to give."

"I'm not."

Maybe he was, but it was embarrassing to admit.

"Let's make peanut butter sandwiches." She grinned. "We'll make them special."

"Just to confirm that I'm a real class act, I have stolen packets of jelly to go with the peanut butter."

"I hope it's grape."

"I have grape. I have triple berry. I have strawberry jam. You name it, and I have a jelly flavor for it."

She stepped toward him. "That's the best offer I've had in a long time."

His stomach dipped at how she smiled, like it came from her heart. "You don't have to say that."

"I mean it."

"I'm sorry our signals got crossed this week. I missed you."

She didn't appear to believe him, but it was the truth.

"I missed you, too," she said quietly. Rosie shoved her nose between them, not wanting to miss out on the action. "I know you're still his best girl." Cassie patted the dog's head.

"Her favorite thing is peanut butter. I think she heard us talking about it."

"Rosie and I have our favorite thing in common." Cassie led the way into the house. "Or maybe a couple of our favorite things."

How was it that some lucky man hadn't claimed this woman? She was beautiful, easy to be with, and had the biggest heart of anyone he'd ever met.

"Are you serious about a girls' night out with your high school friends?" he asked once they'd made the sandwiches and sat at the kitchen table. He'd put a spoonful of peanut butter in the center of Rosie's favorite rubber chew toy, and the dog was happily occupied on her bed.

"I'll at least give it a try. I'm not the person that my high school friends think I am. I wasn't even that person back then. They know the Cassie who had a perfect life. She had parents who loved her and a happy home. Not that I didn't have that in high school, but things changed after my dad's diagnosis. We kept the secret for a while because he didn't like the thought of people at the bank or in town treating him differently if they knew about the ALS."

"That must have been tough."

"It pressured my mom and me to act a certain way. She said to have faith and be the person people wanted to see. That was also tough, and I did not know how to open up to anyone."

"Most people change from who they were in high school," he told her.

"Yeah, but you heard what Cameron said. She remembers me as sunshiny. Happy-go-lucky Cassie. Just like you, but that was a mask I wore. One I still wear a lot of the time, and I'm not sure how to let it go. I don't know that people will like me if I do."

"I'll like you no matter what."

She gave him a smile that didn't reach her eyes, and he wondered if he'd done something wrong. Something to lose her faith.

"I like hanging out with you," she said, "even if it's just for now for both of us."

Aiden didn't need the reminder about their lack of expectations for each other. He wondered what she would say if he told her it didn't have to be just for now.

He couldn't force himself to form the words. If Cassie was worried about how people would react or judge her if they knew who she was deep in her heart, then Aiden had every reason to be terrified. He knew who he was at the core. He wasn't able to care for people in the way they needed.

He would risk too much if he let himself truly care about Cassie. He would end up a black spot on her soul, and she deserved better. He did his best to hide the depressing directions of his thoughts as they cleaned up dinner and took Rosie out to the backyard to do her business.

"Dusk is beautiful this time of year." Cassie shielded her eyes as she looked up at the clouds. "I love this time of night."

He nodded and threw a ball to Rosie, who galloped after it with as much speed as any four-legged dog. "It's going to be an adjustment when the time changes in a couple of weeks and it gets dark early."

Cassie wrinkled her nose. "Yes, but early nightfall has its own beauty. The stars are so bright up here. It's not like that in Denver. There's so much pollution that the sky is dark, like a blank canvas. In Crimson, it's painted by the hand of God. Everything about this place is special."

Just like the woman standing next to him, Aiden thought as he took her hand, grateful for this perfect moment with her.

"Cassie, Dr. Smith would like to talk to you." Jules sounded almost apologetic as she peeked her head into Cassie's office, which was actually Dr. Rooney's office that Cassie had been using.

She wasn't sure where she'd fit in the unlikely event they made her a full partner in the practice. It had seemed like a given only weeks ago, but the outcome felt less certain every day.

"I'm finishing a few patient notes from today. I'll be with him as soon as I'm done."

The receptionist cleared her throat. "He said he needs to see you ASAP because he's got a dinner reservation."

"Of course." Cassie refused to let her irritation at the demand show on her face. "I'll come right now."

She pushed away from her desk and walked across

the hall. If it was so imperative that Bryan speak to her, why hadn't he just come to her instead of summoning her like he was a king on his throne?

"Cassie, we need to talk privately," he said when she entered. "Shut the door."

Although Dr. Rooney was the senior and founding partner of the practice, Bryan had the more prominent office with a view of Crimson Mountain. It wasn't as if veterinarians spent much time in their offices, but she didn't understand why Dr. Rooney wouldn't have had the better one.

Not that it mattered to her. She'd be lucky to have a job there when her mentor returned from his medical leave of absence, let alone her own office. In her heart, she still wanted to believe it would work out. She was a good vet, and Dr. Rooney appreciated the value she added to the practice. His was the opinion that mattered to Cassie.

"What can I do for you, Dr. Smith?" she asked, deciding not to torment him further by calling him by his first name. He didn't like that.

"I was hoping it wouldn't come to this, Cassie, but I think it's better you know now rather than wait for Martin's return. It's not working out for you here. We won't be offering you a partner position."

Even though she'd been preparing for and half expecting this potential outcome, shock reverberated through Cassie.

She reached out to steady herself on the leather chair in front of Bryan's desk.

"Does Dr. Rooney know you're firing me?" Her mouth felt like it was filled with sawdust.

"Don't be dramatic or immature," Bryan admonished. "I'm not firing you. You'll stay on until Martin returns in a few weeks and give him time to get back up to speed."

She shook her head like she could convince him to change his mind. "Why are you doing this? I'm good at my job. I take good care of our patients. I add value."

"You take away from the bottom line," Bryan said, like that explained everything. "Since you've been here, our profit margin has gone down seven percent. We're losing money because of you."

"Why? Because I'm not upselling clients on tests and procedures they don't need? That isn't our job."

"Our jobs won't be here if we can't pay the bills to keep the office running."

"I didn't have this problem in Denver."

"It was a bigger practice. I'm guessing that because there were more vets on staff, they could absorb your mismanagement of time and resources."

"Mismanagement?" Cassie shook her head. "There are alternative practices that I'm trained in—acupuncture and massage—things that you won't let me try with patients. Maybe if you did, then—"

"I've made my decision." Bryan looked down at the notepad on his desk like he was dismissing her.

Cassie refused to be set aside so callously. "And is it only your decision?" she demanded. "What about—"

"Dr. Rooney agrees."

His words hit like a physical blow, and she took a step back.

"He hasn't wanted to tell you because he's focused on getting better." The older vet dipped his chin and peered over his reading glasses at her. "I certainly hope you aren't going to desert him in his time of need."

"Of course not." Cassie narrowed her eyes. "What do you take me for?"

"I take you for a person with no future at this practice."

"Your loss," she countered, proud of how unconcerned she sounded. "There are other vet clinics in town."

"Yes, but I have relationships with most of those doctors, and I'm not sure you'd be a match for any of them. I don't think you belong in Crimson."

"What are you talking about? Are you saying you're going to blackball me?"

"No. There you go with the drama again. You need to learn how to control your emotions. The fact is I'm looking out for you. I want what's best for you. Besides, how will it look if you start working for another clinic when it didn't work out with us? This is a small community. It's not like Denver. You could return to the city."

"I don't want to move back to the city." She didn't owe him an explanation but couldn't help offering one. "The city wasn't right for me. I want to live in a smaller community."

He inclined his round head. "Then perhaps look at Aspen or Vail or even Grand Junction."

"You know I grew up here. My mom is here."

"I've talked to the girls at the front desk, and they said you're not significantly enmeshed in the community."

"Significantly enmeshed? What are you talking about? I know half of this town by name. I'm volunteering for the Harvest Festival."

"Because of your mother."

"I've reconnected with friends from high school."

"That's great. I'm sure you're on social media, so you can keep in touch when you leave."

Cassie swallowed. *I'm not leaving*, she wanted to tell the man but didn't say the words. She felt angry and defensive but also scared that he was right.

What if she didn't belong in Crimson? What if the

only reason people liked her was that she was acting in service and not charging her patients what she should?

She could sometimes be a pushover and reluctant to show anything but her happy, sunny side, just like Aiden and her friends from high school expected.

She was feeling anything but sunny now.

"I'll keep in mind this conversation when planning my next steps," she told Bryan Smith.

"This is for your own good, Cassie. You'll see."

Without answering, she turned and left the room.

"Hey, Dr. Raebourn, could you pop into Exam Three?" Annika, one of the vet techs, asked as Cassie shut Dr. Smith's door behind her. "We have a seven-year-old Weimaraner who came in for a tech visit to get his nails trimmed, but I noticed a growth on his left hip. I want someone to take a look."

"Why not Dr. Smith?" Cassie asked, frowning at the woman.

"He tends to schedule animals for surgery at the drop of a hat." The tech shrugged. "I trust your opinion."

"Too bad Dr. Smith doesn't," Cassie muttered. She entered the room and examined the Weimaraner, who kept trying to lick her face. It was as if the animal understood she needed some extra love today. The dog's owner watched with obvious concern.

"What do you think, Dr. Cassie?"

"I think it's a lipoma, which is a fatty tumor. Weimies are prone to them. We'll do a quick needle aspiration and check the fluid in the tumor to confirm it's benign." She reached out and touched the woman's hand. "I think it will be. If so, my recommendation is to keep an eye on it. We can leave it be if it's not bothering her or impeding her movement."

She cleared her throat as she thought about Bryan's

complaints about her not adding to the bottom line. "But we can do surgery if you're more comfortable removing it. If Applejack were my dog, I wouldn't if the biopsy comes back benign."

Surgery to remove a harmless tumor would cost hundreds of dollars, and it wasn't necessary for a lipoma. No matter what Dr. Smith said about the bottom line, Cassie wasn't about to compromise her values by manipulating a pet owner into spending money without it being necessary.

"If Dr. Cassie says you don't need surgery," the tech told the owner, who'd looked at her for confirmation, "you can trust her. She's just as good if not better than Dr. Rooney."

"Let's confirm that it's benign," Cassie suggested. "And we'll go from there. If anything changes, call me right away."

"That sounds perfect." The owner let out a relieved sigh. "My daughter moved back a couple of months ago after losing her job, so money's tight, but I want to do the right thing for my little Applejack."

"Applejack is going to be just fine," Cassie assured her. They did the needle aspiration, and she confirmed the tumor was benign. As Annika led the woman and her dog toward the reception desk to check out, Cassie lowered herself to the stool in the empty exam room.

She closed her eyes and tried not to let emotions wash over her. She'd find some solution for this, even if her dream of working alongside her mentor wasn't going to come to pass.

She tried to do everything right. She'd been helpful, kind and always put on a happy face. While people in her life seemed to appreciate and expect it, her obliging nature wasn't moving her toward her dreams or goals.

She hadn't even stopped to think about why she wanted the thing she did. Did she want to be the junior partner in this clinic or simply to prove her worthiness to her mentor—just like she wanted to prove to her mom that she was a good daughter?

She rested her head in her hands and focused on breathing in and out. She would find a place where she could not only be herself but valued for that.

As much as she wanted that place to be in Crimson, at this clinic and in Aiden's arms, she would survive no matter what. She quickly stood when the door to the exam room opened. Annika walked in with a spray bottle of disinfectant.

"Sorry, Doc." The other woman smiled. "I didn't realize you were still in here. I'm just cleaning between patients. Are you okay? Do you think that Applejack's tumor might be something more?"

"Applejack is going to be fine." Cassie ran a hand through her hair. "I had a conversation with Dr. Smith earlier that didn't go as I'd hoped."

"Don't tell me he's letting you go, too. That man could not be more of a..."

The vet tech grimaced and began to wipe down the exam table. "Never mind me. I shouldn't speak about things that are none of my business, or so Dr. Smith likes to tell me. This is a steady job, and I need to keep it."

"Of course you'll keep it," Cassie assured her. "But what do you mean getting rid of me, too?"

Annika closed the front hall door and turned to face Cassie fully. "You aren't the first younger vet Dr. Rooney has tried to bring on. We all thought that because you have a personal relationship with him, Dr. Smith wouldn't be able to get rid of you quite as easily."

"Why does he want to get rid of people? The office is

so busy you need another partner. Maybe the way I interact with patients and my billing isn't up to his standards,
but that can't always be his excuse. Can it?"

"I think it's more about his insecurity than you. I'd
love you to look at the clinic's financials to know if what
he's telling you is the truth."

Cassie crossed her arms over her chest. Delving into
the clinic's financial records felt like a declaration of war.
"I don't know if that's my place."

"It might be if you feel like your place is here. I know
Laura had some trouble with how Dr. Smith wanted
things done when she first became office manager. She
figured out a way to get along with him, but I think she'd
be willing to show you the books. At least you'd know if
he was telling the truth."

Cassie dropped her voice to a low whisper. "Do you
have a reason to believe he would lie?"

"I'm not sure." There was a noise outside the door,
and Annika looked suddenly alarmed. "You make your
own choice about it. Just know that we all like having
you here. The patients do, too. I'll be sad to see you go,
Doc, if that's what happens."

Cassie nodded and let herself out into the back hall-
way. She'd never been much of a fighter. But then again,
she'd never believed she deserved fighting for something.
Was this a battle she was willing to take on?

It just might be.

Chapter Fifteen

"That a boy. Easy. Easy."

Aiden was in the ring with Isaac, the troubled palomino, working on the day's lesson plan. They'd had a breakthrough with the horse allowing Aiden to put a halter on him a few days earlier, coincidentally after the night he and Cassie had spent looking at the stars.

Yet Aiden was quickly finding that Isaac's recovery would not be straightforward, which made him even more committed to building a bond with the animal.

"You have a way with that horse."

He turned to see a man he didn't recognize but who seemed vaguely familiar standing at the side of the ring. The stranger was tall and undeniably handsome with dark hair cropped close to his head, a chiseled jaw and commanding air, even wearing a faded sweatshirt and jeans with a hole in one knee.

"I'm just reminding him that he's safe and we're going to make sure he stays that way."

"You seem to have a way with animals in general."

Aiden followed the man's gaze to where Rosie watched at the edge of the ring, a kitten cradled next to her. Two of the little ones he'd discovered in the barn had been adopted before they'd even left the vet clinic, but the tiny black boy hadn't been claimed, so Cassie had planned to transfer him to a rescue organization in town so they could handle his adoption.

Only Rosie had other ideas. She'd gone with Aiden to say one last goodbye to the kitten and immediately bonded, refusing to leave his side when Aiden had tried to leave.

He'd ended up with both animals under his roof when he'd had no plans to take care of either of them.

"I'm lucky that a couple of good ones ended up in my life." He released the horse and moved toward the stranger. "Can I help you?"

"I'm Nolan Tucker," the stranger said, like that should've meant something to Aiden. "You don't recognize me?" The man sounded legitimately amused.

"Should I? Have we met?" Aiden shrugged. "I'll be honest, if it was at the start of my stint on the circuit, I had more than a few hazy mornings where I didn't remember much from the night before. I've outgrown the need to drink more than I can handle."

Nolan scrubbed a hand over his jaw. "I wish I'd been able to manage that trick. It took going cold turkey for me to start having clear mornings." He glanced up, eyes closed like he was offering a silent prayer. "One day and sometimes one step forward at a time, just like your horse. It's been five years, and I plan to keep on this path."

"That's an accomplishment," Aiden said, "but I don't think it's why you're here. If you don't mind me cutting to the chase, what *is* the reason you've come?"

The man inclined his head, and Aiden got the impression Nolan continued to be amused that Aiden couldn't place him. "I've been talking to Morgan Walten about property in the area. Do you know Sara Travers?"

"Sure. She and her husband, Josh, own the Crimson Ranch guest property on the other side of town."

Nolan nodded. "I'm staying with them for a few days. I've got work that's bringing me to the area, and to be honest, I've fallen in love with Colorado, so I'm looking to buy a place. Sara suggested I talk to Morgan before getting in touch with a Realtor because, as a local, he might know of a diamond-in-the-rough property that isn't officially listed."

"Is Morgan thinking of selling this ranch?" Aiden frowned and glanced over his shoulder at Isaac. "I find that hard to believe."

"No. At least not that I know of," Nolan said. "I spoke with Morgan last week, and he mentioned that your family has property nearby. I'm here now to speak to you directly. I drove by the place, and I'm interested in buying—or at least having a conversation about—"

"It's not my ranch." Aiden shook his head, willing his stomach to settle as familiar difficult memories and thoughts of the future threatened to engulf him. "My sister owns it."

"Morgan mentioned that," Nolan agreed, "but he suggested I talk to you first. He seems to be under the impression that your sister would be amenable to selling, but he thought you should have first right of refusal if she is. As I understand it, you're living there."

"For now," Aiden conceded. The uncertainty of what came next only added to the low-grade agitation he couldn't seem to shake. "But I don't have the kind of money it would take to buy that land. Even if I did, I'm not interested in owning it."

"Are you interested in staying on to work it?"

"Who are you?" Aiden asked, studying the man more closely. There was something about him that seemed familiar.

"I see you two have met," Morgan said as he entered the arena. "Are you feeling as starstruck as I do, Aiden?"

Nolan turned. "He doesn't know who I am."

"What am I missing?" Aiden did not like the feeling he wasn't keeping up with a conversation.

"Have you lived under a rock for the past fifteen years?" Morgan demanded. "This is Nolan Tucker."

"Yeah, I got his name. So what?"

"He's one of the biggest Hollywood stars in the world, maybe even the biggest." The weathered rancher turned to Nolan. "Are you the biggest?"

"I suppose it depends on who you ask," Nolan said with a shrug. "It's been a while since I've talked to someone who legitimately had no idea who I am. I like it. It makes me more convinced Crimson is the right place for me."

Aiden suddenly felt foolish. "I know who you are. I've heard your name and seen you on television. I don't go to movie theaters. I didn't realize that you were…well… you." He growled out his frustration. "I didn't put the two together. Sue me."

Nolan grinned, and Aiden half expected a sparkle to gleam from the man's straight teeth. It was stupid that he hadn't recognized Nolan Tucker, at least by name. That showed how preoccupied he was—and not simply from training Isaac.

"Like I told you, it's refreshing."

"What do you think, Aiden?" Morgan tipped his hat. "Would Lila be willing to sell the property?"

"I don't know. You're going to have to ask her."

That was a lie. He did know. His sister would welcome a buyer for the ranch.

"Have you even stepped foot on the land?" he asked Nolan. "What makes you so sure my family's property is the one you want? I don't have a lot of experience with Hollywood types, but I can tell you my sister has been through hell losing her husband. I don't want her taken advantage of or misled because you've got some wild idea to become a cowboy after saddling up on a movie set for a couple of weeks."

Nolan's thousand-watt smile broadened, and he didn't appear the least bit offended by Aiden's gruff assessment of him. That was a point in the movie star's favor.

Morgan chuckled and scratched his beard like he wasn't sure whether to applaud Aiden's words or apologize. "I told you he was a straight shooter," he said to Nolan. "He's also got a hell of a way with horses."

Nolan's smile faded as he nodded. "I'm five years off liquor and drugs, but not many people know the details of the event that pushed me into sobriety. Because it *was* a push—or, more accurately, a fall."

Rosie had gotten up and moved close to Nolan like she could feel he needed a bit of comfort. The kitten followed close behind, and the Hollywood star bent down to pet each animal.

"To answer your question," Nolan told Aiden, his tone amused, "I normally spend more than a couple of weeks on a movie set. This particular film was shot in New Zealand over the course of seven grueling months. We were filming the second in the *Walk through Fire* trilogy."

"Nominated for a bunch of honors," Morgan added.

Nolan grimaced. "I wasn't able to attend any of the ceremonies because I was getting sober in a pricey rehab facility in the desert. Although I kept it hidden, things had gotten out of control during filming. They let me on the back of a horse even though I was downing pills with vodka for breakfast most days. No one cared as long as I could still say my lines."

Aiden appreciated that. He'd gotten banged up plenty over the years before the accident that had ended his career. No one had cared as long as he could still saddle up for the next event.

The air suddenly felt charged with past memories and regrets—both his and Nolan Tucker's. He watched tiny dust motes ripple through the beams of sunlight illuminating the arena, like tiny dancers whirling to music only they could hear.

"If I wasn't still drunk the morning of the accident that propelled me into getting clean, I was certainly hungover. Maybe it would have happened even if I'd had a clear head. But I didn't. I missed a cue and turned the wrong way on the horse. She tripped over a wire, and... it was bad."

Nolan's voice cracked, and he cleared his throat as he pulled out his phone. He held up the device, and Aiden nodded at the photo of a chestnut-colored horse on the lock screen.

"This is Gaya," Nolan said, looking every bit the proud parent showing off his baby. "She's retired from moviemaking and living her best life on a farm outside Auckland. That's where I was filming at the time. We were lucky she didn't have to be put down, but she's lame. I pay for her care."

"And you want to move your pet horse to Colorado?" Aiden was unsure of the response the man was looking for but knew he'd said the wrong thing when Morgan rolled his eyes. Yes, he should play nice with the important Hollywood guy who obviously had deep pockets, but he'd seen plenty of horses and other animals injured during his time on the rodeo circuit. Hell, he still carried guilt over the accident with Storm.

While he could admire Nolan for his willingness to fund the horse's care, he wasn't impressed based on the circumstances.

"I want to create a horse sanctuary. Perhaps not just for horses—a haven for any animal that needs a safe place to spend its last days."

"You want to do that on my family's land?" Aiden couldn't help but laugh. His father had hated any hint of weakness. Eddie Riley would be turning over in his grave at the thought of his land being used as an animal sanctuary, which made Aiden immediately take to the idea.

"Yes, if your sister's willing to sell it, but..." Nolan lifted and lowered his big shoulders. "I can't be there full time. I'll be lucky to spend a total of a month in Colorado during any given year. At least at this point while I'm still a box-office draw."

Aiden felt his brow rise of its own accord. "Do you have a reason to think that will change?"

Morgan scoffed. "It ain't changing. Nolan is in his prime. How old are you, Hollywood?"

Nolan flashed a grin. "Thirty-seven, sir."

"Right. A baby." Morgan slapped him on the back. "You're going to be the Clint Eastwood of your generation."

Nolan glanced at Aiden. "I assume you've heard of Clint Eastwood?"

"Yes," Aiden said, "and I've heard of you. Like I said, I wasn't putting it together. I appreciate the sentiment behind what you're trying to do, Mr. Tucker."

"Call me Nolan."

"Fine, Nolan. But even if my sister is willing to sell you the property, I've got a job in Wyoming I need to get back to."

"You don't owe Wyoming anything," Morgan said.

"I don't owe Crimson anything, either," Aiden countered.

Nolan held up his hands. "Let's not get ahead of ourselves. The first step is for me to find a property. I think your sister's ranch would fit the bill, and if it does, I'll make her a generous offer. Would you be willing to broach the subject with her and set up an introduction?"

Aiden took a step back and let his gaze settle on Nolan Tucker's handsome face. He had a good sense for people simply by observing them. He'd liked this man from the get-go, even after discovering he was somebody famous.

Aiden didn't hold much value in fame and had a feeling Nolan didn't, either. Even though he wasn't willing to commit to a potential position on a nonexistent horse sanctuary, if nothing else, he could help broker a deal that would make his sister financially secure for the rest of her life.

He would take care of her and George, and they would be one worry off his plate.

Maybe there'd be money left over to buy his mother a house. Lila would be willing to do that and also want to give Aiden some of the money from the ranch's sale. Even though their father had left it solely to her, she believed that it belonged to both of them.

As much as that land ran through his blood, Aiden didn't want anything to do with it. It was tainted, from his point of view. But now it could be used for something good.

"I'll set up a meeting with Lila. I assume you're going to want Realtors and lawyers involved?"

"I can't draft a bill of sale," Nolan said. "As far as Realtors, if we can come to an agreement, my preference would be to have someone on my team draw up the paperwork. Your sister can have whoever she wants to review it. I'm not particularly interested in more people than necessary knowing my business."

Aiden nodded, and to his surprise, Isaac approached from behind him and draped his head over Aiden's shoulder.

Morgan whistled low under his breath. "I told you he has a way with animals. Three weeks ago, I thought I was gonna have to put down that horse."

"Any trainer worth his or her salt could have done what I did," Aiden told the two men as he gently patted Isaac's nose.

"Sure," Morgan agreed. "You keep telling yourself that, and I'm going to keep believing you're special."

"I'm not special." Aiden must have said the words with more force than he'd meant based on how Morgan blinked.

Nolan nodded like he understood more than he should. "Morgan has my contact information. I'll wait to hear from you."

"I'll walk you out, Nolan," Morgan said.

Aiden blew out a breath and turned toward Isaac when the other two men left the building.

"I'm not special," he said to the horse.

Isaac nickered as if agreeing with him, and Aiden placed his forehead against the horse's neck and breathed in the animal's musty scent.

As always happened when he was near an animal, he relaxed. Rosie pressed against the back of his legs and whined softly.

Shadow, the cat, chased a mouse across the arena floor.

Aiden might not have been special, but he couldn't deny that this town was. He couldn't deny that he wanted to belong here. He hadn't felt like he belonged anywhere since he'd climbed into his mom's battered old Bronco and driven away that day.

The thought of staying on and committing to something, especially when it involved his family's property...

He shook his head. One step at a time, he reminded himself, just like the movie star had said. One step at a time.

Later that week, Cassie sat on a barstool in the popular local brewery, Tap Room. The lively establishment felt oddly crowded for a Thursday, although she generally had little experience hanging out in bars.

The interior had a rustic feel with knotty pine paneling on the walls and a bar that ran the length of the main room. The red leather stools were filled, as were most of the tables and booths nearby. The shiny mirror behind the bar reflected the hundreds of bottles of liquor that lined the shelves. Everyone, from the man pouring drinks behind the bar to the trio of waitresses serving them to the people talking and laughing in clusters, seemed happy to be there. Just like Cassie.

Anyway, what did she know about the habits of bar patrons? It wasn't as if she had a social life to speak of, and Cameron had said something about karaoke night being popular with locals.

Cassie had never imagined she'd be a person who considered taking part in a karaoke number, but she smiled and nodded as the women she'd considered friends in high school discussed what song they would perform.

"What do you think, Cass?" Molly Haufmeyer—now Molly Enichs thanks to her recent marriage—asked, leaning forward over the high table where the group was congregated. "What's your favorite karaoke song?"

"I don't have one," Cassie admitted with a shake of her head.

"Too bad," Cameron said, sounding legitimately disappointed that Cassie couldn't contribute to the decision.

"Maybe 'Love is a Battlefield'?" Cassie wasn't sure why the old-school female-rocker anthem popped into her head, but the suggestion was met with immediate approval.

"Perfect." Cameron wrapped an arm around Cassie's shoulder. "Everyone loves that song, although I've heard your love life isn't much of a battlefield right now."

Cassie blinked. "I don't have a love life to speak of."

"Come on," Brogan Tewes urged. Brogan had been prom queen their senior year of high school, boisterous and lively—and a bit of a gossip as Cassie remembered it. Apparently that hadn't changed. "Word on the street is you're dating that hot cowboy Aiden Riley."

"He was a weird little kid," Cameron added. "That's how I remember him from grade school."

"I don't remember him at all." Molly took a sip of her craft beer. "But now he's hard to miss. Give us the details, Cass."

Cassie felt her cheeks heat with a blush. She didn't want to discuss her relationship with Aiden—if she could call it a relationship.

"We were friends when I first moved to town in fifth grade," she said, glancing at Cameron. "He wasn't weird," she felt the need to point out, "just shy."

Molly placed her drink on the table and rubbed her hands together. "The strong, silent type. I love it. Go on."

"You're married." Brogan flipped her straight black

hair over one shoulder. "What do you care about the scoop on the cute rodeo stud?"

"Retired rodeo…competitor," Cassie said under her breath, not that any of them were paying attention.

"I love my Tommy," Molly said, crossing a finger over her heart. "But I'm not blind. What's going on with the two of you?"

Cameron nudged Cassie. "Is it serious?"

"We're just friends." Cassie realized how lame that sounded. She half expected the trio of friends to roll their eyes and turn their backs on her for being such a dud when it came to gossip.

But all three women seemed to recognize what she wasn't saying out loud, displaying a perceptiveness that left her heart thudding in her chest.

"Is that what you want?" Brogan asked gently, her soft voice managing to be heard despite the crowd laughing and talking around them.

Cassie started to smile and play off the question. In truth, she barely knew these ladies and had no reason to believe they'd want to hear about her internal war with regard to her feelings for Aiden.

This was a night out, fun and lighthearted. She was sunshine Cassie, not bringing anyone down with her real-life struggles.

But she'd committed herself to be herself, not the pretend version of herself that she feigned because it was more palatable for the people in her life.

"It's what he's able to give." She cleared her throat around the emotion that lodged there. "Plus he's a great kisser and stuff."

"And stuff," Molly repeated, her grin widening. "Let's talk about—"

"Hold on." Cameron placed a hand on Cassie's arm.

"If *and stuff* is what you want, that's great. Aiden Riley is as hot as an egg frying in a pan. But you need to make sure whatever happens is on your terms."

"I've never really set terms," Cassie said with a laugh.

"No time like the present to start," Cameron told her. "I broke up with my boyfriend a month ago because he kept canceling plans to hang out with his mother. I figured if he couldn't cut the apron strings at the start, it wouldn't get better. I'll find a new boyfriend."

"Aiden isn't my boyfriend. It's a *for now* thing."

"Cameron's right," Brogan said, her tone soft. "For now with a hot guy is fun, but if you want more than fun, he either needs to give it to you or you need to move on. Girl, you're worth it. Don't let any man make you feel different."

Cassie nodded, then glanced around at the crowd. There were couples with arms casually draped around each other and larger groups of friends. Why had dating and friendship always seemed too complicated? Tonight it felt easy. She liked easy.

"My Tommy makes me feel like a queen every day." Molly wiggled her hips. "And every night, but that's my private business."

Cassie was saved from saying more when the woman hosting the karaoke night gestured their group forward. She followed the other women up to the stage and tried to stay out of sight.

She couldn't help the thoughts pinging through her brain. She hadn't precisely unburdened her soul to Cameron, Molly and Brogan, but they'd understood without her having to go into details.

Their unquestioning support made her feel like she wasn't so alone. Perhaps letting people in might not be so scary after all.

There was no pushback or judgment that she expected too much or must've been giving Aiden undue pressure. No hint or outright suggestion that it was her problem.

Cassie was prone to believing there was something wrong with her that she had difficulties trusting things might be right. Bryan Smith wanted to convince her she was the issue, but one casual night of reconnecting with old friends had helped her see she might be okay just as she was.

She joined in as the words to the popular song scrolled on the screen in front of them. The women linked arms as they sang, and Cassie once again wondered if she was always destined to be an outsider, even in her own hometown.

Then Molly grabbed her arm and pulled her forward. She linked her arm around Cassie's waist. "We are not putting you in the corner," she said. "This song was your idea. Come up front with the rest of us. You belong."

Cassie smiled, ready to open herself up to being part of a group. She belted out the lyrics along with her new old friends, not caring when she hit a sour note because they didn't seem to care, either.

Maybe that was the point—among friends, she could open herself up to knowing sour notes happened. She had to be willing to risk being real and let people in so they could see the woman she was without her mask.

Could it be the same with Aiden? If she let him in and made it known that she wanted him as part of her life, would he take the risk with her?

There was only one way to find out.

Chapter Sixteen

"A car just pulled up." Nolan sounded none too happy about it. "Would your sister have told her friends that I was here?" The Hollywood heartthrob looked like he wanted to bolt out the back door.

Aiden tried to appreciate the man's point of view even though he didn't appreciate aspersions cast on his sister. "You can trust Lila. You said to keep it quiet, and she'll respect that."

Nolan didn't look convinced, and Aiden couldn't blame the man. He'd never seen his sister act so goofy and starstruck as she had when she'd been introduced to one of the biggest box office stars on the planet.

The more Aiden thought about it, the more he felt like an idiot for not recognizing Nolan Tucker from the start.

It had been so out of context to see someone famous in the Walten barn, and other pressing matters had filled Aiden's mind.

"I'm not up for an autograph session," Nolan said as he

looked out the window. "Wow. Even if the person asking is a knockout." He laughed softly. "I might be willing to deal with it in her case."

Aiden stepped toward the front window and sucked in a breath. "That is not a fangirl, and she's off limits."

Now he sounded like an idiot, but he wasn't going to take it back. His whole body had gone on high alert, watching Cassie exit her car.

"Should I slip out the back?" Nolan asked, amusement replacing the annoyance in his deep voice. "I don't want you to get a bruised ego when your woman sees me. I'm known to affect the ladies." He chuckled like it was a joke.

Aiden should admit that Cassie wasn't his woman. He had no claim on her, but he liked the sound of the description too much.

"I trust her," he told Nolan. "If she's so blown away by your pretty face, then so be it. But I don't think she will be."

Nolan inclined his head, his striking blue eyes taking on an unflinching gleam. "That sounds like a challenge."

"I'm up for a challenge," Aiden countered, then immediately regretted the words. What the hell was he thinking? For one, Cassie didn't belong to him. Even if she did, who would blame her for being dazzled by somebody like Nolan Tucker?

By the time Aiden got to the door, Rosie was already waiting next to it.

"Hey." Cassie stood near her car as if unwilling to approach the bunkhouse. She wore a black tunic-style sweater, jeans that hugged her curves and black ankle boots. Her hair was curled and fell over her shoulders. He had the sudden yearning to sweep her into his arms but didn't move. "Do you have company?" She looked uncertain. "I probably should have called first."

Aiden realized Nolan's rented SUV sat in the driveway. "You're fine. I'm glad you're here. It's good to see you. Come on in. How was your girls' night?"

Her shoulders relaxed slightly. "You just strung together a liberal amount of words." She looked wary again. "Are you nervous?"

"Why would I be nervous?"

"Are you sure you want me to come in?"

"Yes, I invited you." He backed into the house as she moved closer. "Tell me about girls' night."

"It was fun."

"Did Henry McKerlie show up?"

"He did, and…" She paused in the act of petting Rosie. "Hello," she said slowly, her mouth dropping open.

"This is Nolan Tucker."

She tossed Aiden a strange look. "I know who he is, but I didn't know you hung out with movie stars."

"Just me," Nolan said. "Hello. It's nice to meet you. I didn't catch your name."

"Cassie?" The response sounded like a question, which didn't surprise Aiden. Nolan was the sort of man who would make a woman forget her own name.

"Cassie. It's lovely to meet you." Nolan shook her hand with great sincerity. "Are you from around here?"

She nodded. "Born and raised. I recently moved back."

"What do you do?"

"I'm a vet."

"That's amazing. What a service you provide. I love animals."

"Me, too," Cassie agreed, then turned to Aiden. "You love animals. Is that why you guys are friends?"

Aiden shook his head. "We're not friends."

Nolan chuckled. "We might become friends."

"I doubt it," Aiden muttered, earning another laugh from Nolan.

"Well, Cassie." Nolan turned his attention to her with a wink. "You and I might become friends. I'm buying a property in town."

"I work a lot," Cassie said immediately, and Aiden wanted to kiss her.

He lifted a brow in Nolan's direction. "She works a lot."

Nolan inclined his head. "What if I adopt an animal? Can we be friends then?" He reached down to pet Rosie. "Is that how the two of you became friends, or did you grow up together?"

"A little of both," Cassie said, glancing between them. "What about you two?"

"Nolan wants to buy my sister's property."

"Really? Is Lila interested?"

"I think so." Aiden was shocked by the knot of emotion lodged in his chest.

"What do you think?"

Aiden fidgeted under Cassie's scrutiny. "It's none of my business. The land belongs to Lila."

"I should go," Nolan said, reading the change in mood with more insight than Aiden would have expected from a man in his position.

The meeting with Lila had been productive once his sister had overcome the shock of meeting Nolan. She'd had a field day scolding Aiden for not warning her about the identity of the potential buyer he had for the ranch.

Lila quickly took control of the meeting, displaying a deep understanding of the value of their family's land. Aiden realized he'd inadvertently underestimated his sister's capacity to deal with real-life situations. Her grief and despair had seemed so all-encompassing when he'd initially returned to town.

The sadness that had consumed her and made her seem vulnerable and unsure was nonexistent as she grilled Nolan Tucker with questions about his intentions and commitment to being a good steward of the land.

Her voice trembled slightly as she'd spoken about her late husband and how much the ranch had come to mean to him in such a short time.

To Aiden's surprise, she also briefly touched on the history of the Riley family, which was fraught with discord and abuse for generations. She said she no longer wanted the land to be tainted by what had come in the past.

The reason she'd agreed to return to the ranch their father had left her was so that she could build something new with her family.

If Aiden was surprised by his sister's strength and composure, he was even more shocked that Nolan Tucker listened to what Lila had to say. He addressed her questions and concerns with a sincerity that Aiden didn't believe the actor was faking.

As he had with Aiden, Nolan explained his history and the initial plan for how the ranch would be used. The man had given his future a lot of thought.

They hadn't explicitly discussed money, and Aiden had rolled his eyes when Lila told Nolan that her willingness to sell depended as much on the buyer's integrity as the offer's fairness.

Integrity was important, but Aiden wanted to see his sister and mom financially secure.

That was when Aiden had invited Nolan to the bunkhouse for a more pointed conversation about an offer. Lila had simply kissed Aiden on the cheek and thanked him for taking care of her. He had a feeling she knew why this deal was important to him.

But the more time that went by, the more he was convinced that his sister would be fine without him, just like Cassie. He wasn't about to tell either of them that. Not yet.

"How long are you in town?" Cassie asked Nolan as he moved toward the door.

"A few more days," he said. "As I told Aiden, I'm staying at Crimson Ranch with Sara and Josh Travers."

Cassie nodded. "They're patients of mine—I should say their animals are my patients."

"Lucky animals." Nolan turned toward her fully and offered another thousand-watt smile. "I have a few meetings scheduled over in Aspen, and I hope to work some things out with Aiden's sister while I'm here. But I can make time for dinner if you're available to join me one night?"

Aiden had no doubt Cassie would say yes. It would be part of her new "live for the moment" mantra. His heart ached as he realized he wanted to capture and hold Cassie close. He wanted her to belong to him and selfishly wanted to hoard every moment she had to give, but he had no right to ask.

"There's a great restaurant at the base of the ski resort. Cassie knows it," he said, and they both looked at him like he'd grown a horn out of his head.

He understood that he was practically playing matchmaker, even though the idea of Cassie with another man would kill him.

"Maybe a rain check," she said to Nolan, her glossy lips pursing slightly. "I'm swamped at work and volunteering for our upcoming Harvest Festival. Any chance we could convince you to make an appearance? We're raising money for some great causes."

Nolan grimaced but continued to look amused. It had probably been decades since he'd had a woman refuse a date.

"Not this year. I'm trying to keep a low profile until I settle on a property and the sale goes through. If I'm here longer than planned, I'll let you know. You could give me your number just in case." He added another wink for good measure, and Aiden nearly groaned in frustration.

Cassie laughed, low and husky, causing the hairs on the back of Aiden's neck to stand on end.

"Aiden and I are working together on the festival," she told Nolan. "If you change your mind, let him know."

"Fair enough." Nolan turned to Aiden, the gleam in his gaze making Aiden think he took pleasure in being spurned. "I still plan a serious conversation about you staying on after the sale."

Aiden shrugged, trying not to fall to his knees in relief that Cassie hadn't responded to Nolan's advances. "That's a conversation for down the road."

"Got it," Nolan agreed. "Have a good night," he said and walked out the front door.

Cassie sank onto the sofa, and Rosie hopped up next to her. "That was unreal. I'm pretty sure Nolan Tucker just asked me out on a date."

"Why did you say no?" Aiden asked, rubbing a hand over the back of his neck.

Again the look like he was sprouting a horn. "Do you know why I'm here?"

He thought about it and then shook his head. "It doesn't matter why. I'm glad you came over, Cassie."

"I'm here because I had a great time with my friends, and you're the person I wanted to tell about it." She hooked a finger at him, and he ventured closer as if drawn by a magnet. She had that effect on him. "Although I'm guessing my paltry adventures can't possibly compete with hanging out with a movie star."

"Nolan Tucker isn't a big deal to me." Aiden sat next to her on the sofa and took her hand in his. "You are."

"Is that so?"

"Tell me about your adventures." He tugged on her hand until she was pressed against him. "I want to hear every detail and for you to stay all night."

He wanted more, but as she recounted her evening, his heart settled, feeling content. Another night with Cassie would be enough for now.

"It wasn't nearly as exciting as hanging out with Nolan Tucker," Cassie told Aiden, "although I might be a ka-raoke convert." She laughed at the look of abject horror on his face.

"Did someone threaten bodily harm to get you to take part?"

"No. I liked it. I liked everything about this evening. Cameron, Molly and Brogan made me feel like I be-longed—and not because I was doing something for them or they worked for me or anything like that. They seemed to like *me*."

Aiden stared intently into her eyes like he was search-ing for something. "Do you find that hard to believe?"

"I guess I never believed it… I know I'm likable, but that's because I work at it. I smile when people expect me to, and I try to be positive and not too needy. I don't want anyone to think I'm a burden. But tonight, I was honest about some of my struggles and they were supportive. It didn't feel like I was troubling anyone."

As she revealed her innermost fear to Aiden, it felt like butterflies were taking flight inside Cassie's stom-ach. Would he think she was silly?

Her face heated, and she tried to shrug out of his embrace. "I'm making a simple night at a bar way too big of a deal."

"I'm glad you had a good time, but you know I like you, right? Just as you are and not because you feel you have to act a certain way."

The butterflies settled at his words. "That's why I'm here."

His brows rose. "I thought you might be here for post-karaoke canoodling."

"How do you know the word *canoodling*?"

"What can I say? I'm a renaissance man."

"Canoodling is all well and good." She blew out a breath when he looked dubious. "Admittedly, between the two of us, canoodling is amazing. Before we get to that part…you should know I want more."

"I can give you more." Aiden trailed his hand along her jaw and drew her forward for a lingering kiss.

Oh, how easy it would be to sink into the embrace and accept everything Aiden offered. She could again ignore anything but the moment and how this man made her body feel.

It would be easy but not simple. There was more than her body involved. Cassie's heart was as much part of this and wouldn't be satisfied with only the physical aspect, incredible as it might be.

"As it turns out, I'm not a no-strings-attached kind of person," she said after forcing herself to pull away. She felt the change in Aiden immediately.

A surge of tension entered his body as he dropped his hand from her head. "What does that mean?"

"I'm not sure." She frowned. "I'm new to the business of determining what I need and want and going for it. I like you and care about you more than just as a friend."

"I care about you, Cassie, but I'm not the commitment type. You know that."

"I'm wondering if you would be willing to try," she asked softly. "For me. For us. I don't expect declarations or promises, but I need to know..."

What did she need to know? She couldn't see their future clearly, even in her own mind.

It felt like a dozen emotions flashed through his dark gaze at her words—everything from vulnerability to hope to desire to fear.

She didn't want fear to win for either of them. But she'd said her piece and needed to give Aiden a chance to tell his.

"There's a good chance I'm going to screw this up," he said, tightening his hands into fists in his lap.

"There's also a chance you won't," she countered. "I'm willing to take the risk. I need to be with someone who'll do the same in return."

"And if I say no, what are you going to do? You could track down Nolan Tucker and take him up on the dinner invitation. Do you think a movie star will bend to your will?"

"That's not what I'm asking you to do."

His words stung, but she understood they came from a place of fear. She was afraid, too, but she wasn't about to let it run her life. Not anymore.

"If you can't give more, I respect your decision. I might not like it, but I'll respect it."

He got up and took two steps toward the front door. For a moment, she thought he would walk out of his own house.

Then he spun around. "If you want me to attempt to be somebody different, then I owe it to you to give it a go."

Cassie released the breath she'd been holding. "Oh, you stupid, stupid man. I want you just as you are."

She stood and moved to him. "I don't need you to

change." She knew how to deal with frightened creatures who would just as soon lash out as reveal how they were hurting.

That's what Aiden reminded her of now. She took his hand, slowly wrapping her fingers around his. "The fact that you're in this with me is enough. It's more than enough."

He shook his head.

"You don't think so?" she asked.

He drew in a shaky breath. "No, but as long as you do, I'm willing to try."

"That's a start for both of us." She kissed the underside of his jaw. "Don't argue with a woman who knows what she wants. I want you."

He lifted her off her feet and deepened the kiss. It felt demanding and tender, and she met every one of his questions with an answer of her own.

"Are you sure this is what you want?" he asked as he carried her to his bedroom.

"More than anything," she whispered. "Are *you* sure?"

"I'm sure I want you, Cassie."

They undressed slowly as if they had all the time in the world to discover each other. It felt as though Aiden was already an expert on her body, knowing exactly how to hold and caress her to send her to new heights of pleasure. And when he entered her, Cassie felt like she'd found her place in the world in the arms of the man who had captured her heart.

They moved together as if they'd been together and been meant to be together...forever.

Although she told herself not to read too much into it, it had to mean something. How could she help it when being with Aiden felt so right?

Chapter Seventeen

Cassie walked through the backdoor to her mother's bookshop early morning on the Saturday of the Harvest Festival and was immediately greeted by both Spud and Rosie.

"George, I told you to keep those dogs on a leash," Lila said as the animals circled Cassie's legs.

"Sorry, Doc Cassie." George dropped the stack of books he'd been holding and ran forward.

Her heart raced as she looked around the small storeroom but settled again when she saw no sign of Aiden.

"He had to run over to Aspen with Morgan Walten," Lila said, following Cassie's gaze. "There was an emergency with a horse that got loose. They thought Aiden might be able to help track her. He said he'd be back in time for the dance tonight."

Cassie nodded. "I hope it turns out okay." It was foolish to feel hurt that he hadn't told her of his plans. She was a vet and possibly could have added something to the efforts. At least she would have been able to offer support to Aiden. That was what she did best.

"Doc Cassie, I've been teaching Spud some tricks. Rosie can do them, too. Do you want to see?" George asked excitedly.

"Sweetheart, we've got to get this stuff out front before the festival opens," his mother admonished.

"Can I show Doc Spud's tricks first?"

"I'd be happy to see them." Cassie winked at Lila. "And we'll move extra fast after."

"Fine." Lila rolled her eyes with amusement. "One of these days, George, you're going to be too big and smelly to wrap me around your finger with your cuteness."

Cassie knew that wasn't true. Lila adored her son, and now that she was doing better, it was amazing to see the boy also flourish.

"Okay," he said. "But my farts already stink."

Cassie laughed and then dutifully watched Spud and Rosie go through their obedience commands, from sitting to rolling over to shaking paws.

At the same time, her mind wandered to Aiden. It was silly to read more into the fact that he hadn't run his trip to Aspen by her.

He didn't owe her. Besides, she hadn't shared some things with him, like her trip to Aspen a few days earlier to interview for a position at a vet clinic there.

The swanky mountain town was less than an hour from Crimson and might've been her best bet for staying close. She hadn't told anyone, not even her mom or Aiden, about her conversation with Bryan Smith. She felt deeply embarrassed that despite trying so hard, she wasn't being offered the partner position.

She'd spoken with Dr. Rooney, who had been apologetic and as confused as her. He told her Bryan had men-

tioned something about her not being a team player and
insisting on doing things her way.

It seemed ironic that the first time Cassie had held her
ground and made choices based on what she believed
was right in her heart, she'd lost something she dearly
wanted. Yet she didn't regret it.

As Annika had suggested, she'd reviewed the clinic's financial spreadsheets for the months of her employ-
ment, which had left her even more confused. Based
on her initial calculations, she'd been hitting the clinic's
profit margin targets, although that hadn't satisfied Dr.
Smith. Cassie wasn't naive enough to believe serving
animals and creating a profitable practice were mutu-
ally exclusive.

Unfortunately, she didn't have the insight to understand why the figures didn't add up to a successful business model. Laura, the office manager, had offered to
have Dr. Rooney review the income and expenditure
statements and see if he could shed some light on the
calculations.

As much as she appreciated that, Cassie had told the
woman not to bother. She didn't want to add more stress
to her former mentor's plate upon his return, especially
when he'd have to try again to add another veterinarian
to the practice who would meet Bryan Smith's exacting
and inexplicable standards.

"You've done great work with both of these dogs," she
told George when he finished the demonstration.

"I'm going to be a dog trainer when I grow up," he
said, "and a veterinarian like you and an astronaut and
a professional LEGO builder."

"I like your goal-oriented mindset," she said, nodding
with sincerity. Lila mouthed a thank-you from behind

her son's shoulder, and they began carrying the boxes of books and gift items through the store out to the front.

The Harvest Festival included a farmers market in the town square, and most businesses also set up sidewalk sales to entice visitors to do more local shopping.

Cassie's mother was already outside talking with the woman who owned the flower shop next door and two of her book club friends who had come to help set up for the day. It was the reminder Cassie needed that her mother would be okay regardless of whether Cassie stayed nearby.

Better than okay.

Melissa was managing the grief over her husband's death and creating a new life and identity for herself while helping Lila do the same.

It frustrated Cassie to feel insecure and tethered to her past and the person she'd been. Why was it so easy for other people to reinvent themselves when it felt like such a hurdle for her?

But she was trying, and the interview in Aspen had gone well. She would tell her mother after the festival, and if she got the job, then she would share the news with Aiden.

She didn't want to scare him into thinking that she was basing any decision for her future on their relationship and what he would do next, even though she couldn't help but wonder what he was thinking. Would he stay if Nolan Tucker bought his sister's ranch, or would he return to his former life in Wyoming?

George ran toward Cassie's mother, Spud and Rosie in tow on their leashes. Both Melissa and her friend greeted him with hugs. Cassie hadn't seen that kind of happiness radiating from her mother in so long, and she stepped away from the group when her eyes filled with tears.

"Hey, sweetheart." Melissa gave Cassie a hug from behind, a look of concern replacing her smile when Cassie turned to face her. "What's wrong?"

Cassie should tell her about all of it—her struggles with Bryan Smith, his baseless accusations about her not contributing to the practice. She needed to share the interview she'd had in Aspen and how she struggled to open herself up and make friends. The fact that she didn't believe she was worthy of being loved if she wasn't acting a certain way.

There was so much she'd kept inside, but then she noticed the crowd already beginning to gather at the edge of the square in anticipation of the festival's official opening.

She realized now was not the time to burden her mother with worries that could wait another day. "I'm just happy for you, Mom," she said with a smile she hoped didn't appear forced. "You seem to love your life. Dad would want that for you."

"He'd want the same thing for you, sweet girl," her mother responded, clearly more in tune with Cassie's emotions than she'd realized.

"I *am* happy here." That was the truth, if not the whole of it. "I love Crimson."

"I'm not sure either of us thanked you often enough for coming back for so many years. You gave up—"

"I didn't give up anything," Cassie insisted. "I wanted to help you take care of him."

Her mother smoothed a hand over Cassie's cheek, her expression wistful. "You took care of both of us, but it's time to put yourself first, Cassiopeia."

No one ever called Cassie by her given name.

"We named you after the stars," her mother continued, "but neither your father nor I could have imagined how bright your heart would glow. He would want you to do find your bliss now. You don't have to look out for me anymore."

Cassie shook her head. "I'm not sure I know what to do if I'm not caring for people or animals. That's not going to change."

"Being a veterinarian is more than a career," her mother agreed. "It's your calling. But you can still take care of yourself."

"I'm not a kid," Cassie said, although she sniffed like a child trying to hold her emotions in check.

Embarrassment washed through her, but her mother's smile was gentle. "I know that. I'm not sure you were ever a child. You were born an old soul, Cassie. I don't mean I'll take care of you like you can't manage it yourself. I can support you and listen if you need a shoulder to cry on. Heaven knows you've done more than enough for me."

"Thanks, Mom." Cassie hugged her mother and then released her when Lila asked about arranging some books on the sidewalk shelves. "I'm glad to be here today for the festival. Maybe we could go for a walk tomorrow? There are some things I'd like to talk to you about and have your help figuring out how to handle." She was shocked at how pleased her mother looked.

"That sounds perfect. I've been waiting to be needed by you for a long time, my girl."

Those words stuck with Cassie for the rest of the day. She'd spent so much time assuming that the people around her wanted something from her—to be the one to offer support. She hadn't considered that asking for help in return could also bring her closer to the people in her life.

She was self-sufficient, which wasn't a bad thing. But

there was a difference between taking care of herself and being emotionally cut off from vulnerability and sharing her life and heart.

This new path was scary and also exciting. Cassie hoped Aiden would be willing to join her on it.

The Harvest Festival dance was the last place on earth Aiden wanted to be, but that didn't stop him from smiling and greeting people as he entered. The barn was decorated with twinkling lights strung from the rafters, bales of hay and colorful bouquets of autumn blooms.

He should have been there earlier to help set up, but with how things had gone in Aspen, he'd been lucky to make it at all. They'd eventually found the lost mare, who'd slipped from the edge of a washed-out cliff and gotten wedged between the mountain and a log after wandering off from the rest of the herd.

It had taken hours and the coordinated efforts of volunteers, local firefighters and veterinary staff to finally lead the terrified animal to safety. The horse was bruised and traumatized but predicted to make a full recovery. The same couldn't be said for Aiden, who felt like he'd been kicked in the teeth when one of the veterinarians had casually mentioned Cassie Raebourn possibly joining their practice.

He felt like a complete fool for not knowing her plans and couldn't shake the sense of betrayal that Cassie's unwillingness to share her life had triggered in him. But it was the reminder he'd needed that he wasn't built to open his heart to love someone. That path always led to pain.

He glanced around the barn's festive interior, his gaze drawn like a magnet to the one woman he didn't want to see. Cassie twirled on the dance floor with none other than Henry McKerlie. It was fine, he told himself. A dance didn't mean anything, and she didn't owe him her loyalty. What had they agreed to, after all?

Some sort of meaningless exclusivity or an unspoken promise that things might turn into something more.

He wasn't meant for more. At that moment, he wished he were.

His sister waved to him, and he approached Lila where she stood with a man who looked familiar but Aiden couldn't quite place.

"How was Aspen?" his sister asked gently, as if reading his mood. "I was wondering when you'd get here."

"I'm here now." He ignored both the question and her assessing perusal. "Looks like the dance is a success. Things are moving along just fine without me, as I expected they would."

"The dance is a *huge* success because of the time and effort you and Cassie put in to make it so." Lila squeezed his arm. "Both of you," she insisted. He wasn't going to argue with her.

"Hey, I'm Gary." The man standing next to Lila offered a smile. Aiden shook the man's outstretched hand.

"Sorry," Lila said immediately. "I forgot introductions. Gary, this is my brother, Aiden." She looked slightly flustered, her cheeks blooming with pink. "Gary has an insurance agency here in Crimson. He was helpful after Jason's death." She pitched her voice to be heard over the band. "His son is in George's class at the elementary school."

"Yeah." Gary flashed a wry smile. "Our kids recently had a bit of a misunderstanding about a dog, but I think it all worked out in the end. Both boys are better for it."

Aiden blinked as his sister nodded in agreement. "Gary's son, Gabe, found Spud, but George insisted on taking care of him." She glanced back at Gary and shrugged. "My son has a big heart when it comes to animals. Not that Gabe doesn't," she quickly added. "I'm sure George insisted on taking Spud home."

Aiden suddenly realized that because of Lila's fragile emotional state at the time George had rescued Spud, they hadn't told her the specifics of the situation. More importantly, George had been bullied by Gabe Tinmouth.

Now his dad was standing next to her looking...the only way Aiden could describe it was *flirtatious*. That didn't make a damn bit of sense.

"I need to talk to you," he said, inserting himself between her and Gary Tinmouth.

"Oh, they're starting the Electric Slide. Come on, Aiden, you know this one. Gary, do you want to dance with us?"

"He doesn't," Aiden said.

Gary frowned as if Aiden wasn't making sense. "Sure I do." Before Aiden could protest again, the bully's father followed his sister onto the dance floor.

Aiden felt his hands clenched into fists at his side. Could this day get any worse?

He wanted to pull his sister away from Gary Tinmouth but knew better than to make a scene in the middle of a crowded dance floor. Then he glanced to the other side of the barn and saw Henry place a hand on the small of Cassie's back as he led her back to the dance floor.

"Well, aren't you gonna do something about it?" a voice said next to him.

He turned to see Martin Rooney standing there, one thick brow raised in challenge.

"Cassie's dance partners are none of my business."

"Really?" The older man looked genuinely curious. "I was under the impression you two had grown close again."

"There's no again." Aiden drew out every word. "We were never close."

"That's strange because she was mighty upset after you left town with your mother."

"We were kids. It didn't mean anything then. But while we're on the subject of Cassie…" He turned to face Martin. "I thought you were planning for her to join your practice. I know Dr. Smith was giving her trouble, but she was excited about working with you. What happened?"

"What has she told you?" The tic in Martin's jaw belied his casual tone.

"She hasn't said anything, but I heard she might not be staying in Crimson."

Martin looked at the barn's raftered ceiling and closed his eyes like he was gathering his composure. After a few tense seconds, he returned his gaze to Aiden. "The situation is complicated, and it's up to Cassie when and how to share it."

The older vet used a cane as he walked away, and his lack of an answer was the confirmation Aiden needed. This situation seemed simple to him. Cassie had asked him to take a chance on the two of them, but she didn't have enough faith to trust him with something meaningful.

He didn't want to give up, but what was the point of trying? She didn't feel like she could rely on him, which he understood. If they tried to make it work, he would become a dark cloud in her life. His past issues with trust and the fear of abandonment were embedded too deeply.

He didn't deserve someone like Cassie and would eventually dim her light, too. He'd dilute her sunshine with the blackness inside of him, which was too pervasive to overcome.

"Aiden, what's wrong?"

He blinked as Cassie took his hands, so caught up in his own maudlin thoughts that he hadn't seen her approach. "Lila told me about the mare. Did you find her?"

"We did," he answered. "She'll be fine. It's not your concern, Cassie. My life isn't your concern."

She blinked at the force of his words. "I'm still glad it turned out okay. If I'd known, I could have help—"

"I'm sure that would have been convenient for you, looking like a hero to the community in Aspen."

"I don't need to be a hero." She released his hands with a frown, and he immediately felt cold seep into his veins like her touch was the only thing keeping him warm. "I'm glad things worked out, and that you made it tonight even more."

She flashed a bright smile that did nothing to pierce the frozen wall around his heart. "Who would I have to two-step with otherwise?"

"Maybe Henry McKerlie," he suggested, knowing he sounded like a petty ass but leaning into it because it was safe and comfortable.

Aiden knew how to be a jerk. He didn't know how to be the man Cassie needed him to be in this moment or in general. Why had he thought it could be any different?

"Aiden, what is going on? I don't understand—"

"Hey, sweetheart."

Aiden felt a stab of white-hot anger when Henry approached and draped an arm over Cassie's shoulder. It was not the kind of warmth he wanted. Henry's eyes were glassy and unfocused, his words slurred.

"Some friends of mine are here. I want you to meet them. Duke and Boomer are a lot of fun."

"Cassie doesn't need your kind of fun," Aiden said, his voice pitched low.

"Look at the big, bad cowboy sticking his nose in

where it's not welcome. Cassie's a grown woman. She can make her own choices."

"I thought I had," Cassie murmured as Aiden met her gaze, which was filled with hurt and betrayal. The pain he'd caused.

"Come on, Cass," Henry crooned. "It'll be great. I haven't seen these guys in months, and they bring the party wherever they go. My friends are a guaranteed good time."

Henry turned away with Cassie, just as Aiden had thought he wanted. She glanced over her shoulder at him; the loss he felt was more than he could have imagined. Knowing he was bringing this amount of pain to both of them killed him.

So what if she hadn't told him about leaving Crimson? What had he truly done to deserve her trust? What could he do to gain it back?

The words *Don't go* were on his tongue, but she pulled out of Henry's grasp before he could say them.

"I don't want to meet your friends, and I'm guessing you should stay away from them, too. Where's your sister, Henry?" she asked, studying him. Aiden wasn't the only one who'd realized McKerlie was under the influence of something substantial. "We need to get you home."

"No way, Cassie my lassie." Henry flashed a boyish grin that Aiden wanted to knock right off of his admittedly handsome face.

"Cassie, I need to speak with you."

Henry and Cassie shifted as Bryan Smith approached their unlikely trio.

"Not now, Bryan. This isn't a good time," Cassie said pointedly.

"You wanna party with us?" Henry asked.

Bryan looked shocked, as if the out-of-it Henry had

outright offered him a line of coke, but then focused his glare on Cassie. "Laura told me you were sniffing around the clinic's financial statements. You have no right to access privileged information."

"Not now," Cassie repeated.

"You got something to hide from Cassie-Lassie?" Henry's voice was obnoxiously loud as he listed forward.

Cassie straightened her friend's brother, who took it as an opportunity to put his arm around her again.

Aiden suppressed a growl, but just barely.

"Henry, what's going on?" Cameron rushed up to them and grabbed her brother. "I saw a couple of your former friends here. Those losers are completely out of it. You need to stay away from them."

"Hey, Camerarama-Ding-Dong." With his free hand, Henry patted his sister's head like she was a pet.

"Oh, no," Cameron whispered.

"We should get him out of here." Cassie's gaze darted to Aiden's for a brief second. He still didn't understand what was happening, but she needed his help. That much was clear, even if she seemed unwilling to ask for it.

"I want an explanation," Bryan Smith said, louder now.

"Not now, Doc." Aiden moved forward, and Dr. Smith stepped back. Then he turned his attention to Henry McKerlie. "Let go of Cassie."

"Nope," the man said. Stupid, stupid man. Aiden's temper was rising by the second.

"Come on, Henry." Cameron yanked on her brother's arm, but he pulled Cassie closer. This time she was less successful in shrugging out of his grasp.

"I want Cassie-Lassie to meet my friends."

"They aren't your friends," Cameron told him.

"Yes, they are," Henry bellowed, growing more belligerent and unstable. Aiden would bet his last dollar there was more than alcohol in the man's system.

"Henry, let go and listen to your sister," Cassie said, her voice gentle.

Aiden cringed. He was pretty sure she'd used the same inflection on him the afternoon he'd brought Spud into the clinic. Her tone for out-of-control people and animals. He didn't like knowing he was part of that group.

"I like you, Cass-Lass."

"I like you sober, Henry."

He leaned in and planted a smacking kiss on her lips.

Cassie pushed at his chest, but Henry didn't release her. Aiden didn't hesitate. He grabbed the man by the back of his collar and lifted him off his feet.

"You can't do that," Aiden said simply as he dropped Henry to the floor.

"Let go of me."

"Let go of him," a man's voice shouted.

"Oh, no," Cameron said, pressing a hand to her forehead as two deadbeat-looking guys came toward them.

The music had switched to a soft country ballad—the kind of song Aiden would have liked to dance to with Cassie. No one was dancing because all attention had shifted to the scene playing out with Henry.

This was not the way the night had been supposed to go.

"Cassie." Bryan Smith put a hand on her shoulder. "If you're done making a public spectacle of yourself, I really need to speak with you."

"You *need* to stop touching her," Aiden told the older vet as he reached forward and yanked Bryan away.

"I can take care of myself," Cassie said through gritted teeth. "You've made it clear I'm not your business anymore. Maybe I never was."

Had he made that clear? What a mistake. She was his business and his light and the reason for most of the good things in his life.

Henry grinned at Cassie. "These are the friends I wanted you to meet, Duke and Boomer."

"They aren't your friends," Cameron said again, stepping in front of the two men. "Please, Henry, let's go."

"Your wet-blanket sister has the right idea," one of the guys said, leaning around Cameron. "Grab the girl, and let's go. This place is a drag."

"I'm not your girl, Henry," Cassie said.

"You could be." Henry wiggled his brows.

"Leave her alone," Cameron begged her brother.

"Cam, you're the one who wanted to set me up with her in the first place."

"That was before you started acting like a fool." Cameron crossed her arms over her chest. "Henry, please," she repeated. "Don't do this."

"Listen to your sister," Aiden echoed.

Henry flicked him a glance, then let out a beleaguered sigh. "Dude, enough with the scowling. We're trying to have a good time. Maybe if you knew how to have a good time, Cassie-Lassie wouldn't have been so sad at the start of this dance. I'm the one who got her to smile. Let's remember that."

The words hit Aiden harder than a blow could have. Despite looking severely uncomfortable, Cassie didn't correct Henry.

"Come on, Cass," the man said, but she shook her head. "Seriously, don't be a buzzkill."

Henry reached for her, and something in Aiden snapped. All the frustration, anger and fear he felt congealed into a dark shadow inside him. "Take your hands off her."

But when Henry released her and swung wildly. Aiden ducked, then reflexively threw a punch that landed square on Henry's jaw.

"You hit him," Bryan Smith said with a gasp. "You're just like your father."

Hell no, he wasn't.

Henry staggered but remained on his feet. He lunged for Aiden, who dodged out of the way, sending Henry into Bryan. The vet pushed back, which seemed to enrage Henry. Before Aiden could stop him, Henry clocked the older vet. Dr. Smith went down in a heap, and the next thing Aiden knew, he had Henry and his drugged-out friends coming at him.

This was not at all the night he'd imagined.

Chapter Eighteen

Cassie stood outside the Crimson police station the following morning, wondering if she was making a huge mistake. She'd spent most of the night awake, ruminating over how her life had gone off the rails so quickly, and facing the problem head-on seemed like the fastest way to fix it.

But maybe that was lack of sleep and the adrenaline letdown talking.

The day was gray with heavy clouds socking in the town and blocking the view of the mountain peak in the distance.

The changing weather wasn't a shock since the first snowfall often fell in early October at this high elevation, and the cold, whipping wind mirrored her frozen emotions.

At least the cold was a welcome change from the fire that had engulfed her heart as it had pounded with terror and temper in equal measure when the fight had broken out at the dance.

She didn't entirely blame Aiden for the brawl, even though he'd punched Henry. Unfortunately, he'd been hauled off to a local holding cell, along with Henry McKerlie and his lowlife friends, when enough men had finally separated the two sides.

Aiden hadn't seemed bothered by the odds of fighting three people at once and had been holding his own against them.

Cameron and Lila had followed the group out, concern for their respective brothers etched into the lines of worry on their faces. Cassie had stayed behind to calm the dance attendees and get things back on track.

Her mother and the book club ladies had helped, encouraging people to keep enjoying themselves despite the ruckus. The musicians had struck up a lively tune to lure the crowd back onto the dance floor, although Cassie imagined most of the talk had centered around the fighters.

She'd turned her attention to Bryan Smith, who'd been yammering about pressing charges against Aiden. Despite her anger, that was the last thing Cassie wanted, so she'd spent an hour listening to Bryan lecture her about how she was deficient and unworthy of a partner position at the vet clinic.

The rant had done enough to take the edge off his self-righteous-victim mentality. She'd convinced him that pressing charges would bring unwanted attention to the clinic and make people wonder why Aiden Riley might have such negative feelings about him.

The incident with Aiden's dog, Sam, had been twenty years ago, but certain people in Crimson had long memories. Bryan had finally agreed he didn't want any questions about why he hadn't done more to help the dog or its owner.

Lila had texted her that they were keeping everyone overnight and Aiden would be released in the morning. The police chief had found drugs on Henry's two friends, so they were dealing with more-severe charges.

The morning had dawned after an interminably long night, so Cassie was waiting. Although she wasn't sure for what or how Aiden would react to seeing her.

She'd thought about picking up Rosie from Lila's house to have a buffer. She and Aiden knew how to connect around their mutual love of animals.

But they needed to work things out—if that were possible—on their own. She needed to give it *everything* she could before admitting defeat. That was how full her heart was with love for him.

That same heart flung itself against her ribcage when he exited the police station. She took a moment to register the unfairness that he'd spent a night in jail and still looked ready for the photo shoot of some modern-cowboy magazine cover.

His hair was tousled like he'd been running his fingers through it, and the dark shadow of stubble covering his jaw gave him an air of danger. Aiden was dangerous—mainly to her heart.

Cassie was hidden from view by the trunk of a large oak tree, and she watched as Aiden closed his eyes for a moment, took a deep breath, then pulled his cell phone from the back pocket of his jeans.

She could see his thumbs furiously tapping out a message, and a moment later, her phone pinged in her jacket pocket.

She extracted it, and everything inside her stilled as she read the message.

I'm sorry. Can we talk?

Before she could respond, the device began ringing, reverberating in the silence of the overcast morning.

"Hello?" she answered as she glanced up to see Aiden staring at her from the steps of the police station.

"You're here," he said, sounding dumbfounded.

"You're calling me," she reminded him.

"I texted you, too." He was walking toward her now, and she dropped the phone from her ear.

"Are you okay?" she asked as he drew closer.

He shook his head. "Not at all."

Alarm ricocheted through her, a sharp taste in her mouth. "Was it bad in there? Did Henry and his friends—"

"A night in the Crimson holding cell was fine, Cassie." One corner of his mouth tipped up. "Sadly, it's not the worst place I've ever slept. Once Henry slept off the effect of the pill his buddies slipped him, he was remorseful, to say the least. Expect flowers."

She tried to comprehend what Aiden was saying. "From Henry?"

"His memory of last night is patchy at best, but he feels bad for involving you."

"Is that what you were calling to tell me? Was your apology a proxy for someone else? It couldn't wait until he had access to his phone?"

Aiden pressed two fingers to his temple and shook his head. "I'm messing this up already. It's easier for me to talk about Henry." He blew out a soft laugh. "Or Lila or George or a dog or horse we lost. Anything but my feelings."

He lowered his hand and reached for her, his warm fingers wrapping around her cold ones. "But the apology was mine, Cassie. I'm sorry."

She wasn't sure how to respond. Old Cassie would have accepted the words, offered an excuse for him and moved on. But she'd changed, or at least she was trying to. That meant holding people accountable when it was necessary. "For what exactly?"

He made a noise that registered somewhere between a grunt and a groan. "A lot of things. Mainly for being a fool. That covers most of it."

Cassie wrinkled her nose. "Can you be more specific?" She was surprised to see admiration flash in his dark eyes. "I'm sorry for hurting you," Aiden said. "I got scared because I heard about your interview at the clinic in Aspen, and I didn't like not knowing about it. I behaved badly because I was insecure. I'm sorry."

"I didn't even know you were going to Aspen," she reminded him.

"I understand that, and you don't owe me a play-by-play of your life. I haven't done anything to deserve a place as your confidant."

She opened her mouth to answer, but he held a finger to her lips.

"But I want to, Cassie. I want to be your confidant and your support. You can rely on me."

She smiled against his finger. "I'm not very good at depending on people, if you haven't noticed."

He blinked. "I thought it was just me."

She shook her head. "It's me. It's hard for me to let myself be vulnerable, but I want to."

"With me?"

"Yes, you big dummy. Why else would I be standing in the cold across from the police station?"

"I love you, Cassie." He pressed a hand to his chest. "Wow, that's cool."

She inclined her head. "That you love me?"

"That my heart feels so full when I say the words. Like your sunshine is inside of me. Before these past few weeks, I didn't believe I had a heart. You brought me back to life." He frowned at the look on her face that she apparently didn't hide well. "What is it, honey? Did I say something wrong?"

"I love you, too," she whispered, then swiped a hand across her cheeks. "But I need you to understand that I'm not all sunshine. I have bad days and tough moments, and I can be angry when I'm hungry."

"I'll keep the pantry stocked," he promised and wrapped his arms around her. "I want all of you, Cassie. I love you, not just one version. I don't care about bad days, weeks or any challenges life throws us. Let me be your haven, your port in the storm. I want to take care of you the way you do for me."

She drew in a shaky breath, having never imagined hearing those words, especially from Aiden. And she hadn't realized how much she'd needed to hear them.

"I might be taking a job in Aspen," she said against his canvas jacket, which somehow smelled like the forest even after his night confined to a cell.

"They have horses to train in Aspen," he said in response.

She pulled back. "You aren't going back to Wyoming?"

He frowned and tapped one finger to her forehead. "Woman, I just told you I love you. I haven't said that to anyone in, well… I'm not sure I've ever said those words. I'm in this all the way. Wherever you go, that's where I go. You are my home, Cassie, and I will spend the rest of my life working to be yours."

Her heart bloomed with hope and joy as her fear disappeared, the shadows no match for the light in his gaze. "I love you, Aiden."

"I love you more," he whispered. "You've had my heart for twenty years." He gave her a crooked smile that made heat radiate through her body. "I figure that's why I didn't think I had one. You took care of it until I was brave enough to accept your love."

Cassie sighed contentedly, knowing she'd always love this man. He kissed her then, long and deep, and she sank into him. They were finally going to get it right. Now and forever.

Epilogue

A month later, with the scent of snow lacing the cold air and the sun struggling to peek through the clouds filling the sky, Aiden loaded a last box into the back of his sister's compact SUV.

"That's the last of it," Lila said, the thread of emotion in her voice making his chest tighten.

"It's not too late to change your mind, Li."

She laughed and drew him in for a hug. "The ranch is sold, Aiden, and all of our furniture has been delivered to the new house. If that isn't the definition of *too late*…"

"I don't want you to be sad." He drew back and searched her face.

"I'm sentimental, not sad." The certainty in her gentle eyes made him know she was telling the truth, and the worry in his heart eased. "This is the right decision for all of us. Tell me you aren't having second thoughts."

He let his gaze roam over the land he'd known all his life. "It's time to let the past go. This property was never mine, and I surely didn't expect to come back here and face our childhood memories straight on. But I'm glad George called me when you needed help."

"I needed to be pulled from the brink of a grief that would swallow me whole," Lila said. "You saved me."

He shook his head. "I threw you a rope. You did the hard work of using it."

"Using it to play tug-o-war with Spud," she said with another laugh. "I'm rediscovering happiness, Aiden. It's different than when Jason was alive, but I'm finding reasons to smile."

"It all started with Spud." Aiden shook his head. "That puppy was the catalyst of a lot of change for both of us."

"And for George, although I wish you would have told me about what he was dealing with from the beginning."

"I'm sorry, Lila. I should have known you could handle it." He nudged her. "Just like you handled Gary Tinmouth."

Once his sister had discovered the truth of the boy bullying her son, she'd confronted Gabe's father. She'd had a thoughtful conversation with George about being honest with her regarding his challenges or struggles. Aiden wasn't sure his sister would ever truly move past the loss of her husband, but he admired her determination to move forward and embrace happiness for hers and George's sake.

They both turned as the house's front door opened, and Rosie and Spud raced out, followed by George and Cassie.

Aiden was beginning to become accustomed to the warmth that soothed his rough edges every time he saw Cassie. She smiled, and it was like fireworks went off inside him.

Lila wasn't the only one embracing happiness.

"Mom, can we go? Colby is coming over in an hour, and I need to unpack my LEGOs at the new house."

"You bet, bud." Lila took one last look at the house and then squeezed Aiden's hand. "We're done here."

Rosie let out one low whine as they loaded Spud into the car.

"I'm going to miss seeing you every day, Rosie-Girl." Lila patted the dog and hugged Cassie before turning to Aiden. "Bring her over anytime. I love this dog."

"You're going to miss me, too," Aiden teased, earning a wider grin from his sister.

"I expect to see you plenty, little brother. And I love you, Aiden. I'm glad you're staying in Crimson, although I know I'm not the one to thank for that."

Aiden looped an arm around Cassie's shoulders. "Yeah, we have Spud and Rosie to thank."

Cassie let out a gasp of protest, then leaned into him with a laugh. "You're right. It was love at first bark."

"You two are so cute. It makes me want to hurl," Lila said with an exaggerated eye roll. She climbed into the vehicle, and with a quick toot of the horn, she and George pulled away from the house.

Rosie let out a loud woof, then trotted over to Aiden's truck. She sat on her haunches as if patiently waiting for the two of them to get with the program.

"Are we going to keep her waiting? Let's go home, Cassie."

He, Rosie and Shadow had moved into her house two weeks earlier, a level of commitment Aiden had never imagined but which made him happy to his core. He allowed himself to be happy. He'd agreed to work for Nolan Tucker, running the horse sanctuary.

After the night of the barn dance, Bryan Smith had decided that he no longer wanted to be a part of the Animal Ark practice after the community had rallied around Cassie and Aiden. Cassie had grown in confidence and compassion once she'd felt recognized for her contributions. She and Dr. Rooney were currently interviewing to add another veterinarian to join the clinic staff.

Now Cassie linked her fingers with his, and Aiden felt his heart completely melt. It did the same thing every time she touched him.

And when she told him she loved him...

"I love you, Cassie." He pressed his mouth to hers. "I'll love you forever."

"I love you right back, Aiden." She smiled against his lips. "Forever."

* * * * *

Look out for these other great romances
filled with animal friends:

Matchmaker on the Ranch
By Marie Ferrarella

Old Dogs, New Truths
By Tara Taylor Quinn

Seven Birthday Wishes
By Melissa Senate

Available now from Harlequin Special Edition.

Chapter One

Ian Steele leaned back in his full grain leather chair, the one he'd just dropped three grand on, and looked out at the sparkling waters of San Francisco Bay. The light in his office this time of day was soft, golden. The sun filtered in through the blinds in warm rays, making the dust particles in the air look like stars. He'd always liked San Francisco this time of year. It was almost Christmas, but it didn't necessarily feel *Christmassy,* which suited him just fine. He could almost look out the window at the sailboats bouncing over the swells and mistake it for summertime.

There was a soft knock on his door, but he didn't take his eyes off the view below. "Come in," he said evenly.

"Ian, there's a call for you on line one."

At the sound of Jill's voice, he swiveled around to see her standing with her hands clasped in front of her stomach. She always looked apologetic these days, like she didn't want to upset him. He could be an ass, but she was the consummate professional, which was why he'd hired her in the first place.

He smiled, trying his best to put her at ease. But truth be told, he'd probably have a better shot at swimming across the bay without being eaten by a shark. She had the distinct look of someone standing on broken glass.

"Who is it?" he asked.

"Stella Clarke. Says she's from Christmas Bay." She frowned. "Where's that?"

Ian stiffened. It had been years since he'd thought of that place. Maybe even longer since he'd heard anyone mention Christmas Bay. He'd cut that part of his life out as neatly as a surgeon. He was too busy now, too successful to spend much time dwelling on things like his childhood, which quite frankly didn't deserve a single minute of reflection.

"Tiny little town on the Oregon Coast." He rubbed his jaw. "What the hell does she want, anyway?"

His assistant's eyebrows rose at this. Clearly, she was taken aback. Ian was usually smooth as scotch. Unruffled by much of anything.

Clearing his throat, he leaned back in his brand-new chair. He had the ridiculous urge to loosen his tie, but resisted out of sheer willpower. "Did she say? What she wants?"

"She has a favor to ask. She said she knows you're busy but that it won't take much time."

Typical Stella. Exactly how he remembered her. He could see her standing in the living room on the day he'd arrived at the foster home, when his heart had been the heaviest, and his anger the sharpest. Wild, dark hair. Deep blue eyes. Even at fourteen years old, she'd been a force to be reckoned with. Even with all she'd probably endured. Just like him. Just like all of them. She'd been whip-smart, direct, always trying to negotiate something for her benefit.

But he couldn't exactly talk. Now he made a living out of negotiating things for his own benefit. A very nice living, as a matter of fact. As one of the Bay Area's top real estate developers, he'd been snatching up prime property for years, building on it and then selling it for loads of cash. He had people standing in line to do his bidding. The question was, what was this favor she was talking about? And how much time would it actually take?

He looked at his Apple Watch, the cool metal band glinting in the sunlight. Almost noon. He had a meeting across town at two thirty, and he hadn't eaten yet. He could have Jill take her number, and he could call her back. Or not. But for some damn reason, he was curious about what she wanted. And whether he'd admit it or not, he was itching to hear her voice again. A voice that would now be seasoned by age, but would no doubt still be as soft as velvet. He hadn't talked to her since he'd graduated from Portland State. They'd run into each other at a swanky restaurant in the city where she'd been a server. They'd awkwardly met for coffee after the place closed, and it hadn't gone well. At all.

"Thanks, Jill," he said. "I'll take it. Have a good lunch."

She smoothed her hands down the front of her cream-colored pencil skirt. "Do you want me to bring you something back?"

He smiled again. "No. Thank you, though. Why don't you take an extra half hour? Get some time outside if you can. You've been working hard this morning, and the weather's nice. Enjoy it."

"Are you sure?"

"Positive. Go."

She reached for the door and pulled it closed behind her.

He looked down at the blinking button on the sleek black phone and felt his heart beat in time with it.

Picking it up, he stabbed the button with his index finger.

"Ian Steele," he said in a clipped tone.

"Ian? It's Stella Clarke. From Christmas Bay…"

He let out an even breath he hadn't realized he'd been holding. He'd been right. Her voice was still soft as velvet.

"Stella."

He waited, imagining what she might look like on the other end of the line. Wondering if that voice matched the rest of her. If she was that different than she'd been ten years ago. Because back then, the last time he'd seen her, she'd been very beautiful, and very pissed.

At least, she'd been pissed with him.

There was a long pause, and she cleared her throat. "How have you been?" she asked.

She was obviously trying to be polite, but he didn't give a crap about that right about now. He had things to do, and opening a window into the past was definitely not one of them.

"What do you want, Stella?"

"Well, it's nice to talk to you, too."

"I know you didn't call for a trip down memory lane."

"I took a chance that you might care about what's happening here," she said evenly. "Even if it's just a little."

"Why would I care about Christmas Bay?" He had no idea if that sounded convincing or not. Because he thought there might be an edge to his voice that said he did care, just the tiniest bit. Even if it was just being curious as to why she was calling after all this time. Curiosity he could live with. Caring, he couldn't. At least not about that Podunk little town.

"Because you have memories here, Ian."

He shook his head. *Unbelievable.* Of course she'd assume his memories at Frances's house were good ones. Worth keeping, if only in the corner of his mind.

The thing was though, she was actually right. Not that he'd ever admit it. There were some good memories. Of course there were. Of Stella, whom he'd always gravitated towards, despite her sometimes-prickly ways. She was a survivor, and he'd admired that. She was a leader and a nurturer, and he'd admired that, too. He'd seen in her things he wished he'd seen in himself growing up. Things he'd had to teach himself as he'd gotten older, or at least fake.

And there were other memories that weren't so terrible. Memories of Frances. Of his aunt. And snippets of things, soft things, that he'd practically let slip away over the years, because they'd been intermingled with the bad stuff, and tarnished by time.

He gripped the phone tighter, until he felt it grow slick with perspiration. Those decent memories were the only reason he hadn't hung up on her by now. Those, and his ever-present curiosity.

"What do you want, Stella?" he repeated.

And this time, the question was sincere.

"I can't believe I just did that," Stella muttered under her breath.

Sinking down in her favorite chair in the sunroom, she looked over at Frances, who was wearing another one of her bedazzled Christmas sweaters. Her fat black-and-white cat was curled up on her lap, purring like someone with a snoring problem.

"Uh-oh," Frances said, stroking Beauregard's head. "What?"

Stella worried her bottom lip with her teeth, and gazed out the window to the Pacific Ocean. It was misty today. Cold. But still stunningly beautiful—the ocean a deep, churning blue gray below the dramatic cliffs where the house hovered. One of the loveliest houses in Christmas Bay. But of course, she was biased.

She'd moved in when she was a preteen and brand new to the foster system. At the time, she'd thought Frances's two-hundred-year-old Victorian was the only good thing about her unbelievably crappy situation. After all, it was rumored to be haunted, and how cool was that? But she'd also been a girl at the time, and incredibly naive. She had no way of knowing that Frances herself would end up being the best thing about her situation. Frances and the girls who became not only her foster sisters, but her sisters of the heart. Getting to live in the house had been a bonus.

Now, as the thought of selling it crept back in, along with the thought of Frances's Alzheimer's diagnosis, which had changed things dramatically over the last few years, Stella felt a lump rise in her throat.

Swallowing it back down again, she forced a smile. This was going to be hard enough on her foster mother without her falling apart. Selling was the right thing to do. They just had to find the right buyer, that was all. Frances's only caveat was that a family needed to live here. A family who would love it as much as her own family had. As much as all of her foster kids had over the years.

"I asked someone for a favor," she said. "And now I'm wishing I hadn't."

"Why?"

She took a deep breath. "Since *Coastal Monthly* is doing that Christmas article on the house, I thought it would be a great time to kill two birds with one stone. Drum up some interest from potential buyers, and get the locals to stop telling that old ghost story."

Frances leaned forward, eliciting a grunt from Beauregard. "What do you mean? How in the world would you do that?"

It had been a long time. Almost fifteen years. Frances might have Alzheimer's, but her long-term memory was just fine. Stella wasn't sure how she'd react to this next piece of information. Maybe she'd be okay with it. But maybe not.

She braced herself, hoping for the former. "I called Ian Steele…"

Her foster mother's blue eyes widened. She sat there for minute, and Stella could hear the grandfather clock in the living room ticking off the seconds.

"Wow," Frances finally muttered. "Just…wow."

"I know."

"How did you find him?"

"I googled him and he came right up. He's this big shot real estate developer in San Francisco."

Frances sucked in a breath. "You don't think he'd want to buy the house, do you?"

"No way. He hates Christmas Bay, remember?" Still, Stella couldn't shake the fact that he'd seemed to perk up when she said the property was for sale. He'd asked several specific questions, the real estate kind, until her guard had shot up, leaving her uneasy.

"It's been a long time, honey. People change."

She shook her head. "Not Ian."

"Then why call him?"

"Because I thought if he gave the magazine a quick interview over the phone, it could help when the house goes on the market. You want a legitimate buyer, not some ghost hunters who will turn it into a tourist trap. You know people around here still talk about that silly story, and he's the only one who can put it to rest."

Frances looked skeptical. "But would he want to?"

"I'd hope so after what he put you through while he was here. Including making up that story in the first place and spreading it around. It's been years. I'd assumed he'd matured enough to at least feel a little bad about it"

Frances was quiet at that. She'd always defended Ian when he'd been defiant. He'd had this innate charm that seemed to sway most of the adults around him, but Stella had been able to see right through him. Maybe because she'd come from a similar background. Abuse, neglect. Nobody was going to pull the wool over her eyes, not even a boy as cute as Ian.

Suddenly looking wistful, maybe even a little regretful, Frances gazed out the window. The mist was beginning to burn off, and the sun was trying its best to poke through the steely clouds overhead. Even in the winter, Frances's yard was beautiful. Emerald green, and surrounded by golden Scotch broom that stretched all the way to the edge of the cliffs of Cape Longing. As a girl, Stella thought it looked like something out of *Wuthering Heights*. As a woman, she understood how special the property really was. And how valuable.

She truly hadn't believed Ian would be interested in the house, or she wouldn't have called him. It wasn't the kind of real estate he seemed to be making so much money on in the city, at least according to the internet. He and his business partner bought properties and built apartment buildings and housing developments on them, and the Cape Longing land was smaller than what they were probably used to. But after talking to him, even for just those few painful minutes, Stella knew he was more calculating than she'd given him credit for. If he smelled a good deal, even if it was in Christmas Bay, he might just follow his nose. Which was the *last* thing Frances needed.

"So, what did he say?" her foster mother asked. "Will he do the interview?"

"He wouldn't say. I never should've called him. I could just kick myself."

"At least you got to talk to him again."

Stella bit her tongue. *Yeah, at least.*

"Did he say how he was?" Frances asked hopefully. She was so sweet. And it made Stella indignant for her all over again. She'd loved and cared for Ian like he was her own, seeing something special in him, even under all the surliness and anger. She'd told him that often, but it didn't matter. He'd made his time with her miserable, and had ended up running away. He'd disappeared for days, worrying Frances sick, and ultimately breaking her heart when he was sent to live with a great-aunt instead.

Stella had a hunch it was *because* of the love Frances had shown him, not in spite of it. If Ian sensed anyone getting close, he ran. He was a runner. She'd be willing to bet he'd run all these years, and had ended up in San Francisco, still the same old Ian. Just older. And maybe a little more jaded, if that was possible.

Stella liked to think that despite their similar background, one that had helped her understand him better than most people might, she'd turned out softer, more approachable. And she credited Frances for that. Maybe if Ian had stayed put, he might've had his rough edges smoothed out some, too.

She smiled at her foster mother, determined not to say what she was thinking. Determined to show some grace, at least for the time being. "We didn't get that far," she said. "I guess he had a meeting or something."

Frances nodded. "So, he's done well for himself?"

If his website was any indication, he was doing more than well.

"He seems to be."

"I wish things had turned out differently," Frances said. "I wish I could've reached him."

"It wasn't because you didn't try, Frances. We all did."

"But maybe if we'd tried harder..."

Frowning, Stella leaned forward and put a hand over Frances's. Her foster mother smelled good this morning. Like perfume and sugar cookies. She was in her early sixties, and was a beautiful, vital woman. Nobody would ever guess that she struggled with her memory as much as she did. So much so that her three foster daughters had moved back home to help her navigate this next chapter of her life.

In the corner of the sunroom, one of the house's two Christmas trees glittered. The decorations were ocean themed, of course. The blue lights glowed through the room like a lighthouse beacon. Christmas cards from previous foster children, now long grown, were strung around one of the double-paned windows. The old Victorian came alive over the holidays, and its warmth and coziness was one of the reasons Stella loved it so much. She knew it would be heartbreaking to sell it. Frances was right to want a family living here. Somehow, it softened the blow.

"You were the best thing to happen to us," Stella said quietly. "I'm just sorry he couldn't see that."

Frances smiled, but it looked like she was far away. Lost in her memories.

Stella scratched Beauregard behind his ears, before leaning back again with a sigh. Lost in some of hers.

Ian shifted the Porsche into second. This was the first time he'd driven it in the mountains, and not surprisingly, it hugged the hairpin turns like a dream. If he was in the mood, he'd be driving faster. After all, why own a German-engineered sports car if you weren't going to break the speed limit every now and then? But he wasn't in the mood. And getting to Christmas Bay any faster wasn't exactly tempting.

Gritting his teeth, he glanced out the window to the ocean on his left. Then at the GPS to his right. He'd be there in less than half an hour. Plenty of time to wonder about this decision. Yeah, the Cape Longing property might be the deal of a lifetime (*if* he could convince Frances to sell to him), but was it worth stepping foot back inside the little town he'd left so long ago? He wasn't so sure.

Which brought him back to Frances again. And to Stella. Ian could smooth talk anyone. Anyone having second thoughts, or experiencing cold feet, was putty in his hands after about five minutes. Less, over drinks. But true to form, Stella had been immune to everything he'd thrown at her over the phone. The conversation had turned stilted in *less* than five minutes, which he wasn't used to.

Thinking about it now, he bristled. She'd always been different than the rest of the kids he'd known in the system. Foster kids were usually wise, but she was wiser. They were tough, but she was tougher. They had walls, but Stella had barricades. He'd never been able to scale them, and then he'd just stopped trying. He didn't need anyone, anyway. Not Frances O'Hara, not Kyla or Marley, and sure as hell not Stella. So, he'd done anything and everything in his power to test them. He'd stolen, lied, smoked, drank. You name it, he'd done it. And for the cherry on the crapcake, he'd come up with that dumbass story about the ghost, knowing what a headache it would be for Frances. Knowing how it would get around and eventually stick in a town that was known for every kind of story sticking. Especially the bad kind.

But now, he had a chance to rectify it. That's what Stella had said. *Rectify.* Like he owed them something by talking to *Coastal Monthly* for their fluffy Christmas piece. *It's not like it matters,* he'd said evenly. *These days, a story like that only helps sell houses.*

And that's when she'd told him that Frances wanted a family living there. Someone who would love it as much as she did.

When he'd hung up, he'd gotten an idea. Why *not* do the interview?

He'd tracked down the lady writing the article, and she'd practically begged him to come up to Christmas Bay so she could take pictures. And if he got a good look at the property in person, through the eyes of a real estate developer, well, then… What could it hurt? Other than shocking the hell out of Stella, who'd asked him to talk to the magazine but definitely would *not* expect him to do it in person. No way would she have wanted to open up that can of worms. She'd suspect a deeper motivation, and she'd be right.

In the beginning, money had been the driving force. Of course it had. But as he made his way up Highway 101, his Porsche winding along the cliffs overlooking the ocean, he had to admit there was another reason he was doing this. For once, it had nothing to do with money and everything to do with wanting to see Stella again.

Just so she could see what he'd become. Just so he could flaunt it in her pretty face.

He downshifted again and glanced over at the water. It sparkled nearly as far as the eye could see. It was deep blue today, turquoise where the waves met the beach. The evergreens only added to the incredible palate of colors, standing tall and noble against the bluebird sky.

It had been so long since Ian had been up this way that he'd almost forgotten how beautiful it was. Easy, because the Bay Area was beautiful, too. But in a different way. There were so many people down there that sometimes it was hard to look past all the buildings and cars to see the nature beyond. On the Oregon Coast, the people were sparse. So sparse that it wasn't unusual to go to the beach and not see anyone at all. The weather had something to do with that—it was usually cold. But the scenery? The scenery was some of the most spectacular in the world, and Ian had been a lot of places.

Swallowing hard, he passed a sign on his right. Christmas Bay, Ten Miles. Ten miles, and he'd be back in the town where he'd been the most miserable, the loneliest and most confused of his entire life. But also, where he'd caught a glimpse of what love could look like if he'd only let it in. But he hadn't let it in. In the end, he hadn't known how. And he'd been too pissed at the world to try, anyway.

There was absolutely no other reason, other than maybe a little spite, that he wanted to come back here again. No reason at all.

That's what he kept telling himself as the trees opened up, and Christmas Bay finally came into view.

Stella opened up the front door to see a woman in trendy glasses standing on the stoop. She looked the part of a journalist. Her hair was in a messy bun, and she had a camera bag slung over one shoulder. It was a beautiful day, perfect for pictures, but it was cold, and she was dressed appropriately for a December day on the Oregon Coast—rain boots and a thick cardigan.

When she saw Stella, she smiled wide. But her gaze immediately settled on the entryway behind her. It was obvious she couldn't wait to get a look inside.

"Hi, there," she said, holding out a hand. "Gwen Todd. And you must be Stella?"

Stella shook it. "I'm so glad the weather cooperated."

"Oh, I know. I thought it was going to pour. We got lucky."

"Please come in," Stella said. "Frances has some coffee brewing."

Gwen stepped past her and into the foyer. Before Stella could turn around, she heard the other woman gasp. She couldn't blame her. The house was incredible. Three stories of stunning Victorian charm. Gleaming hardwood floors, antique lamps that cast a warm, yellow glow throughout. A winding staircase that you immediately wanted to climb, just to see what treasures waited at the top. A widow's walk on the third floor that looked out over the cliffs, where Ian said he'd seen a ghost all those years ago. A coastal cliché that the entire town had latched on to, but that her family would finally shake free of today. At least, Stella hoped they would. It was just an article—it wasn't going to go viral or anything. But for the locals, for someone most likely to buy this house and live happily in it, it would be a start.

Gwen Todd ran her hand along the staircase's glossy banister. "Oh, it's just lovely. I've always wanted to see inside."

Stella had heard that more times than she could count.

From certain places in town, you could see the house, perched high above Cape Longing, its distinctive yellow paint peeking like the sun through the gaps in the trees. It had been built when Christmas Bay was just a tiny logging settlement, and Frances's grandparents had had to get their supplies by boat, because the mountain roads were impassible by wagon in the winter and spring. As the town had grown, the house had become a fixture, near and far. It even had its own display in the local maritime museum—the fuzzy, black-and-white pictures taking people back to a time when the West was still fairly wild.

And Gwen Todd was clearly a fan. Shaking her head, she looked around, enthralled.

Stella smiled. She understood how Gwen felt, because that was exactly how she'd felt as a girl, walking through the doors of this place for the first time. In absolute wonder and awe. For a kid who'd gone from surviving on ramen noodles in a broken-down trailer on the outskirts of town, to this? It had been almost too good to be true. For the first six months of her new life with Frances, Stella had expected someone to come and take her away at any moment. Or worse, for her mother to get her back. She'd had nightmares about being deposited back into that cruelty and filth. Into that never-ending cycle of neglect and abuse. It wasn't until after the first full year that she'd begun to trust her good fortune. That she'd been able to start opening her heart again. Cautiously, and just a little at a time.

Now, standing here, those days seemed so far away, they were just as fuzzy as the pictures in the museum down the road. But other times, they were clear as a bell, and those were the days that tended to hit her the hardest. When the pain and memories were too sharp to take a full breath. Thank God for Frances. Otherwise, there was no telling where she would've ended up. Or *how* she would've ended up. She hadn't spoken to her biological parents in years. She simply had nothing to say to them.

Gwen looked at her watch, just as Frances walked in holding out a reindeer mug full of steaming coffee. This time of year, Frances served all her drinks in Christmas mugs. She was proud of her collection.

"Oh, thanks so much," Gwen said. "This will help wake me up before Mr. Steele gets here."

Stella froze. Frances froze, too.

"I'm sorry," Stella managed. "What?"

"Mr. Steele. He's supposed to be here at eleven, but I think he might be running late…"

Stella stared at Frances, who sank down in a chair by the staircase. She looked pale.

"Oh…" Gwen set her coffee cup down. "Oh, no. I thought I mentioned that he'd be coming?"

"I don't think so," Stella said. There was no way she'd mentioned that. Stella would've remembered.

"There were so many calls back and forth, I must've totally spaced it. I'm so sorry. Will it be a problem?"

Gwen looked genuinely concerned, but if she'd known exactly how Ian had left things all those years ago, Stella knew she'd be downright horrified. He hadn't stepped foot inside this house since he'd left with his social worker at sixteen. Frances had been crying. She'd stood at the window watching them pull out of the driveway with tears streaming down her face. She'd felt like she'd failed him. Which was ridiculous, but that's how she'd felt, which made Stella furious with him all over again.

She forced a smile to ease Gwen's mind. And maybe her own, too. There was always the chance he'd show up and apologize to Frances for how he'd treated her back then. Or that he'd acknowledge that what he'd said at that coffee date years ago had been horribly untrue—suggesting their sweet and loving foster mother had only taken them in for the money. A disgusting comment that had brought up every single insecurity that Stella had ever had about finding a genuine home. But she doubted he'd do either of those things. She also doubted that he was coming back to Christmas Bay simply to do this interview and help Frances sell her house. No way. He had other motives in mind. Probably like getting a good look at her property, since, like an idiot, Stella had practically waved it in his face.

"It's okay," she said. "We just haven't seen him in a long time. He was one of Frances's foster kids, and he left…suddenly."

Gwen frowned, glancing at Frances, and then back at Stella again. "Are you sure? I feel terrible about this. I wouldn't want it to be awkward for you."

Too late.

Frances shook her head. "No, honey. Don't worry. He's come all this way to do the interview, so that says a lot. Maybe this is a blessing in disguise."

As if on cue, there was the roar of a car coming up the drive. All three of them moved over to the bay window and looked out, like they were waiting for Santa Claus or something. Stella crossed her arms over her chest, annoyed by her own curiosity. She didn't care that she'd be seeing Ian again. She couldn't stand him and his giant ego. And she managed to believe that. Mostly.

Outside, a beautiful silver sports car pulled into view, mud from the long dirt driveway spattered on its glossy paint job. Stella's heart beat heavily inside her chest as she saw the silhouette of a man through the tinted windows. Short black hair, straight nose and strong jaw. Sunglasses that concealed eyes that she remembered all too well. Blue, like Caribbean water. But not nearly as warm.

Letting out a low breath, she watched as the door opened, and he stepped out. Tall, broad shouldered and dressed impeccably in crisp, white-collared shirt and khaki slacks. Like the car, the clothes looked expensive. Tailored to his lean body in a way that she'd really only seen in magazines. So, this was how Ian had turned out. Probably with an even bigger ego than she'd remembered.

Frances looked over at her. "I can't believe how handsome he is. He looks so different."

There were differences. But there were also similarities, and those were what made Stella's chest tighten as she watched him swipe his dark sunglasses off and walk toward the front door with that same old confidence. That same old arrogance that had driven her bananas as a kid. That had driven them *all* bananas.

But there was no doubt he'd grown into that confidence. As a woman, she could imagine feeling safe and secure in his presence. And at that, she recoiled. Nothing about Ian Steele should make her feel safe. He was a piranha, only here for a meal. She'd bet her life on it.

Beside them, Gwen cleared her throat and touched her hair. Probably taken with his looks—something that made Stella want to snap her fingers in front of her face. *Snap out of it, Gwen!*

Instead, she walked over to the front door and opened it with her features perfectly schooled.

He stood with his hands in his pockets, gazing down at her like she was some acquaintance he was meeting for lunch. Instead of a girl he'd shared a home with, a family with, for two tumultuous years.

He smiled, and his straight white teeth flashed against his tanned skin. Two long dimples cut into each cheek.

Good God, he's grown into a good-looking man. The kind of man who stopped traffic. Or at least a heart or two.

Stella stood there, stoic. Reminding herself that it didn't matter how he looked. It only mattered that he gave this interview and went on his merry way again. Got back in his sports car and got the heck out of Christmas Bay.

"Stella," he said, that Caribbean gaze sweeping her entire body. He didn't bother trying to hide it. "It's been a long time."

She stiffened. If he was trying to unnerve her, it wasn't going to work. He might be trying to brush those two years underneath the rug, but she sure wasn't going to. He'd made their lives miserable, and had left a lasting scar on Frances's heart. Something she refused to minimize or forgive. And that slippery smile said he wasn't the least bit sorry about what he'd said over that fateful coffee date. Whether he'd meant it or not, he'd definitely wanted to wound her, probably since she'd stayed and found happiness in Christmas Bay, and he hadn't. No, he wasn't sorry. Not by a longshot.

"Ian," she said. "Exactly the same, I see."

His smile only widened at that. "Now, how can you say that? It's been years."

"Oh, I can tell." She glanced over her shoulder into the living room. Frances and Gwen were talking in low tones, obviously waiting for her to bring him inside. She looked back at him and narrowed her eyes. "I know exactly why you're here."

"I don't know what you're talking about."

"Cut the crap, Ian. Frances wouldn't sell to you if you were the last man on earth."

Rubbing the back of his neck, he seemed to contemplate that. "Oh, you mean because the house is coming up on the market, and I'm a real estate developer, you just assumed I'm here to schmooze..."

"I *know* you're here to schmooze," she whisper-yelled. "But it's not going to work. You're not going to just waltz in here after all this time and get what you want. Life doesn't work that way."

"Oh, I beg to differ. It does, in fact, work that way." He leaned back in his expensive Italian loafers and looked down his nose at her. "Are you going to invite me in, or are we going to stand here and argue all day? I mean, don't get me wrong, the sexual tension is nice, but there's a time and place for it."

She felt the blood rush to her cheeks. "Give me a break."

He smiled again, his eyes twinkling. She wanted to murder him. But that wouldn't be good for the sale of the house, either, so she stepped stiffly aside as he walked past, trying not to breathe in his subtle, musky cologne that smelled like money.

When Frances saw him, she took a noticeable breath. Then she stepped forward and pulled him into a hug. He was so tall, she had to stand on her tiptoes to do it. But he bent down obligingly, even though Stella could tell his body was unyielding. Ian had always had trouble with giving and receiving affection.

Stella couldn't bring herself to feel sorry for him. He'd had plenty of opportunities to be loved. Frances had tried, but he'd only pushed her away. It was what it was.

Still, she couldn't help but notice how his jaw was clenched, the muscles bunching and relaxing methodically. How his gaze was fixed on the wall behind Frances, stony and cold. Like he just wanted to retreat. And before she could help it, there was a flutter of compassion for him after all. Because she could remember feeling the same way a long time ago.

After a second, he pulled away and looked down at her with a careful smile on his face. Not the almost playful one he'd given Stella a minute before. This one was more structured. Like he'd been practicing it a while. Like fifteen years, maybe.

"Hi, Frances," he said. "It's good to see you."

Stella could see that she was having a hard time with a reply. Her eyes were definitely misty. Poor Frances. She'd just wanted the kids who'd passed through her doors to leave happy. She'd wanted to give them a home, whether it was for a few months, or the rest of their childhoods. The fact that she hadn't been able to give Ian any of those things still bothered her. Probably because, despite that carefully crafted smile, his pain was clearly visible. It had been brought right to the surface by this visit. Stella had to wonder if he'd been prepared for that when he'd hatched this asinine plan.

"Ian," Frances said. "You grew up."

"Probably all those vitamins you made me take."

"Well, they worked. Just look at you."

Gwen stepped forward and fluttered her lashes. She actually fluttered her lashes. Stella wanted to groan.

"Oh, I'm sorry," Frances said. "Gwen, this is Ian Steele. Ian, this is Gwen Todd, from *Coastal Monthly.*"

Ian took her hand, appearing just short of kissing it. Gwen didn't seem to mind. In fact, her cheeks flushed pink.

"Gwen, it's a pleasure."

"Thank you so much for making the drive up," she said. "I know it's a long one, but I'm so glad you did."

Stella eyed him, waiting for him to admit to wanting to take a look at the house, even in passing. Otherwise, why not do the interview over the phone? But he didn't.

He just smiled down at Gwen innocently. *Who me? I just want to help with the article, that's all...*

Frances took all this in with interest. If she was worried about Ian's true intentions, she didn't let on. She just seemed happy to see him again. Which, in Stella's opinion, he didn't deserve. But that was Frances for you. Kind to the core.

Clapping her hands together, Gwen smiled. "Are we ready? I thought maybe we could start with some pictures of the upstairs, Frances. Maybe the widow's walk?"

"Sounds good to me."

"Me too," Ian said.

Stella stepped forward, narrowly missing Ian's toe. All of a sudden, Frances's spacious living room seemed as big as a postage stamp. She stepped back again, putting some distance between them, but not before catching his smirk. Of course he was enjoying this. Of course he was.

"The widow's walk is where Ian said he saw the ghost," Stella said tightly. "Are you sure you want to put that in the article, Frances? Maybe we shouldn't focus on that part?"

Frances frowned. "That's true..."

"Well, that's no problem," Gwen said, fishing her camera out of the bag. "We'll just start with a few by the Christmas tree, and then we can go outside to the garden. The sun is coming out. The light should be perfect."

Stella smiled, relieved. As long as things went smoothly, this article might actually end up painting the house in the light it deserved, which was what she'd hoped for in the beginning. And maybe she was just being paranoid as far as Ian was concerned. Maybe after he got a look at the place, he'd dismiss it like he probably dismissed so many other things in his life. After all, this was Christmas Bay, and what she'd told Frances was true. He hated Christmas Bay.

He stepped up to the bay window and looked out toward the ocean. The muscles in his jaw were bunching again, his blue eyes narrowing in the sunlight.

"My God, I'd almost forgotten that view," he said under his breath. Almost too softly for anyone else to hear.

But Stella heard. And even though it had been years since she'd seen Ian Steele, or that look in his eyes, she recognized it immediately.

This was something he wanted. And he intended to get it.

Chapter Two

Ian walked behind Stella, having trouble keeping his eyes off her amazing rear end. She'd been slightly over-weight as a kid, always refusing to get into a swimsuit at the city pool. She'd worn a T-shirt and shorts instead, which he'd thought was dumb. She'd looked just fine, but the girls he knew had a way of obsessing over things like that. If it wasn't their weight, it was their skin. Or their hair. Or a myriad of other things. Even the prettiest ones, who had absolutely nothing to worry about, worried anyway. Stella had been that way.

But he could see those days were long gone. She was no longer the girl in the oversize clothes. She was a confident, stunningly beautiful woman, who was looking over her shoulder at him like she wanted to stick a knife between his ribs.

"Be careful," she said. "The railing is wobbly."

They were climbing the stairs to the widow's walk after all. Frances had changed her mind, and thought it would be a fitting end to the article to have a picture of Ian standing there, looking out over the ocean. A grown man, coming back to the place where he'd spent so much time as a boy. A place that, as a confused, overwhelmed kid, he'd once said was haunted, but that he now realized was only a sweet old house that didn't deserve a dark reputation. The whole thing was a little too cute for his taste, but that's what people around here liked. Stella was absolutely right, thinking this article would help sell the house. That is, if he didn't get his hands on it first.

He smiled up at her, running his hand along the railing. "I remember."

She didn't smile back. Just turned around and kept climbing, her lovely backside only inches from his face. Good Lord, he really was a jackass. But he couldn't help it. She had a gorgeous body, and his gaze was drawn to it like it was magnetized. It wasn't like he wasn't used to gorgeous bodies, either. The women he usually dated were high maintenance, and keeping themselves up was part of their lifestyle. But Stella's body was soft, curvaceous. Something he could imagine running his hands over, exploring, undressing. Her skin would probably be just as velvety as her voice, and at the thought, his throat felt uncomfortably tight.

Taking the last few steps up the narrow, winding staircase, he stepped out behind her on the widow's walk. Frances and Gwen were already standing near the iron railing, looking out over the ocean. He stared at it, too, and for a few seconds, all thoughts of Stella's body were forgotten in favor of the house's property value.

He fished his sunglasses out of his front pocket and put them on. The yard below was spacious and pretty. A peeling white picket fence that was covered in climbing vines and rose bushes enveloped it like a hug. In the summer, the whole space was alive with colorful, fragrant blooms that made the garden look like something out of a fairy tale. In the winter, it was more subdued, but still a beautiful, luscious green.

Beyond the yard was the ever-present Scotch broom that butted right up to the edge of the cliffs that dropped into the sea. Cape Longing was one of the most dramatic stretches along the Oregon Coast, and finding land here that was prime for development was rare. Ian's wheels were turning so fast, he could barely think straight. *Condos.* He could picture a small row of expensive condos or townhouses. Simple, midcentury modern style, with lots of glass and metal. Balconies that overlooked the sea. Perfect for reading, or having a glass of wine, or entertaining in the evenings. Bachelor pads, or a couple's paradise... They could go in any direction, appeal to anyone. And with a setting like this, he could sell them for more than he'd even dreamed.

He looked up to see Frances smiling over at him.

"I hope you have some good memories of being up here," she said. "I know this used to be your favorite part of the house."

He smiled back, determined not to let that get to him. Determined not to tumble back into the past, to those lonely nights when he'd sat up here, looking out at the ocean reflecting the full moon above. Feeling scared and alone, and then ashamed for feeling so scared and alone. He guessed that's where that stupid ghost story of his had come from. Underneath everything, it had been a cry for help, a bid for attention. And now he was going to debunk it very publicly, in this article. If he owed Frances anything, that was it. And then they'd be even as far as he was concerned. She wasn't going to look at him with those doe eyes, and make him feel guilty for seeing a good business opportunity here. She just wasn't.

"I wasn't always easy to live with," he said, "but I do have some good memories of this place."

He was in the beginning stages of buttering her up, but maybe that was a bridge too far. It's not that it wasn't true—he did have good memories. Not that he'd ever admitted that...until now. But he could feel Stella watching him from a few feet away, her gaze like a laser beam boring into his head.

"Oh, really?" she muttered.

He turned to her. She knew exactly what he was thinking. He didn't know how, but she did. Not that it mattered. Frances was the only one who mattered here. It wasn't Stella who would be choosing a buyer, it was Frances.

"Really," he said.

"I'm glad to hear that," Frances said. "So glad."

Gwen was fiddling with her camera, looking like she was trying to get the lighting right. "So, this was where you said you saw the ghost?" she asked, holding the camera up and peering through the lens.

"This was the spot," he said. "Only, you know by now I didn't really see anything."

Gwen lowered the camera again. "So, why did you do it? Why did you make up that story?"

"Because I had a problem with the truth back then. Troubled kid, going off the rails—you know the drill."

Gwen nodded. Behind her, Frances frowned, her expression sad.

Back then, Ian hadn't believed her when she'd said she cared about him. He hadn't believed anyone when they'd told him anything. His mother had lied over and over and over again. About her relationships, about Ian's future with her. About everything. So, he'd learned to lie, too. And he'd learned to use lies to get exactly what he wanted.

Stella kept watching him. Maybe waiting for him to apologize. What the hell—he needed to stay on Frances's good side, anyway.

He let his gaze settle on the older woman with the kind eyes. He'd resented her so much back then. She'd been just another adult forcing him into a mold that he'd never wanted or asked for. *Troubled kid, going off the rails...* But he could never quite lump her into the same category as his parents and everyone else who'd let him down over the years. She was different then. She was different now.

"I'm sorry, Frances," he said. He had been bitter about his time in foster care, and she'd been a convenient target. She'd remained one for a long time, even after he'd left Christmas Bay. But she hadn't deserved his behavior. Today, he found he could say the words, but he still couldn't forgive her in his heart. Even though that was ridiculous, of course—none of it had been her fault. But he still couldn't get past her role in all of it. He'd been taken away from the only home he'd ever known and placed with a complete stranger, and the anger had nearly eaten him alive.

But he could at least say the words. And the words were all he needed right now.

She smiled, clearly moved. *Goal achieved.*

"Honey, you have nothing to be sorry for. It's all behind us now."

It wasn't behind them. Not by a long shot, since he was acutely aware that he was still lying for his own benefit. In this case, that benefit was her house. But he'd said he was sorry, and she seemed to accept it, and in that way, they could move forward. He could pile on the charm, convince her to sell, make a ton of money and leave Christmas Bay in his rearview mirror. This time for good.

"Frances," Gwen said, "why don't you move over to the railing next to Ian, and I can get a picture of you both."

"Oh, that's a good idea. Stella, why don't you get in here with us?"

Stella shook her head. "No, that's okay. This one can be just you two."

"Are you sure?"

"Positive."

Ian watched her as Frances walked over, leaning into his side for the picture. She watched him back, her blue eyes chilly. Her long dark hair moved in the ocean breeze. It was wild around her face, wavy, but not quite curly. Her skin was pale, delicate. Almost translucent, and there was a spattering of freckles across her nose. She was so pretty that he could almost forget how he'd never been able to stand her.

But even as he thought it, even as Gwen told them to smile and say cheese, he couldn't believe that same old line he'd always repeated to himself. He hated Frances. He hated Stella. He hated Marley and Kyla, and all the other foster kids who'd come in and out of the house during his time there. But the truth, which Ian still had trouble with, was more complicated than that. More layered. He hadn't really hated them. The truth was, he'd *wanted* to hate them, and there was a difference.

"Perfect," Gwen said, lowering the camera again. "I think that's about it. I've got everything I need. I'll call you if the gaps need filling in, but I think this is going to be a great Christmas article."

Frances touched Gwen's elbow. "Let me walk you out."

And just like that, Ian found himself alone with Stella. Just the two of them, facing each other on the widow's walk, the salty breeze blowing through their hair. He caught her scent, something clean, flowery. Something that made his groin tighten.

"We might as well not beat around the bush," he said evenly. "I'm going to be honest with you."

"Well, that's a first."

"I'm interested in this property, you're right. I think it's a great development opportunity."

Her lovely eyes flashed. "I knew it. I knew that's why you came."

"I came because I owed it to Frances. And I was curious about the house, too."

"You're so full of it, Ian. You were *only* curious about the house."

She was going to think what she was going to think. There was nothing he could do about it, and he didn't care, anyway.

He leaned casually against the railing and smiled down at her. Something he remembered had always driven her crazy. "Now that I've seen it," he said, "I'm going to talk to Frances about making an offer."

"Forget it. She'll never sell to you."

"Says who?"

"Says me."

"Last I checked, you don't own it."

She glared up at him. "No, but she'll listen to me. She'll listen to Marley and Kyla. And all we'll have to do is remind her that she wants a family here."

"She may have some romantic notion of selling to a family, but in reality, money talks. And I think she'll sell for the right price."

"You're insufferable," she bit out. She was furious

now. Her cheeks were pink, her full lips pursed. Before he could help it, he wondered what she'd be like in bed. All that passion and energy directed right at him. But that wasn't a fantasy that had a chance of coming true any time soon. By the looks of it, she'd rather run him over with her car first.

"Don't assume Frances would just sell to the highest bidder," she continued. "She doesn't need the money. Despite what you've always thought."

She was obviously talking about that idiotic comment he'd made about Frances's motives that night at the coffee shop in Portland. Something he'd said out of bitterness. It had been a rotten thing to say, not to mention categorically untrue. Stella hadn't given him a chance to take it back, though. She'd gotten up and slammed out before he could utter another word. Fast-forward almost ten years, and now here they were.

"I didn't mean that," he said huskily. "What I said back then."

She crossed her arms over her chest.

"And I know she doesn't need the money *now*," he continued. "But what about later? On the phone, you said she's got Alzheimer's. That's why she can't handle the house anymore. Retirement homes are expensive. Care facilities are even more expensive. This would give her a nest egg for her future. She's smart—she's got to know she'll need one."

Stella gaped at him. "Oh, you are disgusting. You're even lower than I thought you'd be when you showed up here, and believe me, that's pretty low."

"How is it low? The way I see it, I'd be helping her out."

"You *would* see it that way." She shook her head, her dark hair blowing in front of her face. She tucked it behind her ears again and took a deep breath. "She wants a family here, and that's the only thing that's going to sway her. Believe me, you don't stand a chance."

He put his hands in his pockets. "Hmm."

"What?"

"I'm just saying, if she wants a family living here, I might fit the bill there, too."

She laughed. "What? Come on."

"I don't have a family. Yet. But eventually I might, and it'd be great to have the house checked off the list." She was right. He *was* low.

Stella watched him suspiciously. "You just said this place is a great development opportunity. You expect me to believe you'd actually live here?"

"I might. For a while."

"Baloney. You're just saying that to get what you want."

"Believe me, don't believe me. Doesn't matter to me, Stella. What matters to me is what Frances believes. And by the way, this whole archrival thing we've got going on? It's only making me want the house more."

"Oh, really."

"Really."

"You'd buy a house out of spite?"

"No, I'd buy a house to make money. I'd sell it out of spite."

She glared up at him. She was fuming. But if she thought she was going to stand in his way, she was wrong. Nobody stood in his way. At least not people who didn't want to get bulldozed.

After a second, she looked away. She stared out at the ocean that was sparkling underneath the midday sun. He couldn't be sure, but he thought her chin might be trembling a little. And if it was, that would be a surprise. A crack in her otherwise impenetrable armor.

"Hey," he said.

She didn't look at him. Just continued staring at the water.

He took a breath, not sure what to say. Taken off guard by her sudden show of emotion. Ian could take a lot of things, and did on a daily basis. But the sight of a woman crying had always unnerved him. Talk about an Achilles' heel. He remembered walking in on Stella crying once when they were kids. She'd been trying to be quiet, so as not to call attention to herself. She'd looked up at him, her cheeks wet with tears, and the expression on her face had nearly broken his heart. He remembered very clearly wanting to cross the room to hug her, to comfort her. To take some of her pain away, just a little.

"You can tell me to go to hell," he said now. "But I'll give you some advice, Stella. Sometimes there's such a thing as caring too much."

At that she looked back at him. And he'd been right. There were tears in her eyes. He had to stop himself before he reached for her, because really, she was a stranger to him. He didn't know her anymore, and he didn't care to know her. He was only here for a business deal.

"She's eventually going to forget all the memories she has of this place," she said. "The only thing that comforts her is the thought of someone making new memories here. For me, as far as Frances is concerned, there is no such thing as caring too much."

He grit his teeth. *There's no such thing...* He wondered how it was that they'd ended up so differently. Her caring too much, and him not caring at all. They were two stars at the opposite ends of the universe. And she still shone just as brightly as she had when she was fourteen. Maybe he was jealous of that. Deep down. Maybe he wanted to love just as fiercely as Stella Clarke did.

She lifted her chin. "So, yes, Ian. You can take your money, and your offer, and you can go to hell."

And she walked out.

"Here's your room key, sir." The woman smiled up at him, wrinkles exploding from the corners of her brown eyes. Her Christmas tree earrings sparkled, coming in a close second to her sweater. She looked like Mrs. Claus.

"Thank you," he said.

"There's a vending machine right down the breezeway, and if you want to rent a movie, we have a pretty good selection of DVDs, but the front desk closes at nine."

He took the key card and tucked it in his back pocket, preoccupied with the events of that afternoon. Frances owned a candy shop on Main Street, and she and Stella had gone back to work right after their meeting with Gwen. That had left him zero time to approach her about the house, so he'd made the incredibly annoying decision to stay in Christmas Bay overnight.

He'd called and asked if he could meet Frances for coffee before heading home tomorrow, and she'd seemed genuinely happy about that. He'd make his move then. Her defenses were already down because of this cheesy article. If he could frame the sale in a way that would tug on her heartstrings, it would be easier than he'd thought.

Pushing down the slightest feeling of guilt, he grabbed a razor, comb and toothbrush from a rack beside the counter and paid quickly, not wanting to encourage any more small talk with the Jingle Bell Inn front desk lady. He'd already had to endure enough nosy questions—what brought him to town, where had he bought a car that fancy, etcetera, etcetera. All topped off with a story about someone who'd stayed here not long ago who drove a Ferrari. The kind Tom Selleck had in *Magnum P.I.* He'd smiled and nodded politely. But inside, he was dying. This was exactly the kind of interaction he never had to deal with in the city. In the city, people couldn't care less why you were staying overnight. They just took your credit card and told you where the best seafood places were.

Gathering his things, he told the lady to have a good evening and walked out the door. The sun was just beginning its fiery descent toward the ocean. The sky was a brilliant swirl of pinks and purples, and the salty breeze felt good on his skin. He breathed in the smell of the water, of the beach, letting the air saturate his lungs. Letting it bring him back, just a little, to the last time he was here.

He'd left Christmas Bay the second he'd graduated from high school—right after he'd turned eighteen and was done with the foster system for good. His mother had made some weak overtures about him coming to live with her again, and letting her "help" him with college. He hadn't been able to tell her off fast enough. This, after an entire childhood of not caring whether he was coming or going, or that he'd basically served as a punching bag for her ever-revolving door of boyfriends.

He slid the key card into the lock, watching the light blink green, then opened the door and walked into the small room with his stomach in a knot. He really couldn't believe he was back here after all this time. He'd never planned on it. His mother had passed away a few years ago, and the only relative still living here was a great-aunt who was in a retirement home across town. He'd gone to live with her after he'd run away from Frances's house. She'd tried to make a connection with him, and had been the only one in his family who ever acted like they cared at all. But he'd kept her at an arm's length, anyway, protecting himself the best way he knew how. The thought of coming back to visit her had never crossed his mind. He'd left. And that meant leaving her, and everything else, behind, too.

Opening the sliding glass door, he stepped onto the balcony with the beginnings of a headache throbbing at his temples. The guilt he'd felt earlier had settled in his gut like a small stone. If he had any chance of convincing Frances to sell to him, he needed to bury that guilt, along with any strange pull he was feeling toward Stella. These people were simply part of his past. They had no place in his future. And if they registered in his present at all, it was only because they were a means to an end.

It wasn't in Ian's nature to let fruit like this slip through his fingers once he realized how ripe it was for the picking. And no matter what kind of bleeding-heart reasons Frances had for wanting to sell her house to a family, he knew he'd been absolutely right about her needing the most money she could get out of it. What kind of local family would be able to come up with the cash to outbid him? What he was doing would only end up helping her, not hurting her.

Sinking down in one of the plastic deck chairs, he watched the waves pound the beach. In the distance, a woman was being dragged along by her golden retriever, the dog barking joyously at the water. Up ahead, two boys in hoodies were playing football in the sand. Other than that, the beach was empty. So unlike San Francisco, where the amount of people on a sunny winter day could make you feel like you couldn't catch your breath. Which, normally, he didn't mind. The hustle was what he liked about California. The opportunities, the possibilities. But the deep breathing you could do up here was undeniable.

He leaned back in the chair and pulled out his phone to do some quick calculations. How much the house might be worth on the market, how much the land alone might be worth and what kind of builders might be interested. Ian had instantly seen a few luxury condos perched on that cliff in his mind's eye. But honestly, it would be a great place for a high end spa, too. Maybe even a small, quaint hotel… He'd been worried the house would be on the National Register of Historic Places, but miraculously, it wasn't. Probably because it had always been a private residence and nobody famous had stayed there. Or maybe Frances's family had never gotten around to listing it. He knew there was an in-depth nomination process. Either way, his initial worry that he'd run into red tape was null and void.

Looking out over the water, he rubbed his chin. The golden retriever was in the surf now, its owner standing with her hands on her hips, looking resigned. She'd lost the battle. Despite his headache, Ian smiled. It was a Norman Rockwell kind of moment. But then again, Christmas Bay was a Norman Rockwell kind of town. Scratch that. It was for some people. For people like him, he remembered how dead-end and limiting it really was. Yeah, Frances would definitely be thanking him after this. Even if he did have to stretch the truth initially, she'd thank him in the end.

He'd bet on it.

"Frances, I'm not sure you realize who you're dealing with here, that's all."

Stella leaned against the counter next to the cash register, watching her foster mother go from window to window with a bottle of Windex and a wad of paper towels. She was just about done, and the glass was crystal clear. It wouldn't last, though. When you worked in a candy shop, you got used to fingerprints everywhere. Even some nose prints thrown in for good measure.

Frances didn't turn around. Just kept spraying and wiping, spraying and wiping. "I know you're worried, honey. But we're only going to have coffee. I'll just see what he has to say."

"I *know* what he's going to say."

"I keep telling you, people change."

"Yeah, sometimes they get worse."

"You still think he's selfish."

"Does the Pope wear a funny hat?"

Frances laughed. "Well. That would be a yes."

"I'm just saying, we spent an hour with the guy, and that was plenty. He's only here to make money. He doesn't care about the house."

Frances did turn around at that. "What kind of person would I be, what kind of foster mother, if I didn't at least hear him out? If I didn't give him a chance to prove himself?"

Stella sighed.

"You're just going to have to trust me on this one, Stella. I know my memory is going, but it's not gone yet, and I need to give him a chance."

Frowning, Stella chewed the inside of her cheek. Damn him. Frances was already being swayed by that big-city charm. By those blue eyes, and that calculating smile. He probably knew exactly how Frances felt about him, and was going to use that to his fullest advantage. But at the end of the day, this was Frances's house, Frances's decision. All Stella could do was try to advise and be there for support.

"I do want you to come, though," Frances said, walking over and setting the Windex on the counter. "Would you do that for me?"

Stella's chest tightened. She hadn't been prepared to see him again so soon. Or maybe ever. The thought of looking up into that smug face made her want to chug a glass of wine.

She licked her lips, which suddenly felt dry. "What about the shop?"

"We'll close it. It's just for a little while."

Well, there goes that excuse.

She forced a smile. "Then of course I'll come."

"But you have to promise not to kill him."

"I can't promise that."

Frances reached out and took her hand, suddenly looking serious. Almost desperate in a way, and Stella knew she was asking for reassurance. And comfort.

"I can't explain it," Frances said, "but I just want him to leave on good terms this time. Things with Ian have bothered me for years. This is a way to fix it, even if it's just to smooth it over. I need that. Can you understand?"

She could. She knew the sale of the house was the beginning of smoothing a lot of things over for Frances. She was settling her affairs, mending broken fences, looking back on mistakes she felt she'd made. And no matter how much Stella mistrusted Ian, she had to respect how Frances felt about him. Her foster children were her children. No matter how long they ended up staying with her. And having one of her children out there in the world, alone, unanchored, was too much for her to take, without at least having coffee with him and hearing him out, apparently.

Stella squeezed her hand. Frances had beautiful hands. Soft, and perfectly manicured, her nails usually painted some kind of fuchsia or cotton candy pink. Today, they were Christmas themed, green with little red polka dots.

"I can understand that, Frances," she said. "And I won't kill him. I promise."

Chapter Three

Ian sat in the sunroom of the old Victorian, with Stella sitting directly across from him. Frances had gone into the kitchen to get the coffee and pastries, insisting that "you kids sit and chat" for a minute.

So far there hadn't been any chatting. Just the chilly gaze of a woman who looked even more beautiful today than she had yesterday, if that was possible. She wore a gray Portland Trail Blazers hoodie and had her dark hair pulled into a high ponytail. Her face was freshly scrubbed, her cheeks pink and dewy. She still looked like she wanted to push him in front of a bus, though. Which was fine. Whatever.

He smiled at her and leaned back in the wicker chair. Everything in this room was wicker. Even the coffee table. It felt like he'd been teleported back to 1985.

"I wasn't expecting you to show up today," he said.

"You seem like you'd rather be doing something else. Like getting a root canal, maybe."

Her lips twitched at that. But if he thought the teasing would get her to relax, he was sadly mistaken.

"That would be preferable, yes."

"Then why are you here?"

"Frances asked me to come, and I couldn't say no."

"Even though you wanted to."

"Exactly. But I promised I'd behave, so this is me behaving."

"Good to know. I'd hate to see you misbehaving."

A tubby black-and-white cat sauntered in with a hoarse meow, and blinked up at him through yellow eyes. Then it proceeded to wind itself around his ankles.

Ian stared down at it. He hated cats. He was allergic. In fact, he thought he could feel the beginnings of a tickle in his nose.

"Beauregard," Stella said. "No."

The cat looked over at her, unconcerned. Then he turned around and rammed his little head into Ian's shin.

"Beauregard." She leaned down and snapped her fingers at him, but he ignored her completely. Ian had to work not to laugh. He didn't like cats, but he did appreciate them. They did what the hell they wanted, when the hell they wanted to do it. If they came to you, it was because you had something to offer. If they left, it was because something else was more appealing at that moment. As a human, he could relate.

He reached up and rubbed his nose. Definitely a tickle.

"Oh, I see you've met Beauregard," Frances said, appearing in the doorway with a tray. "Just nudge him with your foot if he's being a pest."

Ian nudged him, but the cat only seemed encouraged by the contact. He immediately came back for more.

"Oh, dear," Frances said, setting the tray down on the coffee table. "I think you've made a friend."

Ian looked down at him dubiously.

Sitting beside Stella, Frances handed over his coffee. "Black, like you said."

"Thank you."

"Honey," she said, handing Stella a cup. "Here you go."

"Thanks, Frances."

"That's homemade blackberry jam for the scones. Kyla and Marley made it last summer." She smiled over at Ian. "They came back to Christmas Bay, too. They're busy with their own families, but we see each other nearly every day, don't we Stella?"

Stella took a sip of her coffee, eyeing him over the rim of the mug. A Christmas tree, draped in blue lights, twinkled next to her. The ocean outside the windows was gray and misty today. The perfect backdrop to the house on the cliff. It all felt like a movie set, and he was about to deliver his lines. The ones he'd rehearsed last night. The ones Frances wouldn't be able to resist.

He took a sip of his coffee, too, and burned his tongue. Wincing, he set it on the coffee table.

"Frances," he said evenly. "I want to talk to you about your house."

Clasping her hands in her lap, she waited. She'd obviously known this was coming. Stella sat beside her with a tight expression on her face. But whatever warning she'd given Frances, it obviously hadn't been enough to dissuade her from meeting with him today.

Sensing an opening, he leaned forward and put his elbows on his knees. "I'd like you to consider selling it to me."

She nodded slowly. "Is that the reason you came up here? To make an offer on the house?"

"I could've made an offer from San Francisco," he said, pushing down that annoying sliver of guilt that kept pricking at his subconscious. It was absolutely true. He could've made an offer from California, but he'd come up to do the interview, and he'd done it. He'd also come up for the house, but again, she didn't have to know that. Right now he needed to work the seller. He'd done it a thousand times before. Frances was no different.

"I wanted to do the interview for you. But when I saw this place again…" He clasped his hands and looked around. "Well, I really couldn't resist."

"It's a beautiful house," Frances said. "And you have to know what it means to me."

"I do."

"I was raised here. And my parents and grandparents, too. And then all of you kids…"

He clenched his jaw. *You kids…* He still couldn't believe she thought of him as more than just a shithead teenager who'd slept here for a couple of years.

Pushing that down, he smiled. "I know. The emotional value far exceeds the monetary value. But I have to be honest, Frances. That's a lot, too."

"I don't care about the money."

He didn't believe that. Everyone cared about the money.

He licked his lips. Stella watched him steadily, saying *I told you so* with that cool gaze of hers.

Taking a page from the cat's playbook—who right that minute had his sizeable girth spread out on Ian's foot—he ignored Stella and doubled down on Frances. If he wasn't careful, he'd lose control of the room, and he never lost control of the room.

"I know you don't," he said softly. Shaking his head. Milking the moment. "I know you want someone living here who will love it just like you do."

Her kind eyes, which had been slightly guarded a minute ago, warmed at that. He could hardly believe it was going to be this simple. But he went on, not wanting to lose any ground, and not trusting Stella to not interrupt when he was just getting to the good stuff.

"I'm not married yet," he said. "But of course, I'd like to be someday." For such a whopping lie, it rolled off his tongue fairly easily. He just had to keep reminding himself that it could be true. Technically. Anything was possible.

"And I'd love this house just as much as you do, Frances," he finished. That part was downright true. He'd love the massive payday it would bring, and that was practically the same thing.

Stella sat there stiff as a board. It was obvious she was trying to keep her mouth shut, but was having a hard time of it. He was sure he could handle her and whatever she threw at him, but it would be nice if he could get in a few more minutes with Frances before she started winding up.

"I'd love to believe that," Frances said.

Stella cleared her throat.

He ignored that, too.

"So, you're saying if you bought the house," Frances said, "you'd want to live here."

"That's what I'm saying."

"But you haven't been back to Christmas Bay since you left after high school, right?"

"You hate Christmas Bay," Stella said flatly. "Why would you live in a town that you hate?"

He held up a hand. "Now, I never said I hate it." That was also true. He hadn't said it. He'd been thinking it.

"Oh, come on, Ian."

"I have complicated memories of Christmas Bay," he said. "But now that I see it as an adult, it's obviously a great place to raise a family."

Stella made a huffing sound. But Frances's interest seemed piqued.

"Honestly," she said. "I love the idea of someone I know buying the house, over complete strangers..."

He smiled.

"And you really think you'd want to settle down here? It's awfully fast. Or have you been thinking of settling down for a while?"

Stella had been taking a sip of her coffee, but she coughed at that.

"Sorry," she croaked. "Went down the wrong pipe."

Ian narrowed his eyes at her before looking back at Frances. "Oh, you know. For a while now." If he was keeping track, that would go in the whopper column. But it couldn't be helped. She'd painted him into a corner.

"How convenient," Stella muttered under her breath.

"Now, Ian," Frances said. "I'm going to tell you the truth. If you made an offer, I think I'd consider it before I'd consider anything else. But I just can't get past what a change this would be for you, coming from the city. What about your job?"

"Oh, I could work remotely for a while. And I'm used to traveling. That wouldn't be a problem."

"But would you be able to acclimate back into small-town life?"

Ian resisted the urge to shift in his seat. He needed to appear convincing, and squirming around like a fibbing third grader wasn't going to get him anywhere.

"It would be an adjustment," he said. "But I've been wanting to make a change for a while, so..."

Frances nodded thoughtfully. He almost had her, he could feel it. But then again, he'd been expecting it. Ian did this for a living, and he was good at it. Really good. By this afternoon, he'd be on the phone with his office, getting the ball rolling. This should be an easy sale, barring anything popping up with the inspection. But that really didn't matter, either. It was the property he was after, not the house, and he'd pay whatever he had to for it.

He leaned back in his chair, the wicker squeaking obnoxiously under his weight. He felt confident, in control. The guilt that had been plaguing him earlier was tucked away in the farthest corners of his mind, ignored. It was all going to work out exactly how he'd hoped. He'd get a kick-ass piece of land, and Frances, whether she realized it or not, would be better off. Taken care of financially. Sure, she'd hate him in the end, but that was inevitable. He could live with it. He'd lived with a lot worse.

Stella continued to stare at him, her eyes cold. Under different circumstances, he probably would've asked her out by now. Taken her to the nicest restaurant he could find, and impressed her by ordering the most expensive bottle of wine. If she'd been a stranger, he would've done his damnedest to get her into bed afterward, too. He'd push that dark mane of hair off to the side, and move his lips along her jaw, down her throat. He'd work to get her to look at him the way so many other women did. He might even turn himself inside out for that.

But it was only a fantasy. Because she wasn't a stranger. She'd never liked him before, and she sure as hell didn't like him now. Again, he reminded himself that he didn't care.

Still, as he stared back at her, he knew that deep down, where that sliver of guilt lay, he did care. Just a little. Just enough to swallow hard now, his tongue suddenly feeling thick and dry in his mouth.

Frances took a sip of her coffee. Then another, as the clock ticked from the other room. The cat continued purring on his foot, and he thought his eyes felt itchy now. Or maybe that was just his imagination.

"I know you want the house, Ian," she finally said, setting the coffee cup down again. "And I want you to have the house."

His heart beat evenly inside his chest.

"On one condition…"

He raised his brows. Stella raised hers, too, and looked over at her foster mother. Even the cat, probably sensing the sudden stiffness in Ian's body, shifted and yawned.

"If you're serious about this," she continued, "if you're serious about living in Christmas Bay again, I want you to stay for a few weeks. Until Christmas Eve."

He stared at her. Stella stared at her, too.

"If you can work remotely," she said, "that shouldn't be a problem. You can get reacquainted with the town, with the people. Stella can show you around and introduce you. Then, you can truly decide if you want to put down some roots here. And if that's how you feel in your heart, I'll be able to tell. I'll be able to see it written all over your face."

Ian felt his mouth go slack. The house—his great investment opportunity, a deal so sure, he'd been writing up the papers in his head—was so quiet you could hear a pin drop. Outside the windows, there was the muted sound of the ocean, the waves slamming against the cliffs of Cape Longing. He felt his pulse tapping steadily in his neck as he let her words, her surprisingly genius condition, settle like a weight in his stomach.

Well, son of a bitch.

He hadn't been expecting *that*.

Stella couldn't stop gaping at Frances. She knew she was doing it. She must've looked like a sea bass, but she couldn't help it. The shock was all-consuming.

Across the room, Ian was apparently just as shocked. He didn't look like a sea bass—unfortunately he was too handsome for that. But he did look like Frances had dropped a sizeable bomb right in his lap.

He seemed at a loss for words. Stella couldn't blame him. She was in the same boat.

"I'm sorry," she managed after a minute. "What?"

Frances folded her hands in her lap, her Christmas sweater sparkling in the morning light. This one had a sequined snowman emblazoned on the front.

"You heard me," she said evenly.

Ian glanced over at Stella, and for the first time since he'd arrived, he looked taken aback. She had to hand it to Frances. She'd surprised them both. And she'd done it on her own terms. If she was going to sell the house, she was going to sell it to whomever she chose. She was not a forgetful old lady who couldn't handle her affairs. She could still manage just fine, and she was going to prove it.

Stella felt a distinctive warmth creep into her cheeks. She loved Frances so much, but she realized she'd been coddling her for the last few weeks. Treating her like a child. She stared at her shoes, ashamed.

Still, Ian *staying* here? And having to show him around? It was worse than him just making an outright offer. Much worse.

Taking a deep breath, she settled her gaze on Frances

again, this time trying to center herself. "Frances, can we at least talk about this?"

"There's nothing to talk about. I was up half the night thinking about it, and it makes perfect sense."

Ian frowned, clearly wondering how he'd been so close to a deal, only to let this wriggle right out of his grasp. Normally, Stella would be gloating, but she couldn't even bring herself to do that. What a cluster.

"I trust your instincts, Stella," Frances said. "You might think I'm dismissing all your concerns, but it's actually because I've been listening that I'm doing this. By spending time with Ian, you'll be able to gauge his true feelings."

She turned to Ian then. "And I love you to pieces, Ian. I know you probably have a hard time believing that, but I do. However, I need to know you're not just here for the real estate. And this way, I'll know."

Ian swallowed visibly. "Frances…"

"There's really nothing you can say to make me change my mind. It's made up. If you're serious about the house you'll stay, or you won't and I'll find another buyer. It's as simple as that."

Stella watched her foster mother, impressed with her badassery, and at the same time horrified that she appeared to mean everything she'd just said. Ian was going to stay. *Until Christmas Eve.*

That is…unless he didn't. She looked over at him, wondering if Frances had called his bluff. There was always that possibility, and she felt the stirrings of hope in her belly. Maybe she wouldn't have to spend any more time with him after all.

He seemed deep in thought. His dark brows were furrowed, his jaw working methodically. He looked far away, weighing how much he actually wanted the property, no doubt. Was it really worth two weeks of his life? She guessed he already had more money than God. Why did he need more?

But right as she was thinking it, his gaze shifted to Frances, and there was something in his eyes that told Stella her foster mother might've just met her match.

"It's a deal, Frances," he said evenly. "On Christmas Eve, you'll see that I'm the right buyer for this house."

"I'm still not sure what you mean," Carter said, sounding confused on the other end of the line. "You're *staying* there?"

Ian sighed and leaned back against the motel bed's headrest. There was a light rain falling outside, and the ocean churned, grumpy and gray beyond the beach. He really didn't care to repeat himself—he wasn't in the mood. But the fact was, he was going to have to be doing a lot of that in the days to come. Telling people over and over again why he was here. His associates, his employees, Christmas Bay locals. He swallowed a groan. *God.* The Christmas Bay locals. If the front desk lady was any indication of the amount of nosiness around here, he'd have to tell everyone his business. And would any of them swallow his reasons for wanting to come back here? They'd have to if he had any hope of convincing Frances.

He felt his shoulders tighten. And it wasn't just Frances anymore. It was Stella, too. And having to convince her was what had him worried. Plenty.

"Yes," he said, gripping his phone tighter than he needed to. "It's a long story. But in order to secure this sale, I need to put the time in."

"Yeah, but two *weeks*?"

He could almost see his partner leaning back in her corner office chair, the bay sparkling behind her. She'd think this was ridiculous, of course. She'd think Ian was losing his edge if it was taking him two days to make a sale, much less two weeks. But if he didn't secure it, as far as he was concerned, that *would* be losing his edge, and he wasn't about to let that happen. Two weeks was a long time, but it would be worth it in the end. Another notch in his belt, another win for his company. And his bank account. All he needed was for Carter to take over while he was gone and deal with their clients in person. He could Zoom until the cows came home, but some of them were finicky and needed to be handled like high-strung racehorses. Zoom meetings didn't always cut it.

"Two weeks," Ian said. "Just trust me on this."

"Okaaay. Two weeks. I can't wait to hear all about it."

That was a lie. Carter didn't actually care if Ian camped out on the moon, just as long as he made them money. She was just as cutthroat as he was. Maybe even more so, and that was saying something in this business.

"Listen," Ian said. "I'm going to drive down tomorrow and pick up some clothes. So if you need me for anything, I can swing by the office before heading back. I'll call on the way down, okay?"

"Sounds good. Talk then."

Ian hung up and rubbed his temple. The headache from yesterday had turned into a full-blown pain in the ass. What he really needed to do was get in the car and head to the little market in town. Pick up a few groceries for his room. He had a microwave, minifridge and a coffee pot, thank God. He'd be living on macaroni and cheese and granola bars for a while. *Great.* This really couldn't get much worse.

But it could get worse, he knew that. He could put in the time and effort for this property, and by Christmas Eve, he might not be able to convince Stella that he was being genuine. He might not be able to convince Frances to sell to him, and then what?

He scraped a hand through his hair. He'd just have to cross that bridge when he came to it. Right now, he was going to have to gird his loins and head into town.

Lord help him.

Stella watched seven-year-old Gracie, wearing a pink slicker with the hood flopping on her shoulders, run up the beach.

"Don't go too far!" Kyla yelled through her cupped hands.

At that, Gracie turned and waved. She was so cute. Dark hair, dark eyes. Maybe one of the cutest kids Stella had ever seen. And she was about to get a brand-new stepmom. Kyla was going to marry Ben Martinez, Christmas Bay's police chief and the love of her life, next spring. She was positively glowing.

But as she walked alongside Stella now, the wind blowing her shoulder-length hair in front of her face, she looked more worried than anything.

"I'm not sure I like this," Kyla said. "It has trouble written all over it."

Stella pulled her cardigan tighter around her, watching as Gracie bent down to inspect something in the sand, then shoved it in her slicker pocket. Stella hoped it wasn't alive. "Tell me about it. I haven't liked it from the beginning."

"And this was Frances's idea? Actually, don't answer that. It sounds exactly like something Frances would do."

Stella nodded. "I know. She definitely wants to know Ian's serious, but there's also a part of her that wants to show us she's still in control. I'm proud of her. I mean, I'm super annoyed, but you have to hand it to her. It's kind of brilliant."

"So, what are you going to do?"

"What can I do? The only way to know for sure if Ian's serious is to spend some time with him, like she said. And even then, I'm not sure he'll ever be honest with us. What if he keeps up this charade about wanting to live in the house?"

"Then she'll have to trust you when you tell her it's just a charade."

Stella looked out over the water. It was gorgeous today. A little windy—the ocean was choppy and unsettled— but the sun was out, warming everything up.

"That's true," she said. "But two weeks… It seems like a lifetime."

Kyla hooked her arm in Stella's. "I'm sorry you got stuck with this."

"Me too. But Frances is worth it. The house is worth it. I'll just have to keep reminding myself of that every time I have to be within five feet of him."

Kyla laughed. "He's still that bad?"

"Worse."

"But good-looking."

Stella turned to her. "Who told you that?"

"Frances. On the phone this morning."

"What do his looks have to do with anything?"

"Nothing…but just how good-looking are we talking?"

"*Kyla.*"

Her foster sister shrugged. "I'm just saying, you're single…"

"Gross. He's an ass."

"But a good-looking ass."

Stella raised a hand to shield her eyes from the sun, watching as Gracie drew in the sand with a stick. "I guess."

"Listen, you don't have to do this all by yourself. Ben and I can help. Bring him over for dinner or something. Take him to see Marley and the baby. Really lay it on thick. Maybe he'll decide he's in over his head and will give up. I mean, how much Christmas Bay can a person take, if they hate everything about Christmas Bay?"

Stella contemplated this, her wheels turning. "That's true…"

"I bet after a few days, he'll start wondering what the hell he's doing here and will leave early."

"Kyla," Stella said slowly. "You just gave me the best idea."

"Uh-oh."

"He'd *definitely* have second thoughts if he has a miserable time. Remember when Frances took us crabbing in middle school, and we were all hungry and cold, and Marley ended up falling in the water?"

"The infamous crabbing day. How could I forget?"

Stella smiled. *"Exactly."*

"Are you going to take him to the bay and push him in?"

"Don't tempt me. But why should we have to sugarcoat anything? Living in a small town isn't like a Hallmark movie. There are all kinds of things about it that drive you crazy. I'm just saying, I'll show him around. I'll introduce him to people. With the sole purpose of reminding him why he hated it here to begin with."

"Oh, you are *bad.*"

"Not half as bad as he is." Stella lifted her chin as a

flock of seagulls squabbled overhead, dipping and bobbing on the chilly breeze. "He dealt the cards," she said. "Now I'll show him I can play."

Don't miss
Their Christmas Resolution
by Kaylie Newell,
available September 2023 wherever
Harlequin® Special Edition
books and ebooks are sold.
www.Harlequin.com

#3013 THE MAVERICK'S HOLIDAY DELIVERY
Montana Mavericks: Lassoing Love • by Christy Jeffries

Dante Sanchez is an expert on no-strings romances. But his feelings for single mom-to-be Eloise Taylor are anything but casual. She knows there's a scandal surrounding her pregnancy. But catching the attention of the town's most notorious bachelor may be her biggest scandal yet!

#3014 TRIPLETS UNDER THE TREE
Dawson Family Ranch • by Melissa Senate

Divorced rancher Hutch Dawson has one heck of a Christmas wish: find a nanny for his baby triplets. And Savannah Walsh is his only applicant! Who knew that his high school nemesis would be the *perfect* solution to his very busy—and lonely—holiday season...

#3015 THE RANCHER'S CHRISTMAS STAR
Men of the West • by Stella Bagwell

Would Quint Hollister hire a woman to be Stone Creek Ranch's new sheepherder? Only if the woman is capable Clementine Starr. She wants no part of romance—at least until Quint's first knee-weakening kiss. But getting two stubborn singletons to admit love might take a Christmas miracle!

#3016 THEIR CONVENIENT CHRISTMAS ENGAGEMENT
Top Dog Dude Ranch • by Catherine Mann

Ian Greer is used to finding his mother, who has Alzheimer's, anywhere but at home! More often than not, he finds her at Gwen Bishop's vintage toy store. He admires the kind, plucky single mom, so a fake engagement to placate his mother—and her family—seems like the perfect plan. Until a romantic sleigh ride changes their holiday ruse into something much more real...

#3017 THE VET'S SHELTER SURPRISE
by Michelle M. Douglas

Sparks fly when beautiful PR expert Georgia O'Neill brings an armful of stray kittens to veterinarian Mel Carter's small-town animal shelter. Mel has loved and lost before, and Georgia is only in town short-term, so it makes sense to ignore their mutual attraction. But as they open up about their pasts, will they also open up to the possibility of new love?

#3018 HOLIDAY AT MISTLETOE COTTAGE
The McFaddens of Tinsley Cove • by Nancy Robards Thompson

Free-spirited photojournalist Avery Anderson just inherited her aunt's beach house. And, it seems, her aunt's sexy, outgoing neighbor. Hometown hero Forest McFadden may be Avery's polar opposite. But fortunately, he's also the adventure she's been searching for.

**YOU CAN FIND MORE INFORMATION ON UPCOMING HARLEQUIN TITLES,
FREE EXCERPTS AND MORE AT HARLEQUIN.COM.**

HSECNM0923

HARLEQUIN
PLUS

Try the best multimedia subscription service for romance readers like you!

Read, Watch and Play.

Experience the easiest way to get the romance content you crave.

Start your **FREE TRIAL** at
<u>www.harlequinplus.com/freetrial</u>.